Carpet Diem

Also by Misty Simon

Carpet Diem

Misty Simon

KENSINGTON BOOKS
www.KensingtonBooks.com

KENSINGTON BOOKS are published by

Kensington Publishing Corp.
119 West 40th Street
New York, NY 10018

All Kensington titles, imprints, and distributed lines are available at special quantity discounts for bulk purchases for sales promotion, premiums, fund-raising, educational, or institutional use.

Special book excerpts or customized printings can also be created to fit specific needs. For details, write or phone the office of the Kensington Sales Manager: Attn.: Sales Department. Kensington Publishing Corp., 119 West 40th Street, New York, NY 10018. Phone: 1-800-221-2647.

Kensington and the K logo Reg. U.S. Pat. & TM Off.

First Printing: October 2019
ISBN-13: 978-1-4967-2374-1
ISBN-10: 1-4967-2374-0

ISBN-13: 978-1-4967-2375-8 (ebook)
ISBN-10: 1-4967-2375-9 (ebook)

10 9 8 7 6 5 4 3 2 1

Printed in the United States of America

To all the readers who have brought Tallie to life—thank you! And to Daniel and Noelle, who make this all worthwhile.

Acknowledgments

In all my years of dreaming about publishing, and my very vivid imagination, even I couldn't have known how awesome it would be to work with Esi and Norma at Kensington for edits and the entire team to bring these books to the reader in such style. And even before them there are the wonderful women who critique like nobody's business. Thank you to Natalie, Vicky, and Vicki!

Chapter One

Few things in life bothered me more than a person who could not seem to get the hint that I had no desire to interact with them.

Preston Prescott, part of my old crowd, was very high on the list of people I had avoided when I was married to the now deceased Walden Phillips III—or, as I called my ex-husband, Waldo—because it had irritated him to no end.

And like Waldo, Preston was obnoxious and irritating and a plethora of other words I didn't have time to look up in a thesaurus. I had divorced Waldo months before he died, and I was thankful I had gotten out of his circle. Or at least I had tried to stay out of his circle, until people like Preston decided to harass me.

This man irritated me, as in I wouldn't just go to the other side of the street but would gladly take a detour through a swamp in order not to be in the same county with him. But he had unlocked a next level—which I hadn't even known existed—when he accosted me at the Hershey Theater during my first date in over a month with my boyfriend, Max Bennett.

A date I had been looking forward to all week. I'd won tickets on the radio to this play I'd been dying to see. There was no way I could have afforded to buy the tickets. I had winced at the fact that it was possible I would run into some of my old crowd there and I might have to interact with the people I now was not fond of, but I hadn't expected it to come from this corner. I had held out hope that being across the river and twenty minutes away from our small central Pennsylvania town, I might not have to deal with anyone I didn't want to, but that hope was dashed.

I was a theatergoer, or at least I had been back in the day when I was married to Waldo. What else was I supposed to do to get out of the house and not have to talk with him very much? The theater had been a place where he could show me off but not bother me, because he couldn't talk during the performance. Now I had very little money to splurge even on my favorite kind of shampoo, much less go to a play, which meant I didn't get out much.

So when I won the tickets, I was elated. That feeling lasted, and it grew as Max and I held hands and watched the actors work their magic onstage. And then it was time for the intermission. Max asked if I wanted a drink and a snack before the second half of the show, so we entered the lobby to get both.

Our schedules had not been meshing lately, and

it had been weeks since I'd even seen him. I wanted only to enjoy myself with him and concentrate on the two of us, not work. When Max and I ran into many of my old acquaintances in the lobby they were actually nice to me and told me it was nice to see me and to meet Max. I was enjoying myself immensely. And then Preston made an appearance.

"Tallie Graver, who knew you had a taste for anything finer?" Preston said after sweeping into the carpeted lobby in a dove-colored tux with a maroon paisley vest and with a fluffy hunter-green cravat wound tight at his neck.

"Preston," I said in a strained voice, though I wanted to yell. Max stood at my side with his hand on my elbow. Probably because of my dead-flat tone. To say I did not like the man in front of me would be a gross understatement. Choking him with his cravat would have been a blessing.

There were many people whom I didn't particularly like dealing with or whom I wasn't overly fond of, but from the first day I met him, Preston had been right up there with the people whom I always actively avoided. Everything about him was like poison, from his attitude to his high-handedness to his cruel streak, which even Waldo couldn't beat.

And now he had been threatening me on a daily basis, to make sure his aunt, Mrs. Petrovski, did not give me a chance to win the contract to refurbish and clean her mansion from top to bottom. It was a big job for my bigger crew. I'd moved beyond just Letty and me, and now I had a total of five people in my company, which still didn't have a proper name. If my crew was given the chance to clean the Astercromb mansion at the edge of town, it would be a huge boost to the budget and to my ladies. They were thrilled. I was happy, or at least I was until this man had started throwing his barbs at me two weeks ago.

To say things had been unpleasant since I was asked to compete for the job was a gross understatement, as in a massively disgusting understatement of epic proportions. The nasty emails from this man, whom I had always considered a huge nuisance, had started shortly after the announcement was made that I and another cleaning crew, one run by Audra McNeal, would be competing for the job, and these emails hadn't stopped in the two weeks since. He apparently didn't like me any more than I liked him, and he was determined that anyone but me would get this job. Intimidation wasn't going to work, but he hadn't yet been deterred.

Jerk.

In the lobby, I took a moment to look over Preston's shoulder, and I focused on the soaring arched ceiling to regain my equilibrium.

When I looked back at him, he had a hint of a sneer on his mean mouth.

"Nothing more than my name?" he said. "Have you forgotten your manners now that you no longer have Walden to keep you in line?"

Max's hand tightened on my elbow. And for good reason. I needed to be held back from going at this venomous snake right here in the swanky theater. Maybe I could try out some of my recent self-defense course moves and kick him in the eye.

If I was lucky, he'd fall onto the old gold and maroon carpet, where maybe an usher would sweep him up with a broom and a dustpan after the show was over.

I calmed myself as best I could and cleared my throat, imagining him fuming over not keeping me from getting the contract at the mansion. And when I sealed the deal, I'd clean with wild abandon, while he sulked at being bested by yours truly.

"What do you want, Preston? I told you in our last exchange that I have nothing more to say to you. It's going to come down to who's better with a vacuum, and I'm willing to see what your aunt, the actual owner of the mansion, has to say about that."

He laughed. "You may think this is going to be yours, but I know better. I know exactly who's getting it. I'm just waiting for the old lady to call and let you know. I don't even know why they're letting you clean anything. You're not good at what you do, and you're just going to make more of a mess of things." His soft voice and huge smile were for anyone who passed by, but the underlying tone was one of total menace. After shoving his hands on his hips and flaring his designer jacket at the sides, he tapped his manicured fingers on his waist.

The man was a nuisance who liked to control everything, even those things he should keep his nose out of. Why had I ever wanted to be with people like this?

Usually, I wasn't a fighter when it came to jobs. I had no problem bowing out of a disagreeable situation and just doing my own thing elsewhere. But this man had got under my skin, had bothered me all the years I'd been with Waldo. I hadn't had to interact with Preston since I'd left Waldo, and now that I was going for this job, the man wouldn't leave me alone. No matter what he did, I wasn't going to lie down while he walked all over me.

No way, no how.

"Talk is cheap, Preston. If you think you've got this wrapped up, then show me. Stop telling me. Now I have nothing more to say to you, and I'm on a date with my boyfriend, who I am not going to introduce you to. Skedaddle." I cocked an eyebrow at him and waited to see what he'd do. I was goading him, but he was ruining my first evening with Max in a long time, and he had been needling me for days.

He had nothing to say back to that. He just lifted his nose at me before walking away, throwing his tux tails behind him. He stumbled while moving from the carpet to the white marble edging the doorway. After catching himself at the last second, he straightened his jacket, smoothed his lapels, and lifted his nose again. When he looked around to see if anyone had noticed, I just smiled at him. Then he flounced off.

I wasn't proud of that moment, but I was human, and he was being a pain in my rear end.

"Do you want to go?" Max asked, putting his arm around my shoulders.

"No. He will not ruin my night out with you." I hugged his arm and smiled up at him. Spending time with Max was at a premium lately. With his job ramping up, and with his new promotion to head Taxinator, we hadn't seen each other as much as we would have liked in recent months. I was not going to let some bitter trust-fund baby get the best of me on one of my special nights.

But I sighed as he led me through the lobby and to the refreshments. My black heels clicked over the cream marble, and my dress whispered over the floor behind me. I should be incredibly happy to be out and dressed to the nines, especially with Max. Instead, I was mighty tempted to order a stiff drink to make it through the rest of the performance after that confrontation with Preston. I talked a big talk, but being the center of someone's anger like that was a trigger for me. I'd spent years dealing with Waldo's tantrums and having everything be my fault. I did not like going back there.

I got a soda instead of something with a triple shot of vodka, then followed Max to a velvet settee in the old theater lobby. The posh space featured ceilings that were arched and carved. Heavy drapes hung in similarly arched windows that were at least fourteen feet above the floor. The beautiful sconces threw off enough light to make the space intimate, and yet I could still see where I was going. All in all, there was something magical about being here, and especially being here with Max. Preston was not allowed to ruin that for me.

I smiled when Max looked at me, but I tried to avoid eye contact. I didn't want him to see how upset I was.

Tallie Graver, faker. It wouldn't be the first time I'd faked something to make someone happy. But Max was worth it, and leaving early would not make me feel better. It would just make me angry. Angrier.

Max leaned over, and I expected to have some sort of sweet nothing whispered into my ear or to be asked how much I was enjoying the play. Instead, I fell more in love.

"You know there's nothing wrong with leaving. I'm sure everyone else sees your brave face and believes it. Even I believed it for a second. But I know you, Tallie, and if you want to go, we'll just come again another time."

He knew me because he took the time to look and care. He knew me, and he stayed.

I hugged his arm again. No faking necessary, thank God. "No, let's stay. I want to see how this ends. I really am okay."

Or at least I was after Max's words. I had finally found myself an actual keeper.

In the middle of that lovely moment, my phone vibrated in my purse. I'd been waiting for a message from my new hire, Bethany, so I made my quick excuses to Max, who waved me off as I took my phone out of my little clutch purse. It was a text from Bethany, with pictures of the inside of the mansion. At last! I'd bid for the contract without being able to walk around, because Mrs. Petrovski, the owner of the mansion, was an old family friend, and I had figured I could trust her to be fair with me. I still wanted to know what we would be walking into, though, before we got started tomorrow. Mrs. Petrovski had agreed to let us in tonight to look around. I wasn't sure if she was letting the other company in, too, but that wasn't my concern.

Bethany was taking off the first two days of the job to go out of town with her boyfriend, so when

I'd won the tickets, she'd offered to check the place out tonight.

As much as I had not wanted to have an actual company, I couldn't deny that it was nice to have people to help with this kind of stuff now that I had a boyfriend and was building a life for myself. When I'd walked away from my old life, I'd really thought I'd just live upstairs from my dad's funeral home, clean houses, and probably die up there some day. This new direction I was going in was totally not what I had envisioned, and I had to say I was mighty pleased about that

What I was not pleased with, though, was the fact that the pictures had not come through with the text. It was just a series of blank bubbles, with downloading symbols attached at the bottom. I texted Bethany to see if she could email me the pictures instead.

"Tallie Graver! I haven't seen you in days!" I raised my gaze from my phone, knowing that voice. Audra McNeal walked with purpose across the marble floor, her arms swinging and her dress a confection of tulle and silk. She was lovely, and one of the new people in town whom I really liked. She was also the one I was going up against for the contract. If I could have figured out a way for both of us to clean, I would have. From the few interactions we'd had, I thought she'd been a peach ever since she'd moved here. She worked for a company that did commercial cleaning, so I had been surprised to learn that she was going for a job at a privately owned mansion. But it did make a certain kind of sense because it was a big job.

As she came toward us, she had a smile on her face. That at least was better than Preston's sneer.

"Audra!" I yelled across the lobby, as if she hadn't already said my name. I even waved. Whereas a moment ago I had been wishing that the lights would flicker to signal that the curtain was going up soon, thinking that surely the intermission had to be over by now, at this point I'd love a few moments to introduce Max to Audra.

I stood in a swish of velvet and silk to welcome her open-armed hug. "How are you? I didn't realize you were going to be here tonight!" I hooked my arm in hers and turned us toward Max. "My boyfriend's in town, finally, and I want to introduce you. Max, this is Audra. Audra, Max."

Max smiled and held out his hand. Audra took it and shook it with the steely grip I'd first experienced when we met at a chamber of commerce mixer six months ago. With her style and her youthful personality, I'd expected her to be closer to my age, so I'd been surprised when she told me she was only a few years away from fifty.

"Oh, I've been hearing such wonderful things about you, Max. It's so nice to get to meet you."

And now I smiled bigger, because I loved my best friend, Gina, but I was also enjoying opening my friend field up a little bit, and I would love for Audra and her boyfriend to go to dinner with Max and me some night. Her boyfriend had just proposed to her, and it could be a celebration of sorts, the beginning of a great friendship that hadn't yet bloomed but was totally planted.

"So, are you ready to show Mrs. Petrovski what we can do tomorrow?" I asked. "I don't know if she told you, but she's looking to actually sell the mansion, not keep it, like she had originally said. That negates a long-running contract for cleaning services, but one big job is better than none, right? She wants us to come in and clean it out and strip it down so it can be refurbished. The last time anyone touched the place was when they had those decorators come in for that television special."

She choked and then laughed. "I heard about that. It'll be interesting to see what the thing looks like inside. I can't believe she won't let us in until tomorrow. What is this? Some kind of surprise?" It was on the tip of my tongue to offer to share Bethany's pictures when they came in, but Audra was still talking. "No one is going to buy that monstrosity, no matter how much you clean it."

I shrugged, because, really, what else could I do? "I don't make these things up, but I'm glad I have a whole crew now instead of just trying to do it myself."

"Yeah, me too. I guess we'll just have to see which one of us gets picked. I don't quite understand why she's doing it this way. We both gave her references, and we both have good reputations. She could have just picked one and gotten on with it."

She smoothed the waist of her dress with her long fingers and expertly manicured fingernails. I had no idea how she actually cleaned with those things, not that it was any of my business. I knew from my cousin that the lengthy and pointed gel nails were in style, so you could just call me styleless, then. My nails were blunt and short, and they got the job done.

"What time are you getting there tomorrow?" Audra asked.

"She told me eight. You? We're cleaning at the same time, right?"

"Yes, of course. Of course." She flipped her hair over her shoulder, then smiled at me again. "Well, good luck. From what I hear, we might have to ask for at least half the money up front and make sure we actually cash her check instead of just putting it in the bank." She laughed again just as the lights flickered, signaling the end of intermission.

"It was great seeing you," I said, hoping she felt the same way.

"And you. I'll see you tomorrow, and we should really get together while Max is here, if you have time." Her smile widened as she looked at Max and squeezed my hand. Then she sauntered away. I would never be that classy—I never was even when I had all the money—but I appreciated her time and her enthusiasm. You could never go wrong with more friends.

The black dress I had dug far back into my closet for swished against the gold and maroon carpet. I'd pulled out all the stops for this night out, and I still meant to enjoy myself immensely.

I could be doing worse things, like working for my dad at the funeral for Mr. Peterson, which was currently happening at Graver's Funeral Home.

Although, to be fair, work at the funeral home hadn't been as bad lately. I just wasn't going to tell my dad that. He was still pulling for me to join the family business full-time, and I was still pushing back. Working part-time, surrounded by my father, my mother, and one of my two brothers, was

enough for me at this point. And I'd heard that
the shop next to Gina's café could be coming up
for sale, which gave me the hope that I might be
able to finally open my tea store. I wasn't ready fi-
nancially yet, but I had Max, my tax guy, whom I
trusted to help me figure out where to get the
money and how much it was going to cost me.

I held Max's hand and kept an eye out for a Second Coming of Preston, but he appeared to be
holding court in the far corner with a bunch of
other sour-faced men. Perhaps this was their night
out. I couldn't imagine it was a ton of fun for the
crotchety old men, but then, who was I to judge
anyone?

Except that Preston caught me looking his way
and raised his nose into the air. If the indoor sprin-
klers would come on right now, he'd probably
drown.

Man, was it going to feel good to grab that contract.

Max and I stepped away from the small settee
and headed back into the theater for the second
half. We didn't have box seats, but there were no
bad seats in the Hershey Theater, twenty miles
from home. We settled into the plush chairs, and
he took my hand in his, then kissed my knuckles.

I smiled at him and caught Audra waving to me
from her box seat, with her boyfriend next to her.
I didn't know where he was during intermission,
and would have loved to meet him, but another
time was fine. I waved back, then glanced at my
phone one more time.

Nothing new had come in from Bethany. The
photos she'd promised me were still hanging in

the electronic cloud, which I knew nothing about. I'd just have to wait for another ninety minutes to see what we'd be dealing with. As the curtain rose, I glanced back at the box and found Audra standing and dragging her guy with her, with no smile on her face now. The music swelled from the orchestra pit, and I turned back to the stage and to my date. I was so thankful that Max and I didn't have that kind of drama in our lives.

Of course, with Preston on my tail, my dad wanting me to work full-time at the funeral home, and the chief of police giving me the side-eye every time he saw me, I had plenty of other drama in my life. But for tonight I was drama free, at least until I got those pictures from Bethany and finally was able to see what I'd set myself up for.

Chapter Two

After watching the rest of the play with Max at the theater, I'd headed to my apartment with him. Saturday morning came a whole lot faster than I had thought it would following our fun night out. My alarm went off way too early. I tried to get out of bed, but I was caged in by Peanut, the enormous Saint Bernard I'd taken in a few months ago, and Max, who I'd taken in over a year ago. Mr. Fleefers, my cat, who I'd had before either of them and who stayed away from me as often as he could, the little brat, was lying on top of the big dog.

He very deliberately gave me the evil eye when I tried to disrupt everyone so I could get to the bathroom before my bladder burst.

"Up already?" Max asked sleepily, then ran a hand over my rat's nest of a hairdo before kissing me on the cheek.

"I have that cleaning to do today, and then we're going out tonight. I have to get moving if I don't want to be late. And I have a feeling that being late would put me at a great disadvantage. Preston seems to be gunning for me, so I want to be there early. I don't want Mrs. Petrovski to have a single reason to doubt that giving me the job is the right thing to do."

Max smiled at me, then climbed out of bed. After scrambling past him, I walked the three feet to my bathroom. Living above my parents' funeral home meant that I had a small apartment above the dead. It wasn't a bad situation, but it did make for limited space. Quiet neighbors, but limited space.

As I did my morning ritual stuff, I heard Max take Peanut out. One less thing I had to do before leaving for work. Thank God for him. I only wished he was around more. Not only to help with chores, but also because I really enjoyed him. Although the chore help certainly wasn't a bad thing.

Since I planned on grabbing something to eat from my best friend, Gina Laudermilch's coffee-house across the street, to go with the coffee I adored, I skipped making myself breakfast in my tiny kitchen. I was thinking another whoopie pie latte might make this morning sing, but I hadn't completely decided yet. I might need something with a couple of shots of espresso to be able to deal with the chaos that was cleaning a house I hadn't seen with a crew on our maiden voyage.

I'd had nightmares last night about Preston tearing up in his car and blocking the entrance to the house or calling the cops on me and saying I was an intruder. At this point, I didn't think I'd put anything past him.

I got that the job was a big one and was supposed to be long running, so I knew the money was going to be coming in constantly while the refurb was being done. But something about his desperate attempts to get me to back out had my curiosity soaring, and my competitive streak along with it. If I was going up against anyone but my friend Audra, I might find my aggression running high.

That part of me didn't come out often, since I didn't want anything badly enough to compete for it. But right now I felt like I had back in seventh grade, when our last volleyball match had been sprinkled with insults and all I'd wanted was to wipe the smirks off the faces of our opponents from an all-girls' private school.

We'd done that by trouncing them with some seriously hard work. I wasn't afraid to work hard this time, either, in order to secure this job. At this point I'd do the hard work simply to show up Preston.

I kissed Peanut good-bye and then Max. Mr. Fleefers raised his tail at me and stalked away. As I was walking out the door, Max's cell phone rang. I stopped in the doorway to listen to his side of the conversation.

"Yes, sir, I can do that. When do you want me to start?" He paused, and my heart dropped to the vicinity of my stomach. Max was supposed to have a long weekend and be here until Tuesday. If this was work, then he might be on the next plane to some state across the country. This promotion seemed to involve a whole lot of travel, and while I was extremely proud of him, I also missed him.

"Where?" I mouthed, but he shook his head at

me. I glanced at my watch. I had twenty-five minutes to get to the mansion. Fortunately, my car was packed up tight with all the necessities of my business, but I'd be cutting it very close if I didn't leave within the next ten minutes.

"So, I have to cut my vacation short?" Max asked, and my heart hit the floor. I had plans for us to hang out with Gina and my brother, Jeremy, tonight. We were going to have dinner, then go to a movie. I so often ended up feeling like the third wheel with them now with Max gone. Gina still wanted to do things with me, but also with her boyfriend, who happened to be my brother. It wasn't awkward, necessarily, but it did often highlight the fact that I wished Max lived much closer than over two hours away in Washington, DC.

I set my purse down and waited for him to hang up so I could kiss him good-bye now. Knowing how this worked, I assumed he'd probably be on the road before I returned from the mansion. We might have to talk about our relationship soon. While I enjoyed my independence, I also enjoyed him and his company. If things kept going well for him, then I might need to make some decisions.

I gulped at the thought of moving to DC. I had no idea what I'd do there, and I didn't want to leave all my family, but I couldn't expect him to give up his job. This was not something I wanted to be thinking about right now when I needed all my concentration in order to work out how to do such things as stripping wallpaper and cleaning like a fiend.

He finally said good-bye to whomever he was speaking to, and I swooped in on him before he had completely ended the call. *Better to make it quick,*

I thought. I'd see him again. I didn't know when, but it would happen.

"Okay, you gotta go. Love you, be safe, and have a good trip. Make sure to let me know when you can maybe come back up here," I told him. I turned to leave, because I wasn't going to be able to do this for a whole lot longer without at least one tear leaking from my burning eyes.

"That ready to get rid of me, huh?" He tried to pull me onto his lap, and I resisted . . . well, at least for a second. If this took too long, I wasn't above flying down the back country road in my old Lexus, if necessary. A minute late to the mansion wouldn't make or break this job, I hoped. However, Max was more important than showing up exactly on time.

"No, of course not. But I'm trying not to be that girlfriend that nags about you not being here enough or whatever." I had spent too much time before being told I was a nag and so many other negative things. While I fully knew that my ex-husband, Waldo, had just been a jerk, some of those criticisms still stuck in my head. Needless to say, I avoided nagging at all costs.

Max kissed me square on the mouth and then laughed against my lips. "You could never be a nag."

"Oh, you'd be surprised . . ."

"About many things, but not that. Now, I don't want to be the boyfriend who asks too much . . . but the job is actually in Harrisburg, and I was wondering if I could stay here for the next month."

I whooped and laughed and hugged him tight. Then I ran out of the apartment above my parents' funeral home, feeling lighter than I had in a long time. I'd tell him how much fun this was going to be after I went through the mansion and made my list of things to do and who would do them, and then we'd celebrate with my brother and my hopefully soon-to-be sister-in-law. Life was good, so very good.

Of course, I still might have to deal with Preston, if he decided to be a truly poor loser and show up at the mansion, even though he was unwanted, but nothing could dampen my happy right now. Nothing!

With only a few minutes to spare, I ran to my car and hopped in. After cranking the key in the ignition, I put on my seat belt and checked behind me so I wouldn't hit the hearse my dad had parked in close after yesterday's funeral.

Something banged on my driver's side window, and I almost peed myself. I whipped my head around so fast, I nearly gave myself whiplash. My fight-or-flight instinct was set on high fight.

Only to find Gina at the window, grinning like a loon.

She enjoyed catching me off guard, the brat. I debated not rolling down the window and just letting her stand there, but then I saw the to-go coffee cup in her hand and the bag, which surely contained some kind of breakfast goody. I wasn't stupid.

"You almost killed me," I said after I rolled down the window. Then I frowned at her when she laughed.

"I did not. Don't exaggerate. I thought you might like this, since I know today is a big day. When you didn't stop by, I figured you were running late or something had come up." She was perky and pretty and my best friend, and not only because she brought me delicious food and made the best coffee.

Still, I scoffed at her, as you did with your best friends. "I'm not going to be late. I'll get there right on time." She scoffed back, and I ignored her. "Anyway, I was held up because Max has a new assignment, which he has to start tomorrow."

Gina's face fell into a frown. "Bummer. I'm sorry, Tallie. I wish he could stay longer."

It was my turn to grin like a loon. "The assignment is right across the river, so he's going to be here for a month."

She whooped, and I whooped back. "That's awesome. We'll have to do lots of fun stuff to show him what he's missing when he goes back to that small place he has in DC."

I thought about telling her my whole line of waffling about moving down there, but that would take far longer than the two minutes I had left.

"We'll talk after I win the job cleaning the Astercromb mansion. Are we on for dinner tonight?"

"You bet. Jeremy will be there, too. Maybe we can play some games. You haven't been thrashed at a board game in quite some time. I might need to drag out the ones from the back that you don't know how to play."

"I don't think you could dredge up something I don't know how to play. Besides, we're going to the movies tonight, like adults, remember?"

"Ha! I'll consider the game night a challenge for a later date, then, since we have a whole month." She leaned on my windowsill, with her chin in her upturned hand. "Are you really ready to take on this cleaning job? It's a whole lot more than you've ever done before."

"I wish I knew how much more. I'm still waiting for pictures to download into my phone from last night, and Bethany never got back to me about emailing them. I like her, but I'm a little afraid I shouldn't have taken a chance on her."

"It'll be fine. Your girl Letty is a good judge of character, especially since she didn't like her previous employer, Darla. I'm sure everything will work out okay." That previous employer was the first dead body I'd ever found, and it had placed me directly in the sights of the chief of police in our little town when I got involved in the investigation. I'd hired Letty after Darla's husband expected her to fill in for Darla and do everything that Darla had done but with no increase in pay. I'd never regretted that decision.

"I hope so. I've got a pretty reliable crew. We still need a name, but I've got them, and we will be able to pull it off."

"If anyone can, it's you."

I laughed, grabbed the coffee and the bakery bag, then waved good-bye. As I carefully maneuvered my way around the hearse, I made my game plan. Details and plans started coming together as I took a sip of the wonderful whoopie pie latte Gina had made for me.

I really was blessed with the most fabulous people around me. I had Max, who was my heart; Gina, my best friend; and my employee and friend Letty. They were all very important to me. And then there was my family, who alternately made me laugh and groan. I had a crew to clean while I figured out what I wanted to be when I finally grew up. Life didn't get much better than this.

And once I figured out what exactly the mansion needed, I could make some serious headway on making my own dreams come true. I only wished I had gotten those pictures from Bethany. Hopefully, she had actually sent them. I had been leery about hiring her, but Letty had been insistent. We'd just see what happened when I caught up with her in a few days, after her vacation with her boyfriend.

I flew down the back roads, keeping an eye out for any one of the four cops we had in my little town in central Pennsylvania. I did not need a speeding ticket, and I couldn't afford the chunk of time that would be wasted if I got one. I stayed right at the speed limit, just in case.

Thankfully, I made it with one minute to go. Of course, Preston was already there, chatting up the owner, Mrs. Petrovski. I boiled for a moment, until I saw Audra there, too, with her sparkly long fingernails flicking back and forth as she talked and then threw her head back to laugh. They were all laughing at something that was obviously hilarious. Mrs. Petrovski's silver hair glinted in the sun, and Audra's nails nearly blinded me. Perhaps between the three of us, we could just make Preston go away.

Only once before had I been tempted to shove a toilet-cleaning brush down someone's throat, and I would not let myself be tempted today. Preston had irritated me in the past with his shenanigans and his cruelty, and he'd threatened me in the present. My future was in my own hands. I'd like to see him do his worst.

I would be the bigger person. I would get this contract. Audra was part of a huge commercial cleaning company, and so she could have a ton of other jobs in a heartbeat. She'd be fine. Preston, though, needed to step off.

I played it nice and pasted on my best smile before getting out of the car. I did not, however, pass up the chance to flash my biggest smile as I handed Mrs. Petrovski the fragrant and still warm pastry in the bag Gina had given me.

Let the games begin.

Three hours had passed since my jubilation over having Max here for the next month. And that feeling had been tested more than once in those three hours, as I had walked through room after room, making notes on what had to be done and how to do it. Today's task was to clean one room and one room alone to prove our skills, but I had wanted the lay of the land in the mansion before I got down to business.

This would have been so much easier if I had received those pictures from Bethany. They still hadn't downloaded in my phone, but being in the middle of the chaos made it all too real. The only thing I could think of was that every room must have been decorated by someone who was on some serious hallucinogens.

About two years ago, Mrs. Petrovski had allowed a group of designers to come in and do each room in a different theme and style to bring attention to the mansion. The designers had done just that, but not in the way she had hoped for. The interest hadn't lasted, and the mansion had never re-opened either as a house or as an inn.

The room I had been given to clean, which I was currently standing in, was indicative of the whole place. The walls were adorned with several different kinds of wallpaper, all patched together like a quilt. It appeared the decorator had then applied a layer of veneer over every wall and the ceiling.

Somehow the owner expected me to strip off the veneer and the wallpaper throughout the entire room and then clean it so that all the surfaces were pristine. Or as pristine as was possible to achieve in one day, to show off my skills in cleaning.

Since we hadn't even been given a quick glance at the mansion before we were told to clean our one room and ready it for inspection, we had not known what exactly we might be facing. I'd brought everything I could think of with me, just in case.

Thank God for my foresight.

No matter how many times I wanted to walk away from that veneer and wallpaper, I managed to cling to my jubilation and the thought that this job could mean big things for me and Letty and the other ladies.

And no matter how many times Preston came in to heckle me, he couldn't take the shine off my smile. My biggest question at the moment wasn't, what might cover the cracks in the wall, but why on earth was he here in my eye-popping room every ten minutes?

"What do you want?" I asked on his seventeenth visit. Should I go complain to Mrs. Petrovski and ask her to make this irritating man leave? My subtle hinting and my physically bumping him out of the way with my hip this morning had made no dent in his resolve to stay. Maybe if I was more direct, he would disappear.

"Just wanted to see what you are doing." He leaned against the doorway in another overdone vest, this one with peacocks all over it, and what could only be called a cravat. It wasn't a bow tie or a regular tie or even an ascot. It was a full-on cravat. Who did that anymore outside of a Renaissance faire?

Not my question to ask, and I really didn't want to know. Heck, I didn't want to engage him at all. I wanted him gone so I could go back to using my claw-like paper ripper and my vinegar-and-water solution to unglue the stuff on the walls. I was trying to see how hard this was going to be by sampling each wall and putting the details into my tablet.

At this point, I was so dirty, I couldn't even remember if I'd worn a blue or a green T-shirt, and my jeans would probably need to be washed at least two times before I could wear them again. Preston's fashion and neck adornment choices were low on my need-to-know list.

"Same thing I was doing ten minutes ago and ten minutes before that," I answered in hopes that he might go away. "What are you doing here? You aren't the owner. Your aunt is. And last I heard, she had total say over who gets this job. From where I'm standing, you have no reason to be hanging out. I have things to do and no time to spend with you and your inability to give up when you've been beaten."

"You think you've got this in the bag, Tallie, but you don't. You might as well just save yourself the time and the energy and go home to that little boyfriend of yours."

I leaned on my broom. "You must be terrified that I'm going to take this job and run with it. Why else would you keep stopping in when you could be doing something else, anything else, like getting your own job elsewhere?"

He huffed away after muttering something I couldn't hear, and I got back to work. Wallpaper was stripped, and corners were cleaned. The walls weren't as bad as I'd thought, thankfully. Beyond that, I would worry about the other rooms when I got the job.

I wanted to nail this and get Letty and friends into a place where I could really begin to make my own dreams come true. My sole employee for months had told me that her friends were jealous of her setup with me a few months ago and had wanted to know if they could come in under my umbrella. I had said yes and now I handled all the money and the paperwork, and in return I had a small army of top-notch cleaners. Not something I had ever really thought I'd do, but there was a certain sense to it that I could see from both our perspectives.

A particularly cobwebby corner caught my eye. I reached for my special hand duster and realized I had forgotten it in the car. Running down to the car would take only a few minutes. I had exactly nine before Preston decided to check back in with me.

I waved to the owner on my way out, then booked it back up to my room within five minutes. Only to find myself standing in the middle of destruction where there should have been cleanliness. What had been a clean room now had garbage strewn across the floor. What looked like kitchen scraps littered the wooden planks, with coffee grounds mixed in for good measure. Pieces of paper and paper towels and toilet tissue clogged up the corners of the room. Some sort of wood pulp or chips speckled the paper products, and then there were the plastic bags—like someone had emptied the bag collection bin at the grocery store and just dumped all the bags in here willy-nilly.

I'd come into the room I'd left five minutes ago to find that Preston Prescott had done his very best in that short amount of time to mess up everything I'd worked so hard to clean.

He didn't like me; I got that. To clean a mansion that had been sitting empty for years would be a real achievement and a gold star on any cleaning service résumé. He and I had had several run-ins when we'd both traveled in the same circles. I knew he was a jerk. But to be this deliberately cruel, this underhanded, this manipulative was even more than I had thought he had in him.

I had worked on this room assiduously, and Preston had apparently decided that I had done too good a job, because he had come in to mess it up.

His words had been irritating enough, but this was too much.

Without thinking, I stalked out of the room, spray bottle full of vinegar and hot water in hand, and headed one floor up, where I'd last heard him tromping around. He was going to get it and get it good, right in the face. I fumed, muttering under my breath with every stomp of my sneakers.

He'd be lucky if I didn't choke him with his own cravat.

I paused in the hallway outside the room, though, and took a deep breath. Attacking him physically would only be lowering myself below even his level.

Instead, I decided we would have words. Even if it killed me, I would keep my hands and my spray bottle to myself. But we would have words, and then I was immediately going to talk with the owner about the underhandedness going on here. Once I got through the horrible swaths of gauze that some previous decorator must have thought was the height of hallway decorating fashion.

Chapter Three

"**P**reston Prescott, you are in some serious trouble," I said as I stepped into the room and found myself face-to-face with someone who was definitely not Preston. Instead, I found another woman, and not Audra, either. Whereas Audra had blond hair and was shorter than me, this woman had to be almost six inches taller and had jet-black hair. She was willow thin, with an almost elfin face.

Her smile, wavering at the corners of her lips, was filled with nerves. As if she wasn't supposed to be here. So had she been wrecking Audra's handiwork while Preston had been wrecking mine? What kind of shenanigans were all these people up to? I'd never dealt with such ridiculousness, even when I was part of the highbrow crowd.

But the room behind her was far cleaner than any other in the rest of this house, and the cleaning person was much further along than I had been even before Prescott pulled his stunt as Destructo.

"Who are you?" I asked when she just continued to stare at me without saying anything. Her eyes wide with fear, she kept running her hand through the ends of her hair and flicking her forefinger over her thumb. After I posed my question, she rapidly glanced left and right, as if she was looking for someone or for a way out.

"I just want to know who you are. I'm not going to do anything. Are you here to clean?" I said. I even put my hands out to show her I came in peace. Unfortunately, I had the spray bottle still, and that set her back a step.

Not the most effective way to show I came in peace.

But was she with Prescott? Audra? Or was she one of the people who had been shut out of the possibility of this job, and had she ruined my room and then come to ruin Audra's out of spite?

The woman tucked a long strand of inky black hair behind her ear and scuffed her shoe on the floor. "I help Preston sometimes. I was just in here cleaning so Audra could get stuff done somewhere else. He asked me to make sure she had everything she needed."

Audra had help? And Preston had given it to her? We weren't supposed to have help. It was very clearly stated in our contracts that this was supposed to be a solo job, so we could show them what we could do alone. Then we could bring in help later.

Now I was fuming, again. Beyond fuming, to be

exact, though I didn't have the right word to express that.

So not only had Preston threatened me and ruined my room, but now he was also helping Audra? I was absolutely going straight to the owner and getting this whole thing out in the open.

"I'll be back," I said to the woman.

"Oh, please, don't say anything," she begged, grabbing my arm and yanking me to a halt.

I pointedly looked at her hand and then into her eyes. "You're going to want to let me go. Right now."

"Please. Please don't say anything. I don't want to get in trouble. And I don't want Audra to get in trouble with the owner. I need the money, and Preston won't pay me if she doesn't get this job."

"And because you were so afraid you might not get this job, you're the one who messed up my room?"

She blinked five times. I counted as I waited for her response. "Gosh, no. I don't know why anyone would do that."

I couldn't tell if she was being serious or was totally snowing me. I didn't really care. I just wanted to talk to the owner and get this taken care of.

"Let me go." I squinted at her as I jerked my arm out of her grip, but then I felt horrible when I saw tears falling from her eyes and running down her cheeks.

I left her quietly sobbing as I swept out the door and into the hallway, which was swathed in black, red, and white gauze from floor to ceiling. My steps faltered when I was halfway through the maze of fabric.

Was I doing the right thing? I knew how it was to struggle for money. Heck, I was still struggling. And if this woman was desperate for money, then maybe she didn't have any other choice than to work for Audra. And I was going to make things worse by going and complaining to the owner and taking away their chances.

But *I* wasn't going to have a chance if the owner saw the disaster Preston had made of my room, and it wasn't fair to let it slide. I had never been a doormat. I certainly wasn't going to start now.

I picked up my pace and stopped by my own room before approaching the owner. I needed pictures of the destruction to be able to show her. And I needed to come up with the right words to tell her about all the work I had done before Preston and his cravat had come in like a cyclone. Again.

Thirty minutes later I still hadn't found the owner. She'd been right in the living room when I'd zoomed through with my special hand duster, but now that I needed her, she was nowhere to be found.

With my luck lately, I wouldn't be overly surprised at finding her stabbed in the kitchen or shot in the billiards room.

I went through the three floors quickly but thoroughly, even braving the basement and the attic, before buzzing by Audra's room again. This time she was in there, but the other girl was nowhere to be found. I flicked a wave at her since I was still incensed that she had help, thanks to Preston, but I didn't stop.

Finally, I went back to my room, and there was Mrs. Petrovski. The frown on her face spoke volumes when she turned around, and right next to her was her nephew Preston.

I started talking before I'd completely cleared the doorway. "This looks bad. I know it looks bad. But I didn't do it."

With her arms crossed tight at her chest, she radiated disapproval. "Ms. Graver, this is unacceptable. You and Ms. McNeal were handpicked to compete for this contract, and I see no evidence that you've given this room your best attention. You might have money from your previous marriage and feel that it's beneath you to clean, but I take this business very seriously, and you are not."

I opened my mouth to defend myself, but she rolled right over me.

"Because you are not, I'm taking you out of the running and giving the job to Ms. McNeal. Preston brought this to my attention, and I'm sorry that I didn't take his advice more to heart when he first expressed concerns about you being here. I don't need your services. I will not say anything to your other clients about your deplorable attitude. Perhaps they already know it, and that is why so many are moving over and using Ms. McNeal's services."

That stopped my brain in its efforts to come up with a retort. How many clients did she think were moving over to Audra's service? As far as I knew, no one had dropped me in order to hire Audra's cleaning service. We weren't even in the same kind of cleaning business. Audra did companies and huge buildings with multiple suites. I did small businesses, like inns, and family homes. Everyone I normally cleaned for had continued to book me and had kept their regular contracts. Even those whose socks I hated to find in the sofa.

I took a split second to breathe through my first response, which was outrage, and clasped my hands in front of me.

After one more breath, I said, "I'm sorry you feel that way, ma'am. I was making good progress and had cleaned most of the walls before someone"—I looked pointedly at Preston, who responded to my angry glare with a smirk—"came in and destroyed my room. I provide a good and useful service to my many clients. I've never had any complaints."

I went on. "You'll want to check in on Ms. McNeal before you give her the contract, because I know for a fact she did not clean that room on her own. She had help, which was provided by someone else in an effort to discredit me. This person also continued to come into my space over and over again, to ask what I was doing and how I was doing it. If you'd prefer to work with someone else instead of me and my honest crew, then all I can do is wish you good luck."

Preston's sneer and Mrs. Petrovski's disdain had me exiting the room without all my gear. I'd call her later to let her know I'd come back for it after she and her odious nephew were gone, he and his judgmental self.

The whole way home, I burned with anger. How dare Preston do that to me? How dare the owner assume that I was above cleaning? I wasn't, hadn't been in all the time since I left Waldo. And I certainly didn't have money left over from the divorce to do anything, so I could hardly turn up my nose at honest work.

Driving through town, I fumed and muttered to myself and probably looked like a crazy person. That was not so different from the usual, so I didn't worry about it.

I did worry about having to tell Letty and her friends that we had lost out on the job. I had wanted to return triumphant and be able to hand them a job that we could all chip in on together. That obviously wasn't going to happen.

Letty's mom had passed two months ago, and so my friend no longer had to worry about splitting herself between helping the poor woman and trying to clean. Of course she was sad, but after all her mother had gone through, she almost felt relief now that her mother was at peace. We'd done a lovely service for her at my father's expense. Letty had been grateful and had taken on more work as the cleaning side of my life had rocketed due to recommendations and referrals. I hadn't been sure that would ever happen after I had married Waldo, turned into a jerk, and then swan-dived from grace by divorcing him. Re-entering the tight-knit community after the way I had turned my back on them to get married had been iffy after my divorce. But after I had eaten tons of crow, it was almost as if people trusted me again not to be a stupid idiot. I had truly been enjoying that, until Mrs. Petrovski and Preston had decided to throw acid on my parade.

Now I'd have to go back and make excuses and

tell Letty that it was my fault we hadn't gotten the job. That stuck in my craw.

I'd figure something out, though. Something that would make up for it.

I did wish Mrs. Petrovski the best of luck, if not her nephew. However, I had a feeling things were not going to go exactly as she hoped they would. Then again, if Preston had a secret brigade to whom he paid little money but they worked their rear ends off, then Audra could clean a lot faster and make a good living at the same time. Good for her, but Lady Karma was not often a very nice person. I hadn't realized Audra and Preston knew each other, but apparently, they did. Either that or he would have helped anyone that wasn't me. The latter was the more probable scenario.

In the meantime, a sign caught my eye as I drove. My store was for sale. It was no longer just a rumor; it truly was for sale, like, right now. After bringing my car to a squealing halt, I pulled up to the curb to look through the dusty windows. My heart thudded in my chest with anticipation as I climbed out of the car.

Right there next to the front door was a stack of flyers with the price and the details. I grabbed one and clutched it to my chest. So first, I'd talk to Max about my disappointment with the way the mansion cleaning had gone, but then I was going to shout in jubilation about the store being available. After that, I'd get down to brass tacks about how to make it happen.

I might not be able to offer Letty a mansion to clean, but I could have her and her friends work in the tea shop as well as step back from cleaning altogether and just let them take all the cleaning jobs I would no longer be able to handle due to the fact that I'd be running the store.

Then, when my jubilation time was over, I'd go back to the mansion to get my stuff and I'd call that a missed opportunity. Sometimes those opportunities ended up being for the best. And if Preston had had no qualms about messing up a room so I wouldn't get the job, I shivered to think what he might have done if I'd beaten my contender. Burned the mansion to the ground?

I'd experienced one vindictive fire already, and it had not been pretty. Knowing that the person who had set it was crazy had not helped things, especially when I had been caught in a fight for my life.

Was Preston that vindictive and used to getting his way? I didn't know, and at this point I didn't have to find out. Score for me.

Second score for me was when Max opened the door to my apartment on the third floor, above my parents' funeral home, and the smell of garlic and Italian spices wafted out from behind him. Having him here for a month was going to be divine for my mental health and well-being.

Not so much for my hips, but I didn't care.

Chapter Four

After plopping into a chair at my small kitchen table in the apartment, I stroked Peanut's head while she sat patiently waiting to see if I'd drop anything on the floor for her. I probably wouldn't, since I tried hard not to give her table food, but sometimes her big brown eyes just did me in.

Max set in front of me a plate of noodles and various veggies covered in olive oil and garlic and liberally sprinkled with Parmesan cheese. What an amazing lunch after a horrible morning. A basket of delicious-looking bread with melted cheese followed and a glass of soda. This man was a keeper.

Now all I had to do was decide if I wanted to rant about Preston first or bring up the exciting news about the store next to Gina's.

Max smiled at me, and I went for asking him how his day was before I had a spirited back-and-forth on the best and worst day of my life.

"Good," he answered, putting cheesy bread on my plate and smiling at me again. Those dimples, that twinkle in his eyes, the way he looked at me as if I was precious instead of someone to be tolerated . . . I was fully in love, and I had not a single regret about anything that had led me to this very moment with this very man.

"Just good?" I took two more pieces of cheesy bread just in case. I knew for a fact that he was not above cleaning out the food he loved before I had a chance to have a second helping. The underhandedness and trickery that ensued especially when snickerdoodle cookies were around could be astounding.

He smiled at my bread plate with its three cheesy breads and then went on. "Yes, good. I won't be more than fifteen minutes away from the job, and the hours are at my discretion, as long as I hit about forty a week. So we can do all kinds of things." He shrugged as he put his own plate on the table and took a seat. "Or nothing, if we just want to hang out. It won't feel like we have to cram everything into the limited time we have. It's going to be good."

"Not great," I said with a half smile.

"I guess that remains to be seen. You might get sick of me being around all the time. Maybe things have worked out so well up to this point because we aren't in each other's pockets day in and day out. You always know I'm going home, maybe right before I would get annoying." He dipped his cheesy bread into his buttery noodles, then smiled at me as he chewed.

Was he kidding? Maybe he was, and maybe he

wasn't. I couldn't imagine that we'd get sick of each other. I really hoped he was kidding. I'd prove that things worked well between us. I had a month to do so.

When it was my turn to describe my day, I started with the cleaning job debacle to get the yuck out of the way. He made the right noises and told me exactly what I'd already been telling myself. Something better was on the horizon. Things would turn out as they should. Karma was going to come for Preston, and I did not need to be there to see it. I just needed to protect what was already mine and let the rest go.

"Thanks for listening," I told Max. "See, that wasn't so bad, was it? Talking about mundane things."

"Tallie, things with you are always anything but mundane."

"I hope that's a good thing, because the next topic is something I'm very curious about."

"Let me brace myself." He chuckled. "Should I go get snickerdoodles to help us through? Did you stumble across another dead body?"

I launched a balled-up napkin at him. "No, this is really good news, and there are no dead people involved." None at all, not even at the funeral home, if I could plan this right. The tea shop would be my whole job, taking the place of part-time cleaning work and part-time work at the funeral home.

"What is this great news?"

"The space next to Gina is for sale. I want to run the numbers to see what it might take for me to buy the building and open my own tea shop."

Ever ready, I pulled a spreadsheet from my back

pocket. I carried the thing with me often just to remind myself that my current reality of cleaning and funeral-home work did not have to be my permanent reality.

"What's this?" Max reached across the table for the paper, then raised an eyebrow at my many lines on the spreadsheet. I'd tried to think of everything that I might need. I'd done a ton of research into distributors and suppliers, but I had no idea how to put things together to make it work.

I sat on my hands so as not to take the spreadsheet back from him. "My projections. I've been waiting for this space to open, listening to rumors, and patiently hoping the owners would finally put it up for sale. Now that it's on the market, I'm almost happy I didn't get the mansion job. This way I can work toward this tea shop instead."

"Pen?" He stared at the spreadsheet, with his hand out. I could almost see his brain spinning in his head. Was that a good thing or a bad thing for me?

Seconds later, the only sound in the apartment was the scratching of Max's pen across my beloved paper. Two minutes later, I groaned into the silence.

"Really?" I stared at the astronomical amount he'd written on the paper. I would not be able to do this. Ever.

"Really. Now, you could get loans and have payments to get this all done, but you might want to make absolutely sure you're committed to this before you spend that amount. And you'll be eating cheap, cheap food for a lot of years, while it gets off the ground."

I sighed.

He gave me a smile and patted my hand. "It can be done, though. We can make a budget and make sure it happens. It's just going to take some hard work and some creative thinking when it comes to money and your creature comforts."

Yeah, like my Murphy bed, which pulled out from the wall, and my life on top of a funeral home, in an apartment that really seemed a ton smaller with each passing day. Or the old Lexus I drove. Or the minimal amount of clothing I had in my closet. I wasn't sure where I'd cut any creature comforts, because I wasn't sure there were any corners left to cut.

"Oh." I took the paper back reluctantly and was sad that I'd given Max a red pen. It looked like all my dreams were dead or dying. Or bleeding at least.

"Come on, Tallie. I didn't mean to make you sad. If you really want this, it's doable. You just have to decide if it's worth it to you. What will you get out of a tea shop? Do you want it badly enough to make the sacrifices that Gina makes? She works all the time, and owning your own business means little to no traveling, unless you have a staff you can trust, or unless you're willing to close down for the days you are gone."

Apparently, I needed some new lines on my spreadsheet. I'd call them "pros" and "What the heck was I thinking!"

Max touched the back of my hand again. "I don't want to ruin your dream."

"Meh." I shrugged.

My phone dinged. It was Letty texting me to ask about the mansion. I paused to read her text, but I wasn't ready to answer. I hadn't told her we'd lost the job yet. I'd get around to it.

"See? I'm already irritating you." He sat back in his chair with a sigh.

Straightening my shoulders, I folded the paper and placed it next to my plate. "Actually, no, you're not. I just didn't think it all the way through. I still need to do that, and we'll see from there. Thanks for the reality check. I really do appreciate it."

"I feel like I should make it up to you."

I laughed. "No, not at all. A tea shop is not actually my lifelong dream, now that I see the reality of what it would take. At this point, anything that is not working at the funeral home has the potential to be a dream, so just ignore my spontaneous bouts of jubilation when it comes to new ideas."

After leaning forward, he placed his elbows on the table. "I like your jubilation. Are things not going well with cleaning right now?"

I shrugged. "Other than this thing with Preston, it's actually a very good job and business."

"But you don't want to stick with it?"

Good question. "I honestly don't know. I guess I just never saw myself doing this for the rest of my life. It's a good job, honest work. When I was younger, I never really thought about what I wanted to be, only what I didn't want to be, namely, part of the funeral home. Cleaning doesn't make it possible for me to quit at the funeral home, so I thought I'd go big."

"There's time to figure it out. You're in a good spot at this time, right? Or there's always the possibility of working for someone else. Letting them pay all the taxes. Plus, you'd also get paid personal time off and benefits."

"True." But he laughed at the way my face scrunched up. And all this was something I'd have to think about. After the issues and troubles Gina had experienced over the years with a coffeehouse, what did I want with a tea shop? Why a teashop? Definitely things to think about. And I had time to do that. Beyond that, I couldn't commit myself to a tea shop if I was going to be moving to DC at some point in the near future. If things kept moving in the way they were going with Max, that was a definite possibility.

Max's voice brought me back from my own mind. "Then take the time and see where you're at. We can work with the numbers until you've fallen asleep. I don't mind working through them with you. It could be interesting to see what it takes to start up a business."

I'd done it before with the cleaning business, though for the most part, I had just put myself out there with the previous friends I'd had in that upper-crust circle and begged to clean their houses. I had added new tools of the trade as I realized they were needed, but the most expensive thing I had bought was the vacuum cleaner. A tea shop would entail refrigerators and tables and chairs and silverware and plates and cups and food. . . . And I couldn't think about it anymore.

"Speaking of which, I need to go get my vacuum cleaner," I said. "We have time to think about all this. I really appreciate your expertise."

He came across the table to kiss me. "Don't give

up just yet. There might be a way to make this happen for you. We just haven't come up with the right scenario yet."

"I appreciate it, Max. I'm not sure what I want to do, to be honest. I guess I never really thought too much about anything other than my need for money."

He hugged me and kissed the top of my head. "Go get your vacuum cleaner, and we'll go from there. Don't worry about the rest of it now. We can return to this topic when we run out of other things to talk about."

I couldn't do anything but laugh. I doubted we'd run out of things to talk about. And I definitely wouldn't run out of things to think about.

The tea shop would take far more than I was willing to give right now, but it was still in the back of my mind. How much more would take some number crunching, which I didn't have time to do at the moment.

I had to get back to the mansion and get my gear now that everyone had probably left. Audra was getting the job, but it wouldn't start until tomorrow, judging from the information given to me before I got booted out.

The sun was setting on this dreary March day, and I was ready to clear my stuff out of this place and never see it again except in passing. As I pulled up in front of the large powder-blue building, my heart clenched. This would have been such a great opportunity for me and my crew to really show the community that we could do bigger buildings and take on more than private jobs. Recently, developers had started building housing developments on the outskirts of town. Cleaning the model homes that people walked through would be an excellent add-on to our business. I needed an add-on if I wanted that tea shop, or even if I just wanted to cut down my hours at the funeral home. Plus, I wanted to help Letty and her friends. Heck, I needed the add-on to do more than just make ends meet.

Despite what Mrs. Petrovski thought, I was not above anything. And I was far more caring and willing to do whatever it took to help my crew and my situation. I might have been high and mighty long ago—well, more like high and stupid—but those days were over. I'd changed.

After parking in the driveway, I looked up at the mansion. It was a monstrosity, with thousands of square feet and endless potential. The rumor around town was that Mrs. Petrovski was trying to sell it even though it had been in her family for three generations. Maybe someone would buy it and turn it into another bed-and-breakfast. We already had two, but the area could probably handle another. And it was far enough out of the way; there were miles between the other two and this one. It could be magnificent, with its gardens and the lovely gazebo out back. Or at least it would be once it was cleaned out and spiffed up.

Right now there was more peeling paint than not, and weeds had overgrown the edges of the porch. My brother, Dylan, had already told me he'd love a chance to come in and do the yard work as part of his landscaping business. Gina knew tons of teenagers willing to paint for a fair price. I could have made something here, and now it was lost because of Preston and his venomous and underhanded ways.

I wished there was something else I could have done to get the contract for us. We'd figure it out. I would do everything in my power to make sure we did. This house would have boosted our credentials, though.

After closing the car door behind me, I pulled the key for the mansion from my pocket and walked slowly up the stairs. I'd leave the key in the mailbox when I was done and text Mrs. Petrovski to let her know where it was. That was as much as I was willing to do after the way she'd treated me.

The whole place shone in my mind. If only I'd been given the chance to let loose my army of stellar ladies. We could have stripped the wallpaper and cleaned the walls and painted and buffed and made this place shine. The floors would have been clean enough to eat off, and the windows would have shone like they'd just been put in, even though they were over a hundred years old. Instead, Audra had been given the opportunity to clean the mansion, all because Preston hated me, not because she was better than me. Man, did that chap my hide.

But there was nothing I could do about it. I'd placed a call to Mrs. Petrovski an hour ago, and she had refused to answer and had sent me to voice mail after only one ring.

I unlocked the door, then entered the house and called out in case anyone was still here. No one answered, so I figured I was alone.

Climbing the stairs to the second floor, I let my feet drag as I fought the urge to mess up the whole place, like Preston had messed up my room. That would be beneath me, though, and Mrs. Petrovski had other properties. Not that she'd let me do anything, since she thought I was stuck-up.

That too chapped my hide.

Once I got to my room, I entered it and then just stood, looking around. I had done good work before that jerk had come in with his garbage and his viciousness. I had been right to call him a venomous snake last night.

I picked up the bucket and the caddy I'd finally bought for myself. It was just like the one I always kidded Letty I was going to take from her. I took my squeegee and my sponges and my clawed paper ripper and put them in the caddy. I guess I had to be thankful that no one had taken my things or thrown them in the trash.

I had spoken too soon, though, because I couldn't for the life of me find my beloved vacuum cleaner. I looked in the closet and even put on some gloves to go through the mountain of trash on the floor. Nothing. I loved that vacuum cleaner, and I had paid a pretty penny for it.

After resting my head against the window glass to take a deep breath before I screamed, I glanced down and saw my precious vacuum cleaner in the freaking Dumpster below. Had he opened the window and chucked the thing out? *Oh my God.*

After hauling my load down the stairs, I threw it in the back of my car and then scaled the side of the Dumpster. I didn't care if the vacuum was broken. I wanted it, and I wanted to bring my baby home with me. I was furious. Furious enough to want to hurl myself over the side of the Dumpster to get the vacuum, but not stupid enough to actually do it and hurt myself. With my luck, I'd get stuck in there, covered in aged plasterboard and wood shavings.

I carefully shifted my leg over the side of the metal monstrosity. Straddling the metal lip, I judged the distance to the rolled-up carpet to the left of my vacuum cleaner. It wasn't too far from me, and I could jump on the thing to launch myself back up to the lip of the six-foot-tall Dumpster once I had my vacuum under my arm.

I jumped and landed on the carpet on the first try, thankfully, then scrambled across the entire length of the backing to grab the vacuum. I tucked the thing under my arm, then climbed back across the carpet toward the edge of the Dumpster. Keeping the cord in one hand, I pushed the vacuum up and over the lip, hoping I didn't break it as it went down to the ground. I slowly lowered the vacuum over the side of the Dumpster and waited until it softly thudded against the packed dirt on the other side.

I wasn't short, but the lip was just out of reach from the inside of the Dumpster. I could do this. I jumped a couple times on the carpet and tried to launch myself, but I missed when I tried to grab the lip of the Dumpster and smacked my chin on the cold metal. *Ow.* That hurt. A lot.

Resting for a moment, I got my breath back and the stars out of my eyes. Moments later, I crawled back to the carpet and tried again. I could do this. I was not going to get stuck in a Dumpster. If nothing worked, I could always call Max and ask him to come get me out, but I really didn't want to do that. I could do this on my own. I was a big girl. Literally. I did not need help.

After I pulled myself to the edge of the carpet, I got to my feet again. Looking up, I gauged the distance I would have to jump. It was longer than I had originally thought. Of course it was. When did anything ever work out the way I thought it would?

I glanced up at the rim of the Dumpster again and then down at the carpet and saw something I hadn't registered before while I was trying to get out of this mess.

There was a hand sticking out of the end of the carpet. A hand. I frantically searched my mind for what it might be and tried to keep my cool. There had been a mannequin in one of the rooms. I distinctly remembered that. A mannequin that had no arms, to my recollection. *Okay. Not the mannequin.*

Maybe it wasn't really a hand. It could be some kind of glove from Audra's team. Yeah, it could totally be a glove, and I was seeing things that weren't there. I had to be.

Except when I took another step toward the edge of the carpet and the hand, I saw that it was most definitely not a glove. Not unless gloves now came equipped with really long nails that sparkled in the light of the afternoon sun.

Chapter Five

Oh my word!
I clamped my hand over my mouth. Was Audra rolled up in the carpet? Could my newish friend be dead and wrapped up tight like a burrito? *Oh my word!* I did not just find another dead body. I didn't. I couldn't. Karma did not always play fair, and I tried to find the silver lining in any hand I'd been dealt, but I felt my bile rising, like I was going to puke.

Oh my word!

The nails were the clincher. I didn't know anyone else who had those nails. I remembered them from last night, when she smoothed her dress around her waist as she stood in the lobby with us at the theater. And now I most definitely had to get out of this garbage bin. Although I thought I should probably check to see if the hand with the nails was attached to a wrist. Because a dead person was one thing, but a severed hand was something altogether different. And if the wrist had a pulse, that would be even better.

Squinching my eyes closed—I didn't know why I did that, but I did—I pulled the hand a little farther out of the carpet and was thankful that the wrist and part of the forearm were still attached. There was resistance, which meant that the whole thing was attached to the body, or at least I hoped so. Although, really, was that any better? It still meant she was dead.

I could feel myself shutting down inside to be able to deal with being in a Dumpster with a dead body. I'd been near them before, happened upon them, spotted them through windows, seen them on the embalming table and in coffins. But I'd never been on top of one. My self-defenses were kicking in fast to save me from falling over and fainting, which would make this whole thing that much worse.

The hand was colder than I thought it should be if the person in this carpet was alive, but who knew how long he or she had been out here? Today the weather wasn't exactly warm, but it wasn't too cold, either.

I unsquinched my eyes enough to see if the fingernail paint job was the one I'd seen on Audra last night. Hers had been a swirl of purple and blue and a beautiful pink, with what looked like crystals embedded in the paint. This was exactly the same. I wondered how long she had had to sit in the nail tech's chair to get her nails done and how much it had cost to have what looked like real crystals.

Not that I was any kind of expert on how long nails took. And I was definitely trying to distract myself from the fact that I was perched on top of what might be a dead person in a Dumpster, one that I wasn't sure how I was going to get out of.

Okay, deep breath, I told myself.

I refocused with that deep breath, and unfortunately, that was when I saw a tattoo of a clover leaf on the inside of the wrist and the very beautiful, big ring on the ring finger. I knew that ring. I'd been shown that ring just three days ago, when Audra announced her boyfriend had proposed to her. *Oh my God.* I was going to puke.

I scrambled away, waiting to hear anything, like breathing or moaning, when I moved around on top of the carpet. Nothing. I had to go back and check for that pulse. I had to.

Forcing myself to do just that, I crept forward, held the wrist again, knowing I would find nothing, and was not surprised when a pulse did not come through her soft skin.

Oh man.

I had to get out of here and call the police and her boyfriend and her mother and Letty and . . . my God.

I scrambled away from her hand again, knowing that I was not hurting her now, but I did not want to be crouched on top of her like a vulture.

Bumping into the side of the bin, I felt a rung of metal dig into my back. I turned to find myself saved from being stuck in here by some toeholds. Even if they weren't toeholds, and I was not a climber, I was going to get out of this thing now.

I did not want Police Chief Burton out here. I did not want to have to defend myself for finding another body when I wanted to burst into tears.

My friend was dead. This woman's life had been cut short, and she would be missed.

Because there was no way she had killed herself and then wrapped herself in a carpet, or even accidentally fallen into the garbage and had the carpet wrap itself around her. There was just no way, so this was a murder, and I was out here all by myself, with no backup.

I clambered up the side of the Dumpster so fast, I almost threw myself over the edge and down onto the hard-packed dirt beneath me. But I slowed down at the top at the last second and made sure to get a good grip before hoisting my leg over the side. I dropped to the ground and ran to my car. After whipping open the door, I grabbed my phone out of the console, then hit the speed dial for the police station and waited.

"Tallie?"

My cousin Matt. *Phew.* At least it wasn't Burton, who thought I was the bane of his existence. *Great.* But where was Suzy, the receptionist, who usually answered the phone?

"There's been a death out at the Astercromb mansion. The body is in the Dumpster that was rented to clean out the house. I just found it and touched only the wrist to make sure there was no pulse. Please send someone out now."

"You almost sound scared."

"Now is not the time to mess with me, Matt. I thought it was something else. I was trying to get my vacuum, which someone threw in the garbage, and I saw a hand sticking out of a carpet. Send someone now."

"Are you still in the Dumpster?"

"No, I got out, but I don't want to stay out here. What if the killer is still out here?"

"Are you sure she was killed?"

"Uh, yeah. How else would she end up in a carpet?" I was about done with the twenty questions. I just wanted to hang up and go lock myself in the car.

A flatbed truck rumbled up the drive just as Matt said he was going to go and get the guys together to come out to the crime scene.

"Wait, wait, wait. Please stay on the phone with me. A big truck from the trash collector is coming up the drive, and I don't know who this is or why they'd be coming to pick up a big Dumpster that isn't filled yet."

Now he sounded full of business. "I'll talk to whoever the driver is."

I had never been so happy to hand over the responsibility to someone else.

The truck pulled up right in front of me, and the driver and I stared at each other for what seemed like an eternity but was probably about four-point-two seconds. I waved him out of the cab. He frowned at me and then turned the truck off.

"I thought there wasn't supposed to be anyone out here this afternoon," he said as he exited the cab. "I was told that, you understand. What are you doing here?"

I filed that info away in my brain and held the phone out. "We have a situation. I'm going to need you to talk to the police."

He backed away, with his hands up. "Don't want no trouble."

"Well, you just drove into it. Take the phone now or don't, but you're in it up to your eyeballs." And so was I.

In the end the driver talked to Matt, who must have used his idle time to call all the cops. Ten minutes after I placed the call, three cars zoomed up the lane with their lights and sirens blazing. It had taken them longer than I thought it should have, but who was I to judge?

At least this time I wasn't going to have to deal with Burton from the very beginning. My cousin Matt was a much easier prospect than the chief, who tended to roll his eyes at me and pinch the bridge of his nose.

Matt was the first to get out of the cars. The truck driver and I had been making awkward and stilted small talk, and I was incredibly relieved not to have to talk with him anymore. No one loved the cops, but this guy seemed very scared of talking to them, even over the phone. What would he do when faced with them?

"Matt," the driver, Chris Telford, said, holding out his hand.

"Chris, I didn't realize it was you. What are you doing out this way? I thought you usually did the cross-country stuff."

"Picking up some extra shifts to pay that child support. Sorry for being so abrupt on the phone. I don't need no trouble, with this custody thing going on."

Ah, made sense. But if he didn't do anything, then why was he worried? And what about the remark that no one was supposed to be out here?

Matt didn't shake my hand or even nod at me.

He just shook his head and pointed at the Dumpster. At least there was no eye rolling and nose pinching. I'd take it.

"Yes. She's in there." I answered his unspoken question with a soft voice.

I wasn't needed anymore, but I knew better than to try to leave. I used the time to call Letty, but I had to leave her a message that we'd hit a problem, though I didn't mention why or what had happened. I was trying to follow the normal guidelines of staying out of the way, not touching anything, and speaking only when spoken to that I knew Burton would have given me if he was here. Where was he anyway? I had braced myself to be yelled at, and all that adrenaline was rushing out of my body, making this girl a very tired cleaner, even though I hadn't cleaned a single thing in hours. Where had my happiness about having Max in the area for the next month gone?

God, Max. He was going to tell me to keep out of this, and I was going to try. I promised myself to do just that. But Audra was my newly gained friend, or at least that had been the direction I thought we were going in before this whole mansion thing. If I happened to come across any information related to Audra's death, then of course I would not turn it away. I'd helped a lot with the last murder in town, with the one before that, and with the two before that, too, if we were counting. Which I wasn't, but I would see justice here.

Of course Mrs. Petrovski returned my call, and I picked it up, just as I was standing outside her mansion, with the woman she'd chosen to clean it not twenty feet away from me and dead. What would this do to her project? Not that it was any of my business, especially when she'd been so mean to me. She was not happy to be talking to me now, while I was trying desperately to get off the phone before I said something I shouldn't. I'd leave the explanation to whoever had to tell her that the place was now a crime scene. Which would probably be Burton.

I should not have thought of Burton, because then, of course, he appeared, like a bogeyman, when I was still trying to get off the phone with Mrs. Petrovski.

"Yes, I'll get my things out right away," I said into the phone.

Burton glared at me. "Who are you talking to?"

"Mrs. Petrovski," I said, answering his question while also addressing the woman who would not seem to get off the phone. "I have to go. Someone's here asking questions, and I need to give them my full attention."

"What are you doing?" Burton demanded while Mrs. Petrovski squawked, "Who's there? Who's asking questions? I need to know what's going on. You don't seem to be telling me everything. I can feel it and hear it in your voice. I have to have this house ready in ten days for a potential buyer. This is critical."

"Give me a moment," I requested into the phone. Burton must have thought I was talking to him, because his glare intensified, accompanied by a fierce scowl.

I hit the MUTE button on the phone and faced

the man who seemed to think I was always a thorn in his side, even though I tried very hard to just be a rose in his day.

"I'm talking to the owner."

"Of course," he said, stepping into the hard-packed dirt. "Of course."

"Look, it's not like I try to find these things. She returned a phone message I'd left her hours ago, and I picked up before I thought better of it. I didn't mean to."

"No, of course not." His face did not convey what his words were saying.

I harrumphed in disgust. "I didn't. I was here to pick up my things after I unceremoniously got kicked out of the place earlier today, due to false accusations. I went to go get my vacuum cleaner and landed on a carpet and saw a hand. You cannot blame me. In fact . . ." I thought about it for a second and then smiled. "In fact, you can thank me, because if I hadn't found her, she would be in the back of that truck, in a Dumpster, right now, and we wouldn't have ever found her."

"Let's not get too carried away."

I could hear Mrs. Petrovski still squawking and knew I had a limited amount of time to get back to her.

He looked pointedly at the phone and then back at me. I knew what he was going to say before the words rolled off his tongue. "Why on earth did you call the owner before we could? This is not something you can just go around telling people about. Surely you've learned that by now, if not anything else."

I harrumphed at him again. It was becoming an

issue. Of course I knew about that rule. Not that he'd give me credit for it, but I didn't expect him to act that out of character just because I had helped him last time. "As I said, I did not call her, and I certainly was not telling her anything, except that I would take my cleaning equipment out of her house right away, which was a little white lie, I guess. I'm assuming you're not going to let me leave with anything, since this is now a crime scene. I thought I'd let you tell her why. If you want to do it now, I can just hand the phone to you." I held it out to demonstrate my willingness to let him get involved right now, right here.

Shaking his head at me, he put his hand out, and I relinquished the phone. He raised an eyebrow when I stood at his side to show him how to unmute the phone. After hitting the button, he shooed me away with his unoccupied hand, but I wasn't going far if I could help it.

Another shake of his head while he turned his back to me. I could still hear him, though. "Marg, it's James. Yeah, sorry to bother you. No, not a burglary. No, not a break-in. Actually, we're going to have to cordon the place off for a little while. Found someone in your trash can. No, they weren't rummaging around for building materials."

I would have put that a little bit differently, and I knew Burton should have when he pulled the phone away from his ear. It was very easy to hear Mrs. Petrovski yelling.

He swiveled around and glanced at me, then hunched his shoulders and turned back around. "Someone died in your Dumpster."

More yelling, at a volume, I thought, that made

it possible for the next-door neighbors a mile away to hear what she was saying.

"Calm down. Calm down. Yes, I'll get things cleared up as soon as possible. My mom knows what I do for a living. You can tell her if you want to. No, please don't talk to her to get me to move faster. I don't need the threats, ma'am." He pulled the phone away from his ear again, and this time shook his head at it instead of me for once. "She hung up on me," he told me.

I wanted to say that this was not exactly surprising, but I didn't want to get more involved in this moment, because I planned on getting involved in all the ones to come.

After handing my phone back to me, he pinched the bridge of his nose. So typically Burton. I expected an eye roll at any moment. Standing there in his black uniform, with his bulletproof vest underneath, he looked like a grim reaper that might be at the end of his own time. I almost felt sorry for him. Almost, that is, until he looked up at me and glared.

"Why?" he said.

I wasn't sure what his question pertained to, so I kept my mouth shut. He turned and walked away.

Obviously, I had been dismissed. I didn't know what to do with myself. I didn't want to leave, in case they needed me, but I was also positively itching to go back to town and talk with Max about what I'd seen.

Matt walked over as I was considering whether to ask if I could leave and talk with them later, once they got back to the station.

"So what happened?" he asked with his ever-present notepad. He was turning into Burton. I was going to have to stop that before he got too far into the nasty chief-of-police track in his life.

"I saw my vacuum cleaner and wanted to rescue it. When I was in the Dumpster, I saw a hand sticking out of the carpet and wanted to see who it was."

"Did you know who it was before you touched her on her hand?" He scribbled furiously on his notepad. Oh, to be able to see what he was writing! But he held the pad too close to his face.

"Time to get glasses? Your mom is not going to be happy if you have a squint. She'll think that's why you don't have a girlfriend."

Matt rolled his eyes at me. Well, at least it wasn't Burton, not yet, anyway.

"At first, I didn't know who it was, but then I figured out that it was Audra, the woman who was cleaning with me today." I knew who I would've preferred it to be, but I didn't think that was appropriate to tell a cop, regardless if I was related to him.

"Are you certain it's the woman who was cleaning with you today in the mansion?"

"I can't be absolutely certain without seeing her face." Which a) I did not want to do, and b) I knew better than to want to look from my days at the funeral home. "But I did recognize the nails, her tattoo, and the ring on her finger. Her boyfriend just proposed to her a few days ago."

"Do you know the boyfriend? What's his name? Could he be the one who killed her? You know, it's almost always the spouse or intimate partner in cases like these."

And yet it had been a "pseudo-spouse" only once in all my time solving murders in town. I would keep that to myself, though. Points for me. Yet this was me helping without asking for anything in return. I wanted points for that, too. I pulled my phone out of my pocket and thumbed through my screens to get to texting. I couldn't remember the boyfriend's name off the top of my head with everything that was going on, but I remembered Audra had texted me about him. The pictures from Bethany still hadn't come through, but I did have a message I must have missed. It was from Audra and was sent this afternoon, ten minutes before I found her.

Heading out. See you later. Sorry it didn't work out for you.

"No way," I whispered.

"Show me," Matt demanded, Burton right behind him.

"No way," I said again to myself, not them.

"Yes, Tallie, now. You don't want to hide anything from us." Burton reached for my phone, and I automatically batted his hand away, but not intentionally.

I snapped myself out of my haze. "I wasn't saying no way to you. I was saying no way to the fact that Audra texted me thirty minutes ago. She had to have been dead by then, and Chris had to be already on his way to get the Dumpster with his truck. Do you think someone took her phone and used it to text people she knew so that the perpetrator could pretend Audra was alive and so no one would look for her, and then she'd already

have been gone?" I got a chill when I realized how
that could have absolutely happened.

"I don't know," Burton said. And even if he did,
he probably wouldn't have told me. "Look, we're
going to take a look around inside the house while
one of the guys looks in the garbage. I'm leaving
you out here by yourself, so please don't get into
any trouble or touch anything. I want you to stick
around, in case I have any questions, but I want
you to stay out of this until I invite you in. If I ever
do that."

Same old song and dance. I really did not get
why Burton always thought I was purposely causing trouble. And I didn't often go touching things
I wasn't supposed to. Okay, so a few times I had,
but not too often and not without getting results.
There was nothing to touch here, though. I certainly wasn't going back into that Dumpster any-
time soon if I could help it.

They left the truck driver out here, too, and didn't
threaten him if he touched anything. At least not
that I could hear.

I sat on the edge of my bumper and checked my
phone again. Still no pictures and no new info
from Audra. Now that we'd found her, would whoever had done this try to text me again from her
phone, hoping I would think the girl was alive and
well? And merely off to her next job?

Of course I didn't want Audra to be dead and
would have preferred for her to have run away.
However, at least her boyfriend wouldn't be looking for her forever, wondering why she had left.

And seriously, I had to stop thinking about people, because just then another car came tearing up the drive. Caleb Yoder jumped out of the junker, which he'd parked behind the other cars, and ran toward the house.

God, her boyfriend. His name and face had snapped together in my head just as he got out of the car and the porch light highlighted his face. I knew Caleb, but I just hadn't been able to pull his name out of the chaos in my brain after finding another dead body. I felt stupid for forgetting, but in the scheme of things, it wasn't the end of the world.

"Have you seen Audra? I can't get ahold of her, and we're supposed to be on the road by now. She didn't get cold feet, did she?"

I didn't know about her feet, but her hand hadn't been warm, even though she was wrapped up tight in a carpet.

Chapter Six

With Caleb standing before me, I glanced up at the house, knowing I was about to get in trouble and not having one single care in the world. Burton would not want me talking to this guy, but Caleb was here, and so was I, and no one else. Besides, what was I supposed to do? Just smile at him until someone from the force came down and told him his girlfriend was dead? I could have sent him inside to find out, but that felt wrong.

I couldn't do that. I knew I couldn't even if I wanted to, which, in all honesty, I didn't.

"I saw her this morning, but that was it." *Keep it vague and simple*, I told myself. I still didn't know if the person in the Dumpster actually was Audra, and I wouldn't know until they pulled her out. Being vague was about all I had. "When did you last talk to her?"

"Right before she came over to clean. She usually texts me at lunch, and I didn't hear from her, but when she also didn't text me at dinner or show up at the restaurant to celebrate her getting this awesome contract for her side business, I got worried. I tried her a few minutes ago and nothing. I don't know where she is, and I couldn't think of anywhere else to look for her but here."

He stuffed his hands into his opposite armpits and began pacing in front of me. "I went by her apartment, but no one has seen her since last night. I called her parents, but they haven't heard from her, and no one remembers seeing her after she took off for this place. I'm worried. Should I be worried? Why are there so many cops here?"

This kid had to be just about drinking age. How was I going to tell him that his girlfriend, whom he had just proposed to, was probably dead, rolled up in a carpet at the bottom of a Dumpster? Seriously, this was something I most certainly did not want to do. And I guess I hadn't realized until now how truly young he was. Not that I had a problem with a May-December romance. I just was curious.

"Hopefully, we can find her." *What a lie!* And it stuck in my throat and almost choked me. And I had completely skipped over his question about the cop cars. I was not good at lying; but avoiding, I could do.

"Did you see her car here? I thought she might still be here for some reason, and I was running out of places to look."

He answered my question of why he would be here looking for Audra before I could ask it, thankfully. Normally, I was all gung ho to put people on the spot and ask the hard questions, but the sadness and nervousness on this kid's face were making it difficult for me to even think, much less ask questions.

Should I tell him what I had found? Maybe it really should be left for the police.

"I don't see her car," he continued. "Did you? I'm sorry if I'm asking twice. I'm just so anxious."

"Totally understandable, but no, I didn't see her car. There's a barn out back. Maybe there?" And I wouldn't mind getting a peek while I was at it.

I led the way but got only to the corner of the mansion before Burton yelled down from a second-story window. "Do not move. Wherever you're going, stop right now."

Caleb and I both stopped and looked at each other. He was wide-eyed and wondering, and I probably had guilt and anger stamped all over my face.

"Are we going to get in trouble?" Caleb whispered.

"Probably not you, but definitely me."

Sure enough, Burton came out of the house and down the porch stairs like his rear end was on fire.

"What did I tell you, Tallie?"

I shook my head slightly at the man who was a pain in my life more often than not with these kinds of things.

"I told you that you couldn't touch anything until we confirmed that your rival really is dead and it is not just a guess. Now I find you trying to traipse off to God knows where with God knows who." He squinted at Caleb. "Who is this anyway?"

"Audra's fiancé."

Burton's eyes went wide, then narrowed down to slits. "Where were you this afternoon, young man?"

Caleb stood behind me, using my body as a shield against Burton, as he squeaked out, "At home, sir."

"Anyone able to verify that?"

"Burton, knock it off," I said. "He just got here, because he can't find his girlfriend, and they were supposed to be at dinner to celebrate their engagement."

Burton's eyes stayed narrowed for a moment longer and then went back to normal, but with sorrow in them.

"I'll leave you two alone." I backed away. "I think you might have some things to talk about." I headed toward my car.

At that moment, the officer who had been in the Dumpster popped his head out. "I got her out of the carpet, boss, but it's not pretty."

Caleb's whole face went sheet white, and I rushed back to put my shoulder under his arm so he wouldn't fall.

"Audra?"

"Let me check it out before I say anything." Burton's whole face drooped. "Matt," he called out. "Can you come down here?"

"I can stay with him, Burton," I offered and was given the scowl.

"We've got this, Tallie. No need to interfere. You can go when Matt gets here. You and I will talk at the station when I get done."

Moments later, Matt walked away with Caleb. Burton and I stared at each other. Then I watched

Caleb's shoulders shake, and Matt put an arm around him before I looked back at Burton.

"You can talk to us back at the station when we're done here." He started to walk away, as if the conversation was over with his decree.

"I want in on this one." I was very capable of making my own decrees.

"No." He kept walking, as if that might deter me.

"Burton, I'm not kidding." I trotted along behind him. "Audra was my friend, and I was good enough to be your eyes and ears last time." She hadn't technically been my complete friend yet, but Burton didn't have to know that.

"That was last time, not this time. This time I have to run the investigation like the department is supposed to run it. That does not include bystanders or citizens."

"But I found her, and that makes this my concern."

"And now that I've opened an investigation into her wrongful death, she's mine, Tallie." He stopped and put his hand on my shoulder. "I know I tease you a lot about getting a hobby, but this time I'm serious. Remember that death a few months ago? I said it was a death by accidental electrocution, but you were all into everyone's business because you were so convinced that it had to be foul play. But it wasn't. It was really an accident. You need to leave these things alone and go with your strengths. Like cleaning and avoiding your father."

"But we know this one is murder for certain." Yes, I totally glossed over that one time when I thought it was murder and it had been an accidental death a few months ago. I shouldn't have tried to get involved in that case when I had no one at stake in the game. And I had felt like an idiot when it turned out I was totally wrong. But this time I did have someone at stake, and no matter what Burton said, I would get involved. Depending on who the murderer was, it could have been me in that Dumpster.

He sighed, then crossed his arms over his chest. "As always, I hesitate to say this, but maybe you really should consider enrolling in the police academy. I heard they have a new class starting soon. Should be just enough time to get to the gym and make sure you're in good shape."

"Two insults, one sentence. I'm impressed. And you know my mother and father would never go for me being a police officer."

"That doesn't stop you from avoiding being drawn into full-time work at the funeral parlor." Walking away again, he made it absolutely necessary for me to trot to keep up.

He had a point there, but I really didn't want to be a police officer. I just wanted to find out who killed Audra and make sure that they were caught and that they paid for the crime.

"I don't understand why we have this fight every time. You know I can help. You called me in yourself last time. Why can't you just admit that I bring something to the table?"

"It's how you bring it to the table that's an issue. And the fact that you shouldn't be looking into things at all, shouldn't even be in the room with the table much less. Heck, you should be in a whole different house, like the one you have to clean." His face stormed over as he spoke.

"But they often find me." I intensely disliked being on the defensive, but Audra was important, or she could have been once I had gotten to the bottom of why she would have let Preston help her cheat. I was not going to let this go.

He finally stopped walking and looked at me. "It doesn't matter. Don't get involved. Let me do my job, and go hang out with your boyfriend. I heard from Gina's mom that he's going to be in town for the next month. Maybe he can straighten you out and keep you out of trouble."

This time when he walked away, I was too stunned to follow. *Straighten me out? Keep me out of trouble?* Who did Burton think he was?

I had a few more words to get in before he ended our conversation. I strolled up to him, ready to deliver a piece of my mind, but I was interrupted by a commotion ahead of us.

In the midst of my conversation with Burton, I'd lost track of Caleb. Matt had walked away with him and, I thought, had him in hand. But suddenly, Caleb took off at a dead run across the field of decaying stalks of corn next to the mansion. Matt was behind him and was falling farther behind with every step. Two other officers tried to come up alongside the runaway, but Caleb hit his stride in the tall stalks and kept on going. Every once in a while, I'd see a stalk sway, but it could have been the breeze. The clouds above our heads suddenly burst open, and a pattering rain fell. It seeped through my clothes in the seconds it took for Burton and me to make a mad dash for the covered porch.

I was surprised he didn't run after the guy, too,

but Burton remained standing with me, watching intently as things continued to run amok in front of us.

"You're not going to run after them?" I asked.

"No, because then you'll probably just go get into trouble in some other way. I think it's better to stand with you here and make sure you stay where you are."

"For God's sake, Burton, I'm not going to get into trouble." I shook my head in disgust, water droplets spraying out around us. "And you keep saying I should let you go do your job. So go do your job."

"I don't have to do anything more than stand here." He used his notebook to point to the left, and sure enough, there was a disheveled Matt and the other two officers dragging a furious and drenched Caleb between them. He kicked and spat and yelled, but none of them were releasing what I was sure was an iron grip.

"I didn't do it," Caleb yelled.

"We'll figure that out down at the station," Burton responded from the porch, then finally walked away from me. He had the stroll down pat, almost turning it into a saunter, even in the mud created by the rain. "Read him his rights, Matt, and we'll go from there. Why don't you put him in my car? We'll get this taken care of and get back to our regular day."

Back to their regular day? What did they normally do? And this was serious business.

While Matt put Caleb into the back of the squad car, I ran up to Burton, not caring about getting more soaked than I already was. "And just like that, you think it's solved? What about the Dumpster? The corpse? You don't even know how she was killed."

"I'm sure Caleb will tell us all about it. And I'll have the guys comb the area for any evidence, while I take the significant other down to the station and get some answers."

"You think you really have the guy?"

"I know I do. It's almost always the spouse or, in this case, the almost spouse." He remained stone-faced, and I sighed.

"So it's all done. No mystery here, huh?"

"Nope, no mystery, so go on home to your soon-to-be-something and let us figure out how it went down and why it went down. You can read about it in the paper in a few days."

He seemed awfully sure of himself as he walked over to his car and got in, with Caleb still yelling in the backseat. That was going to be a long ride back to the station, and a noisy one.

Not my problem, I told myself, and now I really could spend my days with Max. Do fun things without worrying about murder in the area again. And if they got a confession and finished up their clue gathering today, then I could go about my life and not worry. If all the ladies on my team were available tomorrow, I'd gather them together and tell them I'd failed, or at least my reputation had, and we could brainstorm other ideas on how to get them all working.

All was right in the world. But why did it feel so wrong?

On my way home, I tried to talk my way through why I didn't have to worry about this. Burton would figure it out. He was positive Caleb had done it, and he had years of experience behind him. He should know.

It was weird that Caleb had shown up at the mansion, though. Why would he think that was the right place to look for Audra since she should have been done for the day once she got the contract? And he was so young. I hadn't realized he was that young. He'd mentioned that he hadn't received Audra's normal texts at the normal times and that she hadn't answered his phone calls. So on a hunch he'd shown up at the mansion. Why so late in the day? He'd said he talked to her parents, ran by her apartment, and then came right here. Had he really talked to those people, or had he just said that to get me to tell him whether I'd seen her car or to give him any info he wanted?

Plus, there was a barn that I hadn't searched. Maybe there were clues to what happened in it. The carpet had to have come from somewhere, and Audra had to have been killed in a space big enough to roll out that carpet. There were a few rooms in the house that could have worked, but if the barn held all the stuff the Petrovskis had collected throughout the years, then there was a very good chance it could be where she was killed. I certainly hadn't seen any blood on my walk-through of the house earlier.

As I maneuvered around the hearse in order to park, I tried to put the whole grisly affair aside. There wasn't anything I could do about the death of a friend at the moment, and perhaps taking an evening to chill would bring new ideas about what had happened and who had done it.

In an effort to give myself a break, that night I

laughed with Gina and Jeremy and Max, roared with laughter at the movie we went to, and was stuffed when we got home. Every time I thought of that hand in the Dumpster and the way Audra had been lifeless, I tried to submerge the images. There would be time to think about it all after I put all my effort into remembering that life was precious and should be lived to the fullest, because you never knew when it might end.

But after our night out, when I was maneuvering again around the hearse, my cell phone rang. Parking quarters were tight, so I didn't even glance down at the phone. I'd pick it up once I had pulled the parking brake. I had to back up my car and pull in another three times before the parking job was finally done. Breathing out a huge sigh, I promised myself I'd park the big boat of a car better after I drove it for tomorrow's funeral.

"You need to get that?" Max asked from the passenger's seat.

When I picked up my phone, I saw Letty had called. I hesitated with the thing in my hand. *Should I call her now? Wait to hear from Burton? Talk to Max first?* I paused. *Or none of the above?* I thought when her number came across my screen again and my familiar ringtone sang in the silent car.

"I guess so."

He kissed me on the cheek, then opened his door. "I'll go get the fur kids settled and see you upstairs."

On the last ring before the call would have gone to voice mail, I answered. "Hey, Letty."

"What is going on, Tallie? I just heard from Yolanda that they have Audra's boyfriend in custody and that girl is dead. I also heard that we didn't get the job." Her quick indrawn breath was the beginning of a sob fest that lasted for about three minutes. She eventually got herself under control, though I doubted it had anything to do with the empty platitudes I was murmuring over the phone.

"I'm sorry, Letty. I don't know what's happened, and I don't have all the details." I fiddled with the gear shift, wishing there was something more I could say.

"How do you not have all the details? You always have all the details, even the ones the police don't have." She wailed that last part.

"They think they have the right guy, since the boyfriend came to the site and started running. I was told not to get involved."

"Are you kidding me? Tallie Graver not get involved? Who are you, and what did you do with my employer?"

I chuckled because it sounded like that was what she wanted me to do. "What do you know about the boyfriend, then? Do you think he did it?"

She hummed across the line. "I know that despite the ring, things had not been going too well. But he's a sweet kid. She was the wild one. I can't imagine him hurting her, and certainly not rolling her up in a carpet and throwing her away in the garbage."

"How do you know that?" I was usually pretty quick with the information around town and was part of the gossip chain, but Letty had to have an insider that was better informed than my own.

"My friend Yolanda is filling in for Suzy down at the station while Suzy's on vacation."

"Oh." That was all I could say, because my brain was positively whirling with the possibilities. Would Yolanda give me more than Suzy, who had a very big loyalty to Burton, ever had? Could I get the info without having to fight everyone?

I admit I had been surprised when Caleb bolted, but I wouldn't be surprised if he just hadn't been able to process the information in, and so he had run to get away from it all. I didn't think he'd murdered Audra, though. However, I also didn't know him.

But Letty knew Yolanda, who could get info about the boyfriend's interrogation and Audra. If she could tell me what I needed to know, then maybe I could look into it. At least just for the moment. Maybe just a little, to make sure I wasn't missing anything and neither were the police.

"I have a bad feeling about this," I said to Letty, wanting to make sure that she understood I was on her side.

"Me, too, so I'm going to ask you something that I never would normally."

I braced myself. Was she going to ask me to beg for this job? The one that was supposed to launch our unnamed company? How was I going to tell all those women that I was yanking the rug out from under them? Should I start looking for other jobs to replace it now? I gulped. "Go on."

She paused for a moment and then blurted, "I need you to put on the nosy hat and do your thing. We need to figure out what happened to Audra, and we need that job, and I can't rest until we do. Will you please go and find out who did this?"

"I was planning on it, but my hands could be

tied on both the figuring out the murder part and the job part. I might be able to get the job, since Mrs. P has no one now, but the murder could be beyond my capabilities." It was one thing when I was the chief suspect or when one of my closest friends was accused of being the murderer. It was also easier to be involved when I was specifically asked by the police to look into things. But with Burton already having a suspect and thinking the case was all wrapped up, I wasn't sure how much I could do other than make sure they weren't making mistakes, because they didn't have all the info. "Why is this so important to you?"

There was a beat of silence where Letty choked up again. She took a deep breath and then sighed it out. "Caleb is family, Tallie. He's my nephew, and I can't let him go down for something I know he didn't do."

Chapter Seven

The next morning, bright and early, I got up and did exactly the wrong thing. I knew I shouldn't be back on the road to the mansion. I should be at my apartment, figuring out what to do with myself for the day, since I had set it aside in anticipation of winning the mansion contract. Last night was filled with fun and a great movie. I had felt like a normal person out on a normal date with my boyfriend, my best friend, and my brother. No worries about murders or murderers. But then Letty had called after we'd gotten home. And fun and games had turned into concern. Max and I had talked murder and mayhem, while I'd braced myself for the fact that if I looked into this I'd have to endure most of the people in my life telling me to get a real hobby instead of searching out clues.

Eventually, Max and I had fallen asleep and I'd put the murder aside to rest. But all along I had known that I couldn't let Letty down, so today was different. I was on the case, whether Burton wanted me or not.

Last night I'd had nightmares about the killer getting away. I'd tossed and turned as I ruminated about Letty's request and my promise that I would do whatever it took to help find the killer. So yes, I knew I shouldn't get involved, acknowledged it, then shunted it aside and kept on driving.

As I drove to the mansion, I hoped that it would be unoccupied. I still had the key from yesterday morning, and as long as I didn't touch anything, I would be fine. I just couldn't get over the look on Caleb's face and Letty's words that he wouldn't have done this. She knew because he was her nephew.

Of course, as soon as I rounded the last corner, there was Matt leaning against his police cruiser, with his arms tightly crossed over his chest. I started rummaging around in my brain for something I could say I had left behind yesterday, to give me a reason to be back where I was obviously not wanted.

My vacuum was still here, the one I had pulled out of the Dumpster before I realized I was standing on top of my friend wrapped in a carpet. Okay, that would work. Heck, I would make it work if I had to.

"You know, when Burton said I should stick around in case anyone came back who could be suspicious, I don't believe he was thinking of you, but I guess he could have been," he said as I emerged from my car.

I put on the injured face and went with my gut. "Matt, come on. I'm just coming back for my vacuum. I remembered I'd left it here, and I can't be without it."

"Yeah, not working. Besides, Burton took that in as evidence, just in case it's the murder weapon, along with all your other cleaning implements. Try again. Better yet, don't try at all, because it's not going to work." He shook his head, then just gave me a look. He was probably waiting for me to lob the next lie at him. I wasn't going to play that game.

"Look, you and I both know that Burton and all you guys really have a lot on your plate. There's more going on here than an angry boyfriend. How did he kill her? How did he get her rolled up in the carpet? How did he carry her out of the house in the carpet? Heck, how did he get the carpet into the Dumpster? She wasn't small, and she had to be heavy as deadweight." I winced since I had not meant for it to come out sounding that way, and yet it was true.

"All questions we already have under consideration. I'm not quite sure why you always seem to think we can't do our jobs, Tallie. We were doing this long before you came in and started being the unmasked avenger. We'll be doing this long after you finally get that hobby everyone keeps encouraging you to get."

"My God, the notepad was enough yesterday afternoon. Now you actually sound like Burton. Your mom is not going to be happy with that. *I'm* not happy with that."

"Burton is a good guy, if you'd ever give him a chance. The only reason he's always irritated with you is that you don't let him do his job without your nose completely up in all his business."

I crossed my arms over my own chest, mirroring his stance. "That's not true. When Darla died, I tried to give him all the things I'd found and the information that was coming to me, and he brushed me off, until I found the money and the killer for him. With Gina, I was not going to let him take my friend to jail when I knew she hadn't done it. And with the home inspector, he was the one who came to me, asking me to look into things, because he was on leave. I've given him any number of chances. It's not that I think he can't do his job. It's that I think I can help."

Blowing out a breath, Matt finally uncrossed his arms and stuck his hands into his pockets instead. "And you have to look at it from his perspective. You're making him look like a fool every time you solve one of these things and he doesn't do it himself."

"I never intend that." Well, sometimes I had, but I certainly wasn't going to admit it.

"Then back off."

I couldn't. "You have the wrong guy. Letty knows this Caleb, and she is certain he wouldn't have killed his girlfriend. He'd just proposed to her, and they were going to dinner to celebrate. Plus, why would he come back and act surprised and then run and yell if he'd already known she was dead?"

"Because he didn't think we'd find her that easily. Remember, the truck was supposed to haul away the Dumpster before anyone got here. You thwarted that."

"Yeah, I did, and the only thing I got for my help was a pat on the head and a kick in the pants."

He scoffed while I frowned. "That's not true."

"It most certainly is. Burton figuratively patted me on the head and told me to go home to my boyfriend." Now I pulled my crossed arms tighter over my chest. At least I had him talking, which meant he wasn't running me off the property. Maybe I could get some information this way and find out what they thought they had on the poor kid that made them so sure he was going to confess to killing his girlfriend.

Matt, the devil, laughed, pushing himself off the cruiser and tucking his thumbs into his belt. "Classic Burton. More than anything, he's just trying to keep you out of trouble, Tallie, though you seem to find it no matter where you go or how you get there. You're a part of this town, and he's fiercely protective of it. Every time you get involved in one of these things, he gets his nose out of joint about you getting hurt."

"And yet last time he didn't have any problem setting me up to be the whipping boy."

"He most certainly did." Matt shifted his stance to lean back against the squad car. "He agonized over that. In the end, though, he didn't have another choice, because of the dirty cop we were dealing with."

I highly doubted Burton agonized over anything. Especially me. It was time to change the subject. "So why are you all so sure that Caleb did this? Did he confess?"

"You just can't let it go."

"I'm a concerned citizen."

"You're a nosey parker."

My mouth dropped open as I stared at him. "I haven't heard that term in forever!"

Clearing his throat, he shook his head at me. "My grandmother said it the other day to my mom, and it stuck in my head. But it's you to a T. Why can't you stay out of these things? It's not like we haven't done our job before."

"You said that before, and I'll tell you again. It's not that I want to do your job. I would be horrible at your job. Giving citations and dealing with nasty people all day, having to wear a bulletproof vest, and pulling people over for things I do every day? No thanks. But this kind of thing just seems to make sense in my head . . . when I see all the clues and people tell me things, whether they realize it or not."

He took me in for a second and got an intense look in his eye. "Why don't you go to school and become a private investigator? If you had a license, then Burton would trust you to be discreet. And while we're not always happy to have you on board, you at least would have some real reason to be in the middle of things."

I took a step back. Not literally, but in my mind I leaped back from that possibility. It was one thing to help in an ongoing investigation or to make sure an investigation got moving, but I certainly didn't want to get paid to spy on cheating husbands or to find bad people—or even good people. I was not made for a life of fighting crime. I might not have always known what I wanted to be when I grew up, but I had known it wasn't that. No thank you.

"While I appreciate your vote of confidence, I'm going to have to say no." I shrugged and hoped he would take that as the end of the conversation. I was going to have to come back at another time to look for any clues to help with proving someone else had killed Audra and why. I debated briefly about including Matt in it, then thought better of it. He might not be willing to let me in the house, and if he did and we couldn't find anything, then I might look like an idiot.

He shrugged. "Whatever. At least that way you'd be a professional instead of the amateur sleuth you seem determined to be. You're not doing yourself any favors by being involved when Burton doesn't want you here."

"Believe me, I am fully aware of that." I wrestled some more with the thought of asking Matt to walk the house with me. Now that the notion was in there, I couldn't seem to shake it loose. This was the guy I used to hop in the creek with to catch crawfish on camping vacations. We shared a grandmother, though not the one who'd called his mom a nosey parker. Surely I could ask him for a favor and not get laughed at. Plus, I knew he was going to school to get his degree to advance in the police department. It would only boost his chances of getting on the fast track to a promotion if he was able to catch a break in a case. Right? Right.

I cleared my throat and looked around the driveway. I didn't know why, but I just had this feeling that Burton was going to come tearing up the drive and yank Matt away from me, then send me to jail for interfering.

"Just say whatever is on your little bird brain.

And then get moving. Burton's due here in an hour or so, and I want to do a walk of the perimeter for him before he gets back from talking with Caleb at the station."

It was on the tip of my tongue to offer to go with him when his radio crackled alive. Matt, being the professional he was, turned his back to me and started to walk away. Me, being the nosey parker I was, followed him and ignored him when he tried to shoo me away.

"Go ahead, boss, but I've got ears here."

"Tallie?" The tone of voice was not unfamiliar. "What's she doing there?"

"The usual," Matt responded to Burton.

"Whatever. I don't have time for her at the moment, and maybe she'll come up with something useful. Caleb has an alibi, an airtight one, and he swears he didn't kill the victim. We're at square one. I'm sending out some guys to make sure all the evidence is collected that we need and then to try to get some answers. There's pressure to open the mansion back up. I don't want to hear about it anymore, but now we have to start all over again."

"Pressure from whom?" I asked, wanting Matt to ask for me over the radio.

But Burton must have heard me, because he answered with a crackle. "Your future employer, Tallie. Mrs. Petrovski wants this place open right now, for some godforsaken reason. She's putting pressure on my superior to get it open, and apparently, she's decided that you're cleaning it."

"Your superior?"

I noticed Matt didn't push the TALK button on his two-way this time. "His mom."

"Oh," I said and snickered, because I knew that pressure all too well. Mrs. P and Burton's mother ran in the same circles, so Mrs. P must have pulled out the big guns to make sure that she could have access to her house for that potential buyer she'd referenced earlier.

"So get in there and get evidence, Matt. And, Tallie, do whatever it is you're going to do, because no one ever listens to me anymore, anyway." He signed off, and Matt and I shared a look.

"Things aren't going so well for him?" I leaned back against my car and waited for Matt to respond. I didn't know if he'd actually answer me, but it was worth asking.

"We had a big drug bust go down and found opioids in the area. He's angry. We almost had a kid die on his watch. He's trying to handle that with our diminished force, and now with this murder, things are going to take some maneuvering to get it all done."

He probably shouldn't have told me that, but I hoped he knew he could trust me. "All right, let's make a deal. Let me help you so I can be involved, and we just won't bother Burton with how much I'm actually doing. He said I could help, even if it was grudgingly, so let's take him at face value. That way, I can do my thing, you can do yours, and Burton can feel like progress is being made, so he can concentrate on other things without worrying about us."

Matt cupped his hand against the back of his neck. "I don't know, Tallie. He sounded like he was saying you could help only because he's frustrated and defeated. Under normal circumstances, he would not want you in on this, and you know it. And what if he changes his mind? I don't want to get into trouble. I'm trying to move up in the department, not be busted down to traffic control."

" 'Doesn't want' doesn't mean 'doesn't need.' " I focused on that one thing. I could help. I knew I could. And this way, everyone could get what they needed. Including justice for Audra and freedom for Caleb, with no doubts haunting my cousin. Even if Caleb had an airtight alibi, that didn't mean they wouldn't keep looking at him if they couldn't find someone else.

"I'm not going to touch that one." His eyes looked tired, and I didn't want to press, but I knew I was going to, anyway.

"Just let me help like I normally do. I won't look for anything in particular, but if I find something, I'll give it to you. How about that?"

"This is a bad idea. I can feel it in my gut. What if you get hurt? Burton would never forgive me."

Why did they persist in making this so hard? "It's a good idea, a brilliant one even, and Burton is going to think you're amazing for solving this thing for him while he does his thing. Think about it."

"I will . . ." He trailed off, looking over my shoulder. I didn't want to turn around, just in case it was Burton coming to yell at me.

In the end I couldn't keep myself from looking, though. As always. I'd rather know about the attack, so I could brace myself. But instead of Burton, it was a shiny, brand-new sports car in bright yellow. It pulled up to us, and Preston Prescott leaned out the window.

"Tallie, I was told I might find you here. And

Matt. Good!" Preston climbed out of his car, all smiles and shooting his cuffs. "I'm glad you're here, too. Aunt Marg wants me to help in any way I can. She wants this taken care of before the news gets out that there's been a death in the house and the press is here to cover the thing. So what can I do first?"

Matt looked at me with a grimace; I looked back with a smile. Things were about to get interesting.

"Well, Preston, if you could look through the house with us to see if there's anything missing, that would be great." I spoke first because I knew Matt was going to try to send him off with a wave and a handshake. This might not be the way Burton would want this handled, but surely we could rule out any fingerprints that belonged to Preston, anyway, since this was his aunt's property. And if Mrs. Petrovski really was going to offer me the job, then I wanted to rub Preston's nose in the fact that I would be here working, despite all his attempts to derail and discredit me.

Before Matt could do more than growl low in his throat, I hooked my arm through Preston's and walked him up to the front door. "Let's start downstairs, and we can go up from there."

"Tallie, if I could have a word with you." Matt stood his ground and tried to stare me down.

Good luck with that, cousin.

"Come along, and you can talk to me while we hunt through the rooms and make sure nothing is missing." I was taking a chance that Matt would not follow me and would instead call Burton, to have him haul tail out here to stop me, because he was nervous that Burton didn't actually want me to help. I was also taking a chance of contaminating the scene and possibly messing up evidence. I wasn't stupid. But I wanted to know if anything was missing in the house, though I had no reference for what had been in there before, since I'd never gotten those pictures from Bethany.

I sincerely wished I had.

Preston, surprisingly, did not shake me off or even make angry faces at me. He was going right along with the plan, as if we had always gotten along. I'd work my mind around that later. He waited at the front door for me and then produced a key to open up the mansion.

"Wait!" Matt yelled from the spot he had yet to move from. "At least let me call this in to Burton. I don't want to get my ass handed to me for not following protocol. Just give me a second."

I sighed but complied, stilling Preston's hand to prevent him from turning the knob on the door. "It really would be better if we wait to get the okay. I don't want to mess anything up. I just want to know what happened."

"What are we looking for?" Preston asked, shooting his cuffs again. Was this his thing? I didn't remember it from back in the day, but then, I didn't remember a lot from days gone by with Preston. Only that he'd been a pain. We should have been the best of friends. He'd been a partyer, and so had I, living the high life, not taking responsibility for much, and going from one inane thing to another.

I actually had no idea how Preston made money. Maybe he was just a trust-fund baby. I knew his family had money, as evidenced by the fact that they had let a house the size of my parents' three-story funeral home go to rot and were able to afford to clean it up from the ground to the attic. Obviously, I would have loved to benefit from that money at this point, but dealing with him was not my favorite thing to do in any circumstance. He had always gotten on my nerves and made me feel like I didn't belong. With trying to trash my chances at cleaning his aunt's mansion, he hadn't exactly changed my mind about him. And now that he was acting like we got along, I didn't quite know what he was aiming for. It could be anything. I wasn't going to take him seriously no matter how nice and accommodating he was being. At least he wasn't wearing a cravat today, so that was one less thing I had to overlook in his laundry list of faults.

"Anything that is missing or has been misplaced. When was the last time you were here before yesterday?"

"Wow. I wouldn't even know. Other than yesterday, it's been a long time, as far as I can remember. No one ever really comes out here anymore." His eyes widened to the size of a turkey platter. "Are you sure it wasn't some domestic dispute? I've also heard that some kids have used this as a hangout. Maybe we shouldn't go in, after all. Or do they have the killer in hand?"

"Uh, we're just looking around with Matt while you're here. I don't know if they have anyone yet." Of course, that was a lie, since the police had no one in custody, but I didn't think I should tell Preston that.

He backed away from the door. "I don't think I want to go in there. What if we touch something we're not supposed to? I don't want to be scrutinized for prints or falsely accused if I touch the one thing I shouldn't."

I sighed, because really what else could I do? I did understand, but I also knew that the longer we waited, the more time we would lose in the effort to find the person who murdered Audra and put him or her behind bars to face justice. Audra had been a sweetheart and shouldn't have had her life ended so soon. I didn't know why someone had felt the need to kill her and wrap her up in a carpet. I might never know, but I at least *wanted* to know who had done it. I had Letty depending on me for closure, after all.

Matt chose that moment to join us at the wide front stoop. "Okay, look, Burton is on board, barely, with us doing this. But we all have to wear gloves, and please, don't touch anything that you absolutely do not have to touch. Doorknobs and whatever are fine, but don't be running your hands over anything. The crime-scene guys are on their way back over here to go over everything once more, but it would help to know if anything in particular is missing."

He sounded doubtful, and I wondered how much he'd had to fight Burton to get him to agree to this. It was one thing for Burton to have me help because he was in a bad spot. It was something else entirely to have another person come in to the house with Matt and me. Maybe I should offer to clean Burton's house for free. Then again, I knew what a messy bachelor he was, and I didn't think I wanted to put myself in the position of having to pick up his dirty clothes.

In we went. The house was spacious, and so this could take hours, but I had nothing else going on at the moment, since I had scheduled the whole day to be here cleaning. I had a funeral to drive for tonight, but that was it, and Max was at his job across the river.

Once I'd told Letty what was going on, I'd also told her to please call everyone and tell them they had the day off. I would be juggling schedules for the next few days to find other jobs for them to do so they didn't lose money, but there was nothing that could be done about it until this was taken care of.

Room by room, we went through the house. Preston was surprisingly pleasant as he explained that he didn't see anything missing or anything that had been moved. I made absolutely sure I didn't touch anything, but of course I ended up tripping over a wrinkle in a rug and falling against a wall. Face to nasty wallpaper would not be a favorite place of mine if I was to list a top ten places I liked to find myself. Fortunately, the gloves kept me from touching anything with my bare hands when I hit the wall, but the wall gave just a little under my weight. I knew having Max here to feed me had increased my poundage a little, but not enough to make a wall give. At least I hoped not.

I pushed on the wall, but nothing happened. I pushed again and still nothing. *So weird.* But Matt and Preston had already moved on to the next room. I put the info in my mental bank, then scrambled to keep up with them. It was something I might need to talk about with Mrs. Petrovski. If she had actual rot in the walls, behind the wallpaper, then she might have a bigger job than even I would be able to handle. Cleaning, yes. I could do that. Even the cleanup after construction, if asked. Replacing structural walls was totally not on my résumé.

I whisked into the second bedroom upstairs in time to hear Preston say, "There should be a rug here."

Sure enough, there was a dusty outline on the floor. Outside the outline, the floor was dull, but inside it, it was highly polished. Turning in a circle, I looked for the window. As I did so, I wondered if the opening's dimensions would allow the killer to toss Audra, wrapped up in the carpet, out the window and into the Dumpster. Not that I really wanted to think about that, but the logistics kept bothering me. I had a hard time imagining how one person could have done this. Maybe there were two killers . . .

And the window was right there, the sill low enough that the carpet could have been tipped downward and then released to fall into the waiting Dumpster below. The Dumpster sat empty now, as the police had taken out all the debris, and the coroner had taken away the body, along with the carpet. The new coroner would take care of the body and would hopefully do a better job than our last one.

I peered down into the Dumpster. The thing was clean, and the truck that was sent to pick it up had gone away empty.

"Hey, did anyone ever find out who sent that truck out here?" I asked.

Matt was talking, and he stopped in midsen-

tence. I'd been listening with half an ear to his and
Preston's conversation, but nothing had been said
that I needed to pay attention to. Preston had just
been saying over and over again that nothing was
missing, as far as he could recollect. Nothing except the carpet, anyway.

"I'll make a note." Matt took out his notepad
and did just that, frowning as his pencil ran over
the curled paper.

Maybe a career change to private investigator
wouldn't be such a far stretch. I asked the questions and thought the thoughts of someone trying
to get to the bottom of a mystery. I had no idea
how much schooling that would take or if I would
have to do some kind of internship, but it might
be worth looking into. It wasn't the tea shop I'd
dreamed of, but maybe it would be better. And
then I'd be able legally to get all up in Burton's
business. Wouldn't that chap his hide?

I was smiling over that when Matt and Preston
moved into the next room. I felt a little like a puppy
when I trotted along behind them, but I didn't want
to be left behind. So far we hadn't found anything
of note. Everything appeared to be where it belonged, and everything was accounted for, other
than the rug.

I didn't know why I had thought that some huge
sign was going to pop out of a wall and say HERE.
HERE IS WHERE BAD THINGS HAPPENED. AND THIS IS
WHERE YOU SHOULD LOOK TO FIND OUT ABOUT THEM.
But I had, and being proven wrong was disap-
pointing. Usually, by this time I would have found
a scrap of paper with a cryptic message or a clue of
some sort. Here there was nothing.

Finally, we made it through the rest of the house, and my disappointment did not recede. I'd fought to get us into the house, and then we'd found nothing at all. I might have just used a card that I wouldn't be able to use again.

We met the crime-scene guys out front, and Preston offered to go through the house with them again, just in case they needed anything.

I didn't stick around to listen to their answer. I decided to head home, make myself something to eat, and then try to figure out what my next move would be, because at this point I had a dead body, no viable suspects, no known motive, and not a single question to ask or anyone to ask it of, except the person who had done this.

I guess there was also why, but without a who, the why wouldn't make sense.

I bade farewell to Preston and Matt, and returned to my car. When I got behind the wheel, I decided to call Letty before I left the mansion. She didn't pick up, so I cranked my engine over and headed home. I had a few hours until Max would be home. I would use the time to look up Audra and would wait for Letty to call back.

Chapter Eight

I entered my apartment and inhaled the delicious smell of something both sweet and bacon-y wafting through the air. And there was my man, standing in my small kitchen, at the stove, with one of my aprons tied around his waist. This one at least didn't have ruffles.

"So you're going to get involved in another murder?" He turned from the stove and gave me a raised eyebrow when I closed the door. Leave it to Max to point out the obvious.

"It's not like I go looking for these things," I said, sidling up to him and sneaking a piece of bacon from the paper towel to his right. Crunching away, I silently relished the fact that foodwise, having Max here for a month was going to be awesome. He liked to cook and was very good at it. I liked to eat and was also very good at it. A match made in heaven. It wouldn't necessarily be so good for my hips, but who cared? "Wait, what are you doing home? I thought you were going into the office."

"They told me to wait for the moment and they'd call me in this afternoon."

Bonus for me. Now I knew what to do with my day.

The bacon was delicious, and I had to say that for once, I was happy that my apartment was small, because the smells of a good breakfast permeated every corner. Peanut was happy, too, and she paced throughout the whole place with her nose in the air and her tail wagging.

Yet I kept thinking that I just didn't know where to start this time. I didn't know Audra that well. We had been on our way to a better friendship, but it had been a budding friendship, not a solid one. I didn't know her boyfriend well, though Letty could help with that. I wasn't sure about where Audra came from, since she hadn't lived here her whole life. I felt unequipped this time, as I hadn't before.

On the other hand, I had a lot going on with Max, and I should be able to trust that the cops could do their job. At least that was what I was telling myself while I stood and ate a piece of cinnamon-sugar toast. It was not the cheesy goodness of the bread Max had made the other day to go with his pasta, but it was still good.

Max shepherded me toward the small table and got out plates for the quiche that he had pulled out of the oven and that smelled amazing. I wasn't ready to sit down, though, as I munched on my toast.

"Who are you going to irritate this time? And what are you doing home? Aren't you usually out chasing down clues by now?"

I scoffed, then told him about the whole morning, following up on new developments with Caleb and Preston and Matt. "I just feel so bad for Letty. She seems really shaken up by this." I tried to sneak another piece of toast while Max dished out the quiche and then placed my slice on the table.

"No more bread, or you're not going to eat the main dish." He pulled out my chair for me and held it for me while I sat before he got his own plate of quiche and put it on the table.

I waited for him to join me at the table with a big bowl of fruit before I continued my thoughts. "I am never going to be able to eat all this."

"Leftovers are even better. Now, what's going on?"

I admired my quiche as I filled a little bowl with fruit. "Caleb is her nephew, and she says there's no way he could have done this. My understanding is that life had not been overly nice to him when he was a teen, and Letty used to work with him at the youth center. Now that he is in his twenties, Letty has been trying to get him to get his life in order, and she was really helping him get back on track before he was dragged down to the station."

"That's horrible." He crunched into his bacon, and I was taken in again by his face and the set of his chin, his eyes. I didn't know what I had ever done to deserve someone like this, but I was happy I'd done it.

"She wasn't exactly happy about him dating a woman that was significantly older than him, but she'd started to like Audra, at least a little. And now Audra is dead, and Caleb has apparently been through the ringer with the police."

"Also horrible."

I continued with my thoughts, just to get them all out of my head. "But they have to let Caleb out of custody now, because they have nothing to charge him with. Burton was completely convinced that he did it, and the kid took off running during questioning at the mansion. I guess I could have seen him being guilty . . . I guess, but then, that's no longer a factor. Burton is not happy that they're back to square one." I cut into the quiche, and it looked divine, with ham and eggs and cheese. I tried not to think any more about all I didn't know regarding this murder, or I would get myself all up in a tizzy. Not knowing where to start was eating at me.

"Burton doesn't seem to be happy very often in general. What's different about this time?"

"I guess nothing much. It's just that this is a really busy time for the department, with a lot of things going on, and they're trying to cut the force."

"Are you going to do a search to find her on the internet? There should be something, since no one is without some kind of online trail anymore."

"You know it." I just didn't know where to start. Looking at my plate, I thought of a few different ways, then glanced back up at Max. "So when are they going to pull you in for work?" I asked. "I thought you said this morning you were leaving shortly after I did. You're supposed to be working across the river."

"I went there and got turned back. They're not ready to start just yet."

"Can you tell me what's going on? Without having to kill me after?"

He laughed, as I intended him to. "Nothing too intriguing. And I don't have all the details yet, so there's really nothing to share. You know I can't say anything, anyway."

"I know, but that doesn't mean I'm going to stop asking."

"Fair enough, and no matter what it is, if it gets me a month with you, then I'm not going to complain."

We shared a smile and then a kiss, and then I got down to eating the rest of my breakfast. I wouldn't say this quiche would ever replace my snickerdoodle cookies, because, come on, that was the difference between sweet and savory, but I could definitely get used to coming home to this. And him.

We talked a little more, and then my phone started dinging rapidly, like a trolley on a collision course. Who was texting me so much, and why?

I grabbed my phone, not sure if I was going to get a barrage of questions from my mother about Max's stay, if Gina and my brother Jeremy were fighting, or if Letty needed to talk through her crying.

But when I picked it up, I had seven messages, all from Bethany.

"Whoa!" I held the phone up and pressed the MESSAGE button. Max stared at me from across the small table.

"What's going on?"

"I have no idea, but I'm getting a flood of texts from Bethany. Hold on." On my telephone screen the blank squares where there should have been pictures stared back at me, and then they started to fill in slowly, like someone was unrolling a poster over and over again.

All the pictures I'd been waiting for, almost panoramic shots of each room, with multiple pictures of some of the rooms to show me what we might need to do, and then a list of things she recommended we have on hand. The time stamps on the pictures were coming across wonky, but the images were rolling down the screen like a movie. Some of the pictures were of the room I'd been standing in when I'd seen my vacuum cleaner. There was a picture of the Dumpster in which I had found Audra less than twenty-four hours ago. From the way Bethany had shot the picture, I could see that the thing was empty. We'd put the sawdust and the drywall in there during the first part of the morning, but the carpet hadn't gone in there until after everyone supposedly went home.

So who had fiddled with the carpet, and when? Obviously, not before Bethany took the pictures, since that carpet was in the picture of the upstairs bedroom. A room that had looked different when I was in there. I mentally went through each room and compared the images in my mind's eye to the photos to discern if anything else was different.

There was a half wall in one of the rooms in the photos, but I didn't remember seeing a half wall in any room I'd gone into, and I'd been in all of them. What was it doing there, and how was I going to get back into the mansion to check it out?

I was about to burn up with curiosity when I looked up from my phone. Max was staring at me, with his glass of juice halfway to his lips. "Something new?"

"Uh, yeah, but I'm not sure what to do with it."

"Show me, and we'll figure it out."

I turned my phone toward him and waited.

"Pictures of the house, I presume."

"Yes, Sherlock, pictures of the house. The thing is that when I was there this morning, that particular wall did not exist, and that carpet in the third picture is the one that I found Audra wrapped in."

"So I take it you're about to 'undecide' that you aren't getting involved in this case beyond some research, and you will, in fact, interfere?"

I asked the hard question. "Are you going to be mad if I get involved? This is a working vacation for you, and I don't want to miss out on time we could be spending together, but I need to find out what happened to my friend." If it had been one of my girls in my crew, I would have done the same thing. They all belonged to me now, no matter if I had originally wanted them or not.

He looked me over from my head to my hand that was holding a piece of cinnamon-sugar toast tight enough to make it crumble. After taking the bread from my hand, he laid it on my plate and brought my hand up to his mouth. "Tell me what we need to do."

After a sigh of relief, I got down to business. "I really want to get back into the house, but I'm not going to be able to do that until they give me the all clear, since it's a crime scene." I chewed my lip until it hurt. "What if we do a background check on Caleb and another on Audra, just out of curiosity, until Mrs. Petrovski calls to ask me to clean?"

"It's a good plan. Can we finish eating first?"

"Absolutely." I dug back into my food, with my brain whirling at about forty times its normal fast pace. Audra's killer wasn't the boyfriend, at least as far as we knew at the moment. Why would he kill her, roll her in a carpet, then come back hours later and act surprised to find her there? I understood that many criminals weren't very smart, but that was beyond stupid.

But how did anyone get her rolled up in a carpet and then downstairs, then into the Dumpster, anyway? Yes, when I was there with Preston, I had thought she could have been tossed out the window, but later I had remembered that the carpet had been very neatly arranged at the bottom of the Dumpster. And you'd have to be seriously strong to do that, especially by yourself. When I'd talked to Caleb yesterday, I had noticed that he was tall and lanky, not muscular at all, really. And he'd looked so sad that she was gone, so lost because he wouldn't see her again. Maybe that was why he had run, which Burton had mistaken for guilt.

But who else would they look at? I knew from Matt that there had been a big drug bust in town the other night, or at least big for our small town. A lot of our police resources were wrapped up in that. Would Burton have time to give Audra's murder case everything it deserved? Would he try to

find someone and charge him or her without looking too deeply, because he wanted the case wrapped
up so he could get back to his other work? I shook
my head at myself. No matter what Burton had
ever done to keep me from getting involved, he
was a good cop and would never take the easy way
out just to close a case. He'd always been fair and
thorough, even after I'd handed him information.
Why was I doubting him now?

Burton would get justice for Audra even with so
many other things going on. I could make his job
easier by finding out information he might not
get. I could then very carefully pass it on to make
sure the right person was caught. I had to have
faith in him *and* in myself.

He was a good cop. I was a good nosey parker.

My phone rang, and Max and I both stared at it
for a moment before I picked it up. It was Burton's
ringtone. Here was the moment.

"Tallie, you can go back in whenever you're
ready. We've got our guy, and I already told Mrs.
Petrovski that you're clear to clean. Can you be
there in an hour? I'll meet you to do one last walk-
through, and then the house will be released."

I had a bad feeling about this all the way around,
but I agreed to meet him. I didn't even ask him
whom he had taken into custody in the hour or so
since I'd last heard from him. Maybe if I got there
a little early, I could poke around without Burton
and look for that vanished half wall. Maybe then
I'd feel that I had a place to start. After I hung up
with Burton, I finished my food in a hurry.

"Do you want me to go with you?" Max asked.

I winced, not wanting to tell him no, but knowing

that he could be of better use here. He must have caught the wince, because he patted my hand.

"How about I look up the backgrounds of the deceased and her boyfriend while you go into battle?" he said.

My sigh of relief was small, because I didn't want to seem ungrateful or too grateful. There had to be an in-between there.

Before I could try too hard to find it, I decided to head out to the mansion. Now would be the time to see if I could find that extra half wall. I had a feeling something was going on there, and it had to have something to do with Audra's death. I could be totally wrong, but I also could be totally right.

Since I had an hour, I decided to stop in to talk with Gina and get Burton a coffee. Perhaps that would make him happier to see me. I doubted it, but it was worth a try. I'd have to make it quick if I wanted to look around the mansion, yet the gesture of coffee for Burton might go a long way toward him not being angry with me in the long run.

When I entered the Bean There Done That, it was hopping. Coffee scented the air, along with the distinct aroma of fresh-baked cinnamon rolls. I wanted all of them, and I heard my stomach rumble even over the dandy electronic music Gina had playing in the background. I had just had an amazing breakfast, but apparently, my stomach was like Pavlov's dog when it came to food.

After sidling up to the counter, I waited for Gina

to finish with a customer. She smiled, she laughed, and she counted out change faster than anyone I had ever seen, and all with an air of happiness and serenity, which I didn't think I could ever pull off. The tea shop was out, because I would never rock it like Gina did.

When she turned to me finally, the smile faded a little. "Oh, Tallie, you're back. Did you decide that you need me to don my deerstalker?"

I crossed my arms on the counter and groaned. "Why does everyone automatically think I'm going to get involved in an investigation just because someone died under suspicious circumstances?"

She simply raised her perfectly waxed eyebrow at me, threw her towel over her shoulder, and crossed her arms. "Really?"

"Tallie!" Mama Shirley came bustling around the corner and into view. I braced myself to deal with Gina's exuberant mother, because this could go either way. That tone could mean she was happy to see me and wanted me to do something for her; or it could mean she thought I had done something wrong, and she'd been waiting for the opportunity to take me to task.

"What are you doing here, young woman?" She, too, raised an eyebrow, threw a towel over her shoulder, and crossed her arms over her chest. Despite the dyed blond hair on Mama Shirley and the black hair on Gina, they looked almost like twins. I would never tell Gina that, because she'd cut me off from my lifeblood—coffee. Or, more specifically, whoopie pie lattes.

"I am, um, getting my mid-morning coffee and

then ordering some to take to Chief Burton, who is opening up the mansion to be cleaned after the death there."

"I heard about that. Good, good. I was going to tell you to get your rear end out there. I know you don't want to own a company, but now that you do, you need to take care of it like it's your baby. Not that you and Gina are providing me with any grandchildren to bounce on these old knees, but at least it's a step in the right direction. Now, if we could just get your Max to move up here and your brother to finally do the right thing by my daughter."

Oh so many things in her little speech that I did not want to touch. Correction. *Wouldn't* touch. At all. As in ever. Maybe I'd just stop by the gas station for a coffee on my way out to the mansion. I needed to get out of here now.

"Now, what are you having? I'll fix it myself, since I know what Burton will want, and you're pretty predictable."

Gina hid a smile behind a cough and waved to me. I'd see her tonight possibly, if our schedules meshed, and I'd take her to task then. Mama Shirley wasn't the only one who could bring down the hammer.

"Actually, more than coffee, I was wondering if you could help me out. What do you know about the Petrovskis? I'm wondering why Mrs. Petrovski is totally set on selling the mansion right this minute, so much, in fact, that she demanded Burton close up the investigation and release the mansion so that it can to be cleaned *now*."

Mama Shirley leaned in, as if she was about to

tell a secret. I mimicked her, hoping that she was about to lay something exquisite on me.

"I have no idea. I thought that was your area of expertise. I don't really know about the rich people around here."

"That's ridiculous," I said back quickly. "You know more than anyone at all around here, and I need info if I'm going to convince Burton that he isn't insane for thinking I can help."

She pursed her lips. "I'm not one to gossip."

Thank God I hadn't been drinking anything when she said that, as I would have snorted it out my nose. I barely kept myself from rolling my eyes. Gina did that for me behind her mother's back.

"I heard there might be some trouble in the financial arena for them and the Petrovskis need to sell things off, or they're heading for financial ruin. She's got a lot of property that she appears to be preparing for sale."

It could be very bad for my checking account and my crew if Mrs. Petrovski's check bounced. Maybe I would follow Audra's tip to cash any checks immediately.

"But what would Mrs. Petrovski's financial trouble have to do with Audra's murder? Surely having someone die at her house will make it more difficult to sell the mansion. You have to disclose that kind of information to a buyer, and everyone in town probably knows about it by now."

Mama shrugged. "You asked for information. I gave it to you. That's all I've got right now. I'm going to bingo tonight, while you young people are frolicking around. I can keep my ear open for more than the winning numbers if you want me to."

She eyed me, and I eyed her back. Because often these things came with a price tag. I went for it, anyway. "Okay. Let me know if you hear anything at bingo."

"Sure thing, sweetheart. Now let me go do my job, so you can do yours."

Was she talking about cleaning or finding another murderer?

I knew which one Burton would prefer it to be, and I was sad that I was going to have to disappoint him. Well, at least a little. But he needed me, and he'd asked me to contribute, so I was going to take my own advice to Matt and take Burton at face value. I just hoped I wasn't going to regret that.

Chapter Nine

I had stayed too long at the Bean. I was perilously close to being late to meet Burton within his deadline. While exchanging information with Gina I'd forgotten about searching for that half wall. It was probably better that I hadn't had time to go into the house without Burton anyway, since it would have only angered him. Still, I rushed along, once again hoping that no one had set up a speed trap. But I didn't see a single cop out on the road. In fact, I didn't see any at the mansion, either, when I pulled up. I found myself all alone in the driveway: the Dumpster was gone, and no other car was parked anywhere for as far as the eye could see.

Exiting my car, I tried to decide what I wanted to do. I did want to check for that wall, but I didn't want to get into trouble for overstepping the boundaries Burton had so frequently set up in our previous interactions.

He should have been here by now, though. From my dash clock I could tell that I was only three minutes early, but time could be relative when dealing with the cops. He might have had another call come in that he had to deal with or paperwork that took precedence over meeting me at the mansion. So then the question became, should I call Burton and ask if I was late or if he was running behind? Should I get back in my car and come back when he was ready to meet me again? After more thought, I realized it would be a much better idea not to touch anything I shouldn't which could possibly hinder the investigation, if it was still ongoing. Then again, I wanted to find that extra wall, and this might be a great time to do it.

Before I could make a decision between what I wanted to do and what I should do, my phone rang. I didn't recognize the number, but I picked up, anyway.

Mrs. Petrovski's voice rang loud and clear over the phone. "I will not say I'm happy about this, but I want to offer the job to you. You will clean another property until the ridiculous hold on the mansion for an accident is released, and then you will clean and take care of the mansion quickly. Two weeks tops for everything. I expect exemplary work for my troubles."

I wasn't sure where to start. I didn't need any favors, and I certainly didn't want a woman who thought I was incompetent and needed to be hustled along paying me with a chancy check. I also didn't know why she was saying Audra's death was an accident.

Then again, I had a crew to think about, and

this was what I had wanted, anyway. Beyond that, I wondered why she didn't know—though I knew—that Burton was releasing the hold on the mansion at this moment. I was quick to answer her after I let those thoughts run through my head for a split second. "What property do you want cleaned, and when should we start?"

She harrumphed. Yeah, this was going to be a fun contract all the way around.

"I'm still deciding between two properties. You may start first thing tomorrow, and I will tell you which one I've decided on. Both are three stories and need a thorough cleaning. I reserve the right to refuse to let you clean the mansion if your first property is not done to my satisfaction and within the time frame I requested."

Think about the crew, I told myself as I bit my tongue. "Of course, and we do an excellent and exemplary job every time, Mrs. Petrovski. Shall I pick up the keys tomorrow, once you decide which house you want done first?" Apparently, I also got formal when I was biting my tongue.

"Where are you now? We can meet so I can give both sets of keys to you."

Should I tell her I was at the mansion, waiting for Burton to get here, so that I could go through the house again? If he hadn't told her yet, then I should keep it to myself.

"I have an appointment in five minutes. I can call you as soon as I'm done. Then we can set a time and a place."

"That will be fine, though I do want to note that you're already not fitting into the schedule I have set out."

I barely kept myself from harrumphing. "Duly noted. I'll call you in an hour."

The phone went dead without a good-bye, but that was absolutely okay with me.

I'd call Letty and ask her to meet me in an hour and a half. That way I could have some time with Burton before I pulled her and the girls in for cleaning duty. I'd be cutting it close in terms of the meet-up night with Max and my friends, but there wasn't much I could do about that at this point.

After leaving Letty a message, which I hoped she would get, I headed to the front door, though I still hadn't decided what to do about entering the house. Or at least not consciously, as I slid the key into the lock. Squealing tires behind me for the second time in one day stopped my hand.

What now?

I should never ask myself that question.

I turned to find Burton striding up the drive-way, hand on his gun belt. It wasn't like I was a threat or anything. Or was there a threat inside that I didn't know about? Had he gotten a call about the mansion, and was he trying to save me?

I doubted it.

"You're early," he grumbled. I forced myself not to look at my phone for the time, because I knew that wasn't true.

"I haven't gone in yet, even though I have a key. I'd like brownie points for that."

That got me a gruff laugh that could have been equal parts disbelief and actual mirth. "Fine. Brownie points for you. It doesn't quite offset the fact that you're in the negative as far as brownie points go so anything you earn now is only going to maybe get you to zero instead of negative seventeen, but I guess it's something."

Laughing and joking. *Be still, my heart.* "You wanted me out here, and I'm out here. What's the deal? Am I cleaning? I didn't see any death stuff to clean up when I went through the house before. Or did I miss something, and do I have to clean that up too?" I'd never had to do that. With Darla's murder, the house had already been cleaned; with Waldo, I hadn't had to touch a thing. The other crime scenes I'd found had been cleaned also. From the little I knew, I didn't believe there was blood to be cleaned up here, but since most everything was being held close to the vest, I guessed that anything was possible.

A brief thought flitted through my head that maybe I should start offering to do the cleanup for the police department. With my new crew, it could be one more service we offered. It could also be advantageous to be on the scene if another murder happened in town. Then I thought about how gross that would probably be, and immediately dismissed the thought. My true calling would show up. I knew it. I just had to wait.

"All you have to clean is the house itself and nothing related to the crime. There was no blood to speak of, due to the fact that, we believe, she was strangled. I'm just waiting for the confirmation from the coroner on that point, so don't worry your pretty little head over it. Now, any evidence as far as the aftermath is going to be in that carpet." He paced and then paced some more. From previous experience, I knew to wait him out. He had something on his mind, and my probing would not net me anything more than he was willing to say in his own sweet time.

But my time was going to run out before I had to talk to Mrs. Petrovski, and I wanted to find that secret wall before I even mentioned the thing to Burton. I'd learned my lesson on bringing things to him without a solid backing of information to support my theories.

Finally, he stopped in front of me and pulled on his bottom lip. I waited as he stared at me, wanting to look away, but not wanting to seem like I couldn't maintain eye contact.

"There's something fishy going on here, Tallie, and I don't know what it is. Something feels wrong about this whole thing, and I just can't put my finger on it."

Okay, then. What did he expect me to say to that? If I offered to listen to his theory, I knew the chances were good that he might tell me no and shove me back into my car. But if I didn't say anything, then I might miss an opportunity to legitimately help find my friend's killer, instead of sneaking around behind Burton's back, like I usually did.

So I went for the truth. "I'm not sure what to tell you. I think there's something fishy, too, and it just feels like there's more going on here than we know about. I was planning on looking around inside the house, but I don't know what I thought I would find. Have you done a background check on Audra? On Caleb? I don't even know who her friends are or her family."

He sighed, and I understood. The previous times I'd looked into a suspicious death in the area, someone shady had appeared on my radar right at the start of my investigation, so that by this stage, I'd already made significant headway toward determining who the perpetrator was. This case just seemed to have stalled, and it had been only hours since Audra's body had been found in the Dumpster.

"Where is the Dumpster?" I asked. "Did you guys have to take that to the crime lab to go over it more thoroughly?"

"If by *crime lab*, you mean the parking lot behind the police station, then yes. I'm not sure where else we could have put it, and it was a bear to get down the alley, but the truck driver managed."

"Did he say who had called him to pick the thing up in the first place? He seemed pretty adamant that he was expecting no one to be here yesterday afternoon and that he had been told he could pick up even if nobody was around to give the okay. Why would whoever ordered the pickup make a point of telling the driver this? The only thing I can come up with is that the person who ordered the pickup didn't want anyone to find something in that Dumpster, so he or she wasted no time in sending a driver and chose an hour of the day when nobody would be around to interfere. Also, I was thinking, why would he or she have called to have a half-empty Dumpster picked up? Those things are not inexpensive, and now Mrs. Petrovski's going to have to pay to have another one dropped off."

"It's a little scary that our minds work on a similar track."

Scary for me, not him, in my opinion. But I kept that to myself and waited for him to continue.

"Do I dare ask if you've called the Dumpster company and pretended to be from the police department to find out who called in the pickup?"

"Of course not!" But I should have. *Darn it!*

"Don't sound offended. I'm not the chief for nothing. I can see on your face that you wish you had."

Things were not going to go well if he could read my face now. I'd have to work on my stoic look. I tried it out now, and he just laughed again.

He went on. "Look, this is not going to be an easy one. As far as any background checks, the girl was a peach. She did her homework in school, she was an honor student, and everyone I have talked to loved her. She did no wrong and had no enemies. I have nowhere to start and no idea why someone would have killed her, wrapped her in a carpet, and then, we're guessing, shoved her out the window. We've found no prints on the carpet, but that can be difficult with the fibers. And it's not like we don't know where she was before she was killed. As far as we can tell, she never left the mansion."

Should I mention that the carpet had been too neatly arranged to have fallen in the Dumpster from the second story? Or had it? Maybe the murderer had dropped it out the window and then had gone to arrange it.

And should I tell him about the half wall in the pictures? Should I show him the pictures? I felt like I wanted to keep it to myself , too, until I could say for certain where it was and what it was, but sharing could go a long way toward making him believe I just wanted to help, not steal his sunshine.

Indecision must have shown on my face, because he stared me down. "If you have something to add, please let me know. I don't want this to become a cold case. Her family is sick with grief, her boyfriend wants justice, and the local population would look far more kindly on my depleted department if I can solve this in as little time as possible."

"I thought you had the person in custody and that was why we were out here. All wrapped up. Just waiting for me to clean."

"I lied. Or I didn't lie at first, but it ended up being a lie. Yolanda told me someone came in and confessed, but when I entered the interrogation room, it was Gerald Sweets."

I groaned. Gerald came out of the woodwork every once in a while, claiming to have done all manner of things, like he shot Lincoln and was part of a gaggle of geese and was the first to discover coffee. Personally, I thought he was lonely, but he wouldn't talk to you if you approached him. Just sit with his eyes closed, in the criss-cross-applesauce position, no matter where he was, and hum.

"Yeah, so back to square one again."

"But you always yell at me for getting involved and tell me that I should go get a hobby. I want to believe that you actually want my help this time, but I'm struggling with the concept."

Rolling his eyes, he moved his gun back and forth in the holster before crossing his arms over his chest. "It'll be like any other tip that gets called in to the station. I am not against you helping. I'm against you getting yourself involved where it's not your business. It's one thing to hand over information you think will help the investigation. It's another thing to actively go out and find that information and then act on it yourself and bring me the finished product, instead of letting me do my job."

Okay, so now I was going to have to show him the pictures and hope he'd invite me along to check out this wall.

I dug into my purse for my phone, and he put his hands on his hips.

"Did you actually listen to what I just said, and now you're going to be a concerned citizen instead of a vigilante?" He laughed again, but this time his laughter had less disbelief and more mirth. Hey, I could learn.

I thumbed on my phone just as a car came trundling up the driveway. It should have been Letty, whom I'd ask to meet me here to go over the schedule before I called Mrs. Petrovski back. Instead it was Preston. Again.

I put my phone back in my purse. I was not going to show the photos to anyone but Burton. I wanted those brownie points, so I could wait until Preston left before getting them.

"I was hoping I'd find you both here. Burton, how are we doing on the investigation? Is the house ready to be opened?"

"As I told your aunt about an hour ago, we're wrapping things up." With his expression completely neutral, Burton looked the nephew over.

"Excellent. I know Aunt Marg must be pleased with that. She just asked me to come out and see if there was anything I could do to help."

"I don't think anything needs to be done at this point. We're opening the house to let Tallie and her crew get to cleaning so your aunt can sell."

"And that's it? Did you figure out who did it, then?"

"We're still in the process of investigating."

As the two men talked back and forth, I watched them like I would a tennis match. Would Burton take Preston up on his offer to help, and dismiss me? Preston would be able to confirm where the carpet had been and would know if there were any hidden doors or walls, wouldn't he? But I felt stupid asking, so I kept my mouth shut.

"How long do these investigations usually take? Will it hold up the sale of the house?"

"Not that I'm aware of, Mr. Prescott. It's just a matter of an extra day at this point. I understand your aunt has a buyer coming in, and I believe Tallie will be able to do a fine job of cleaning things up with her crew."

Another compliment. I thought I might have to swoon.

"Okay then." Preston shot those cuffs of his. This time his outfit was a swirling pattern of watercolor peacocks on a pale yellow background. Where did he get these shirts? "Let me know if there's anything I can do. I really want to help out my aunt and, honestly, myself. The sale of this house makes so much sense for our family. It's been vacant for a number of years and seems to just be sitting here, doing nothing but costing us money for taxes. I have a business proposition I'd like my aunt to entertain, but she won't even listen to me until this monstrosity is off the books." He finally looked at me.

"If you could get this done as soon as possible, I'd really appreciate it. I'm running out of time to buy into an incredible opportunity."

With that, he got back in his car and zoomed off down the drive. Burton and I looked at each other for a moment.

"A business opportunity that can't wait? Do you think he's up to his elbows in something he shouldn't be?" I asked.

"You have such a vivid imagination. Do you always think everyone is up to something?"

"Well, when we used to run in the same circles, you could always count on Preston to have some kind of scheme up his sleeve. I think he depends on his aunt for a whole lot more than familial niceties. If I remember correctly, she pays a lot of his bills. Or at least she used to."

I bit my lip, because I could ask Mrs. Petrovski without actually having to have a reason to do so. There would be an opportunity when she handed over the keys. I'd just pretend to make inane conversation with her and subtly slip in a question or two about how involved Preston seemed to be in this project. Or maybe I'd be able to address obliquely the opportunity he had mentioned by asking if it was something that Max might be interested in.

She might not like me a whole lot, but she didn't really know me. At least not the new me. If I turned on the charm, I might be able to have her eating out of my hand. It wouldn't be out of the question for me to be in a position where I could ask her, in a subtle way, if Preston was self-sufficient. I could handle that without it seeming like a police matter and without making her think anything of it other than I was being nosy. If Burton asked her such questions, she'd want to know why he was doing so and what it had to do with anything. I'd be gathering information under the guise of looking for gossip, but he'd have to be official.

All that ran through my head in seconds, with Burton still looking at me.

"It's scary how I can almost see your brain working. I don't think it has anything to do with the case, but if you want to ask dearest auntie if she pays Preston's bills, then go for it," he said.

"It could explain why she has to sell so fast. And I could ask Max to look up any tax records, without it being an official inquiry, too."

He just shook his head, but he didn't say no. I was taking that as a yes.

"You were going to show me something on your phone," he said with some resignation back in his voice.

I took my phone out again and was almost afraid to show him the photos, in case it seemed like I was being too fanciful. He already thought I was suspicious of everyone. What would he think when I showed him a wall that shouldn't be there?

I had to chance it, though, just in case.

"These came in about an hour ago." Letty was waiting on me and I didn't want to leave her hanging for too long but I really needed to show Burton the pictures. She would understand when I explained the situation to her. She could then at least talk to Mrs. Petrovski enough to find out what she wanted cleaned in the other property while I would hopefully be looking for this wall that had vanished. If Burton let me tag along.

I handed him my phone and stood back while he scrolled.

"What am I looking at?"

"Mostly pictures I asked Bethany to take the night before the murder, when she came out here to look over the job. Mrs. Petrovski did not let anyone in the house before she told us to come try out for the job of cleaning this place up. Then, for whatever reason, she opened up the house for us the night before we competed for the job, but I had won tickets to a play in Hershey. So Bethany offered to drop by the mansion, take pictures, then send me the images before she headed out on vacation with her new boyfriend. She got accepted into college, and they were going to celebrate."

He studied the pictures and stopped about halfway down. I watched as I stood by his side, and was gratified to see that he had paused on the picture with the extra half wall. Then he scrolled down a little more and stopped at the next picture, the one with the carpet.

"What room is this in?" he asked, pointing at the carpet.

"I'm pretty sure it's in the upstairs bedroom."

"Not where we thought she had been killed." He said it more to himself, but it was information to me, so I stored it in my brain. "Something is wrong with this one." As he pointed at the wall, I nodded.

"That half wall is not there right now. I've been over this house multiple times, and I haven't seen a half wall anywhere."

He bit his lip. I so wanted him to invite me in, so I could find out which room this was and where the wall had disappeared to, but we were in a pretty good place right now. I didn't want to press my luck, in case he sent me home to go get that hobby everyone seemed to bug me about constantly.

"Any idea what room this might be?" he asked.

I shrugged, because I had been racking my brain to figure it out and had had absolutely no luck. "I'm thinking it almost has to be upstairs, near one of the bedrooms. I don't think Bethany ran from one floor to another, all over the place, taking pictures. She had promised to be methodical, so I would know what we were getting ourselves into."

He bit his lip again, and I wanted to prod him, ask him if I could go with him, and demand that we go right now. But I waited, and then I congratulated myself on my restraint when he said, "Let's go find this thing and figure out what it's hiding."

Chapter Ten

I was in! I was so in, and I loved that he was going to let me go along on the search. I would, of course, let him take the lead, so he didn't think I was being too assertive or trying to take over his investigation. But I couldn't wait to see where this wall that looked all wrong was and find out if there was anything hidden behind it. I only hoped we could actually find the wall, since I knew I had not seen it in any of the rooms, which I'd toured numerous times now.

Burton opened the front door with his own key, then removed some leftover crime-scene tape from inside the doorway as we entered the house. Every footfall seemed to echo in the quiet.

I couldn't help myself as I catalogued the furniture and where it might have to go. It was sometimes a hazard of cleaning houses that I knew were going to be sold. I had a lot of relatives in town that did a lot of different things so I was always on the lookout for opportunities for those relatives. I doubted Mrs. Petrovski was going to sell the house furnished and if I could offer her a solution, then maybe she would look more kindly on me for being so helpful. I could call a moving company. Mrs. Petroski might think to sell the pieces individually, but if she needed the money fast, then she might want to consider doing an auction. I had a cousin in Carlisle who could make that happen for her, and quickly, if she was so inclined. I made a mental note and then jogged to catch up with Burton, who had already moved to the wide staircase leading to the second floor.

"Since the pictures were taken at night, and some of the rooms are poorly lit, I can't tell which rooms they are, other than by keeping an eye out for hideous wallpaper and decrepit furniture. Since every room seems to be an eyesore and there are so many of them, I'm not sure which is which. They all seem to blur together after a while. We can't tell the direction, since the sun wasn't out, just the moon."

"The furniture isn't decrepit," I said, affronted. "That's some serious antique merchandise here that people would pay a pretty penny for."

"Whatever. I prefer my furniture to be made in this century, and by machine, if possible."

"Well, now, Burton, I had no idea you were so modern."

"There's a lot you don't know about me, Tallie, but that's for another day. Let's get moving on this room."

I couldn't shake the feeling that someone was watching us as we moved from room to room. So far none of the rooms we'd toured contained the wallpaper and the furniture featured in the photo with the half wall. The mansion was huge, and I was afraid I was going to miss my friend and my boyfriend time if we didn't find this half wall fast.

A car horn honked out front. I took the opportunity to look out the window and was so thankful it was finally Letty, and not some other person who wasn't supposed to be here. Glancing at my watch, I realized she was early and I had about ten minutes to call Mrs. Petrovski back before my hour was up.

"I'm going to run down and talk with Letty about how things have changed. I'll be right back. Don't find it without me," I said.

He harrumphed. I chose to take that as an indication that he agreed to this.

Running down the stairs was not my best option, but I wanted to get back to the hunt as soon as possible. I was out of breath when I hit the foyer. After pulling open the door, I stood there, huffing and puffing.

Letty laughed at me, with one hand on her petite hip and her other hand carrying her ever-present caddy of supplies. "Should I even ask what you were doing?"

"Ha, ha, ha. Burton and I are here checking out a few things, but I'm actually going to need you to move on to a different house. If you'll give me a minute, I'll call Mrs. Petrovski to see which house she chose and confirm the address. I'm sure she'd love to have us clean now, instead of waiting until tomorrow morning. She's being hypercritical of my scheduling abilities." Plus, I had to offer something because this conversation had now put me over the one-hour call time and I was going to be in trouble.

Letty put her caddy down on the floor as she stepped in and then pulled the door closed behind her. "Wait, are you saying that Burton's actually going to let you help this time? You don't have to do all that behind-the-back stuff and sneaking around? I could have sworn he would have changed his mind when the time actually came to start moving on the clue finding and the investigation beyond what they've done so far, which looks like a lot of nothing to me."

"Letty! I do not sneak around or do anything behind anyone's back. And keep your voice down. Burton is just upstairs."

"Really? Come on. It's not a bad thing, necessarily." But she ruined her words by snickering. "Hey, at least this time you won't have to explain yourself."

"I already did that," I grumbled.

"Seriously, though, Tallie. I appreciate this. I need to know what happened to Audra, and I need justice. I'm afraid they're going to pull Caleb back in if they can't figure out who did it, and that kid has had a hard life. He needs a break, not more troubles. I'm not as brave as you are, so I'm going to have to wait to see what you find out."

"I've been told to be a concerned citizen, not a vigilante."

"And are you going to listen?"

"Of course I'm going to listen. Now you listen, Letty. I'm glad we called everyone in, though I feel bad that they have to go to another house. But when they all get here, just have them wait a minute, while

I get Mrs. Petrovski on the phone. We don't need to worry about cleaning here just yet, because we have other things going on. Burton is going to want to do some more investigating. I need to call the owner and find out if she has another Dumpster on the way. I'm late with that call as it is."

"It would be better if she did." Letty could be so very practical.

"You and I know that, but maybe not Mrs. Petrovski. I'll ask Burton when I go back upstairs," I said. "I hope it can be here this afternoon. I don't know if she called him to see if it was okay to bring one in or if we should just pile debris outside, to be sifted through."

What a mess that would be, especially because wallpaper didn't always come off in strips.

"Well, that's something at least. Okay, then we'll get people moving with the cleaning, and we'll go from there." Letty's forehead crinkled, which made me worry that this might be too much for her.

"I know you don't like being in charge, but I need you to do that this time. Sorry for putting you in this position."

"Oh, Tallie, it's not that I don't like being in charge. It's that I don't want to have to handle the money aspect." She smiled and turned away to open the front door. I didn't know how she knew someone was standing there, but sure enough, two of my other ladies were hovering on the front porch, armed to the teeth with vacuums and caddies that matched Letty's. Maybe I should have some custom made with our logo. Of course, first, I'd have to come up with a name for my motley crew, but that would come to me soon enough.

Right now, I had to call Mrs. Petrovski, then find out if Burton had found the hidden half wall, and if I'd missed the big reveal, I couldn't allow myself to get angry.

I dialed Mrs. Petrovski and then ended up having to leave a message. Either she was in the middle of something else, or she was angry enough at my tardiness that she refused to pick up. Either way, I left her a nice message about getting in touch with me so that we could meet up to get the keys for the other house and discuss what she wanted done.

Despite the fact that I wanted to run back up the stairs after I hung up, I took them one at a time and carefully. No use landing on my face on the landing.

"Yoo-hoo! Burton!" I called from the top of the stairs. A crystal chandelier hung from the ceiling a few feet away from the second-floor landing, and it illuminated the foyer below.

He peeked his head out of a room on my left, looking slightly disgruntled. Okay, then, he hadn't found the hidden wall yet, or he wouldn't look that unhappy.

"Trouble?" I asked.

"You took your phone with you, and I have no idea what room matches which picture. I have no eye for room details. Which do you think it is?"

I felt a blush run up my neck and face. While I hadn't intended to take the phone, he also hadn't asked for it. I'd just have to brush off his brusque comment and soldier on.

After taking the phone from my back pocket, I thumbed on the screen, then went hunting for the pictures again. I'd gotten a new phone recently, and the thing was trying my patience at every turn. But at least the picture quality was stellar when I finally found the pictures I was looking for.

"We're looking for animal-print wallpaper and a shaggy rug in brown." I didn't remember seeing a room like that, and I'd looked through a lot of the rooms more than once.

It occurred to me that these could be the wrong pictures, or that Bethany had accidentally sent me pictures of something else, like an old apartment she was looking at downtown above the chocolatier. A ripple of panic went through me. What if I had sent us on a wild-goose chase and made a big deal out of nothing? Man! I should have kept these things to myself, until I'd checked it out alone, and then given it to Burton as a done deal. Now I was going to look like an idiot. I hated looking like an idiot!

"Um . . . ," I began, but I couldn't find the right words to say I might be mistaken.

"Yes, Tallie? I don't have all day. I have background checks to run and a bunch of evidence to process. Spit out whatever you're going to say."

Biting my lip, I looked at the floor and didn't look up again. "I'm sorry, but I think this was a mistake. Bethany might have sent me extra pictures. I don't know. All I know is that I don't remember seeing a room decorated like this, even though I've been through the house a number of times."

He sighed instead of harrumphing. I considered that much better than yelling. He ruined it by pinching the bridge of his nose, like he did when he was truly irritated. "I have things to do. Go ahead and go, then, we'll come back another time."

"I am sorry. I'll be out of your hair. Mrs. Petrovski wants us to clean another house in town until the police investigation is wrapped up here," I offered.

He sighed again. I so wished we could have found that wall!

"Fine." He clamped his hand to the back of his neck. "Go clean to your little heart's content in the other house for Mrs. Petrovski. If you think of anything, please call the station as a concerned citizen instead of going after it like that vigilante we talked about earlier. And call Bethany while you're at it, to make sure those pictures are all of this house, not of somewhere else."

I still didn't look up. "Sure thing."

I listened to him walk out of the room and then let my shoulders finally drop from where they'd been hovering at my ears.

Someone knocked on the doorjamb less than a minute later. I glanced up just to check out who it was, then looked back at the phone in my hands.

"What was that all about?" Letty hooked her thumb over her shoulder in Burton's direction. "On his way out to his car, Burton was grumbling about people wasting his precious time and about how trying to do something nice always bites him in the rear. I thought you guys were looking for something in particular. Did you find it?"

I gave one of those mirthless laughs that sometimes accompanied defeat. "I thought I had a break in the case and a wonky extra room in the house that I needed to find. Turns out that it's possible I was completely wrong. And now Burton is angry with me."

Letty put her arm around my shoulder. "I'm sure you'll figure it out. Besides, it doesn't hurt Burton to get out of the station every once in a while. Plenty of people call in tips that don't lead anywhere. If it had been anyone else, he would still have had to check it out."

I shrugged, but not so hard that I removed her arm. "Do you know this room?" I showed her the picture on my phone, thinking maybe I just hadn't remembered it in the thirty-five-room mansion. I didn't know why I thought she would, since she hadn't been in the house before now, but I was out of ideas.

Surprisingly, she nodded. "Sure, that's on the first floor, next to the laundry room."

I sputtered, "But how do you know that? I sent Bethany to take the pictures so we would know what the place looks like. Did you go with her?"

Letty shook her head at me. "No, I didn't go with Bethany. Darla loaned me out to the Petrovskis a little over a year ago. And I still have nightmares about this whole house and can visualize the rooms like they're chasing me, with their yucky wallpaper and funky carpets. That carpet was a pain in the rear end to clean. I'll never forget it. I guess I could have told you that, but I really wanted Bethany to get signed on to help us, and I didn't know if the house had changed."

After being stunned into silence, I tore out of the room and down the staircase, and then threw open the front door, hoping to catch Burton, but he'd already gone. I wasn't going to call him until

I knew for certain what was behind door number one.

I heard Letty hit the steps behind me and waited in the foyer for her to catch up.

"What are we looking for?" she asked, out of breath. She was much tinier than I was, so it soothed me just a little that she also was running short on breath after those stairs.

"This room. Can you show me where it is?"

"Of course."

I followed her down the hall to the left and around several corners, until I felt like I was in a maze. Doors appeared along the hall in intervals, and I wondered how on earth we were going to clean this monstrosity, even if we had all the time in the world.

She opened a door on the right and stepped back. "Voilà!"

But it wasn't voilà; nothing in the room matched anything in the picture. The carpet was burgundy and had a flat weave, like an industrial carpet, with no shag in sight. The wallpaper was a subtle muted cream and gold, with a fleur-de-lis design and white trim. The floor was speckled around the edges of the carpet. I couldn't tell if it was paint or bits of paper, but I ignored it for the moment in my excitement to find out if this was the right room.

I showed her the picture again, and she bit her lip. "I could have sworn this was the right room. I remember thinking that the carpet was going to be a pain to clean, and I hoped we would just be allowed to throw the thing out. In fact, I don't remember any room looking this nice. They're all decorated outlandishly, and this one is almost tasteful."

She looked around, and I did the same thing. I, of course, wasn't sure what I was looking for, since I didn't remember being in this room before at all, but there had to be something. I scuffed my feet along the floor through the scraps of paper and dirt. Nothing was making sense and normally things at least made a little sense.

"I don't know what the deal is, but we'd better get ready to clean at that other house for Mrs. Petrovski. We're running out of time for today, and I don't want everyone thinking that we're skipping out on helping by just walking through rooms. Why don't you go check on everyone while I try to get Mrs. Petrovski on the phone again to see where she is? I thought she'd be here by now."

Really, I wanted to tackle the bathrooms here, which hadn't been used in heaven knew how long. I did some of my best thinking while I was elbow deep in tub scrubbing.

As I headed back to the foyer, I was greeted by two smiling faces along the way and a ton of empty rooms. I really should have looked more thoroughly into this job before I took it sight unseen. I sighed and headed out the front door and down the porch stairs. For such a huge house, there were few bathrooms, but the ones that were here were dirty, not just dirty, but totally neglected, with soap scum and black marks everywhere. Thankfully, the marks weren't mold and rust. I was going to clean one of those bathrooms just to get the juices flowing, after I spoke with Mrs. Petrovski and cleared it with Burton.

I placed both calls. I cleared it with Burton, and even though he still wanted to see about evidence, he had no problem with my cleaning a bathroom, thankfully. He even offered to let me come over and clean his two bathrooms if that would help me. Funny guy, that Burton. I also got a grudging okay from Mrs. Petrovski to clean one of the bathrooms, at least until she could get here with the keys to the other houses.

And then I selected a bathroom, got down on my knees, sprayed the interior of the tub with one of those industrial cleaners, and got to work. Scrubbing the black muck around the rim first, I ran through everything that had happened so far. Audra was dead, rolled up in a carpet and moved out of the house. So how did it get out to the Dumpster? And why had she been killed?

As far as I knew, she was a nice woman who had just been starting out in life, getting engaged to her boyfriend and cleaning for a big commercial company. She had done a great job at the few places I'd heard about, and she'd always shown up on time. We'd not yet achieved official friend status, we hadn't talked on the phone or shot each other texts throughout the day, and we hadn't gone out for drinks. But we'd been getting to know each other, and I had a feeling that we would have done all those things if she'd lived longer. It was sad that her life was now over.

Then we had the actual killing. I still didn't know how exactly she had been killed. Strangled? That was what Burton thought, but he couldn't confirm it until the coroner gave him his report. Shot? But if she'd been shot, then wouldn't there be blood somewhere? The floors themselves appeared to be clean, and the walls, though weirdly decorated, didn't have any signs of blood spatter on them.

I moved from the black marks to the green streaks running down to the base of the tub and used a special scrub brush for those. They came right off. My sense of accomplishment was huge when I could actually see the way the tub was going to gleam when I was done with it.

Burton wasn't against me working with him as a concerned citizen this time, but I didn't even have anything to offer, especially not after the mix-up with the pictures. Again, I wondered briefly if maybe the pictures were of the apartment Bethany was looking at. Letty thought they had been taken here at the mansion, yet neither of us could find the room in one of the photos. But the ceilings in the photos looked the same as those in this house. They had a swirly pattern, which gave them a texture I loved. And the wood flooring in the photos matched the actual flooring in the mansion.

Where could that room be, though? Could it be in a part of the house I hadn't seen? But what hadn't I seen? As far as I knew, I had been in every room and had seen every nook and cranny. Nothing was hidden from me. And even if I hadn't been everywhere, I was sure Burton and his crew had done a thorough search of the entire place before letting me and my crew back in.

A knock sounded behind me. I turned to find Letty standing in the doorway, with an expectant look on her face. Was there something I should have done that I hadn't yet? I ran over our conversation in my mind and determined that there wasn't.

"Yeah?" I said.

"I remember the room. I remember where it is, and it is right where I showed you. You got a minute?"

"Of course I do!" I lumbered to my feet and gave the gleaming tub a nod of approval. Of course, it made the rest of the bathroom look like it hadn't been touched in ten years, but whatever.

I followed Letty back downstairs and around the corners to the room with the fleur-de-lis wallpaper.

"Where? What?" I said.

"See this outline on the floor?" She kicked some of the bits of paper on the floor out of the way, and I could definitely see a straight line in the wood.

"Yes."

"There was a larger carpet here, and these flecks of paper were not here. Despite how long this place has gone unused, this room is still relatively clean, except for cobwebs and stuff. There isn't paper on the floor in any other room, but there is in here. It's not much . . . It looks like someone ripped wallpaper off the wall and then hastily cleaned up the big pieces, leaving the smaller ones."

I looked around again, this time knowing what I was looking for and finding it. There were definitely little pieces of animal-print wallpaper on the floor. And the outline on the wood from a missing larger carpet became more distinct the more I looked at it. Like someone had removed the carpet that had sat here for years and had replaced it with the smaller burgundy carpet, leaving a five-inch outline on the weathered wood.

So I knew where the carpet had gone now, and I was aware that there had been pieces of something in that Dumpster with me. The questions then were, where was the hidden wall, and how was I going to go about finding it? Because I was not calling Burton back over here until I had an answer to every question he might ask.

Chapter Eleven

Thirty minutes later I still hadn't found the wall. I'd tapped on every square inch of this room that I could reach. I was running out of time, and Burton would be coming back soon. He'd texted to say he had a few things to look over in the mansion. What was I going to tell him?

And twenty minutes later, there he was. "We're out, Tallie. I have other things to do today and not enough time to do them all. Have you found anything?"

I had to shake my head and admit that I'd found nothing.

"It's okay. Maybe there really isn't a half wall, and the photo has a strange shadow. Or just the way Bethany took the picture made it look like a half wall. I tried to call Marg, and she had no idea what I was talking about."

I didn't know what to do with his niceness. Normally, he'd blame me for taking up his time or wasting his time, like he had an hour ago. But now he just looked tired and defeated. I didn't know what to do with that, either.

"It's going to be okay. We'll figure this out. I promise," I told him. Not that I could really do that, but I wanted to assure him, because I didn't want him to feel like all was lost. It was still only day two.

Burton flicked the curtain at the window. "Marg just pulled up. I don't know what she's going to say. Probably that I'm not working fast enough. I've been up for almost twenty hours."

Helpless, that was how I felt. I just wanted to go clean something and maybe try to figure out who the murderer was, so Burton didn't have to worry anymore.

That was a very strange feeling, considering that normally, we were at each other's throats. But not this time. He was looking older than his age, which made me feel worse. Even mad. He usually didn't look even his age, but now he looked older, a little depressed, and a lot defeated.

"We'll figure this out, Burton. I promise," I repeated since he hadn't responded to my first try at reassurance.

"*I'll* figure it out, Tallie. It's my job. Remember, you're just a concerned citizen," he said as we both turned toward the door, having heard Mrs. Petrovski calling out to see who was in the house.

"Get ready," I muttered right before Mrs. Petrovski entered the room.

"Tallie and James. I'm glad I found you here. We have work to do. Tallie, I need you at this address." She handed over a piece of paper, along with two sets of keys, then turned her back to me. I guessed I had been dismissed. It wasn't the first time. It probably wouldn't be the last. But still . . .

I looked at Burton, who shrugged and pretty much dismissed me himself.

Great. Now they both had decided I was not worth talking to.

I left the room, but stood just outside it to listen in on their conversation and see if I could glean any info I did not already have. What happened next really was what Burton had predicted. Mrs. Petrovski berated him for not moving fast enough— at a pace that pleased her—and for not closing this investigation. For not taking her needs and the needs of the community into consideration. In her mind, Audra's death was an unfortunate accident that needed to be swept under the rug.

I could just imagine Burton's face getting redder and redder, and I thought I should definitely not be there when it came time for him to walk out of that room. I'd be the first person he saw and probably the one he took his frustration out on. I did not need that today, or any day, really.

As I made my way through the house, I collected Letty and my other crew members and gave them the piece of paper with the address of property we were to clean and the keys. I would follow along soon enough, but first, I had to place a call to Max to see how things were going with him. Once the ladies left the mansion with their gear, I pulled out my phone and dialed Max. He picked up almost immediately. After the pleasantries were out of the way, I got down to business.

"Okay, so I don't know what this wall thing is,

and I pretty much made a fool out of myself in front of Burton. Mrs. Petrovski wants us to clean another house while she's waiting for this one to be released, and I had a crazy idea that I should start offering cleanup after murders and suicides to the cops. I dismissed the idea almost as soon as I had it, because it wouldn't just be socks crammed into a couch, but some pretty gruesome things. So that's out."

"Wow. All I did was read some papers and use a ruler to make sure I was on the right line of a column of numbers."

"You're funny."

"Seriously, Tallie, I don't think death cleanup is the way you want to go with your life. I understand it can be lucrative, but you might want to consider what exactly you'd be cleaning up and the extra equipment you'd need to acquire before doing something like that. You have a hard enough time being near dead bodies. Do you really want to be near parts and pieces instead?"

"That's pretty much the whole thought process I went through as soon as I considered it. Plus, the ladies might be even more grossed out than me." I smiled, even though Max couldn't see me. "Moving on, then. Will you be home for dinner tonight?"

"Yes, and I have a recipe I want to try out, so get ready to eat."

I groaned. My pants were not going to be able to handle me after a month of this. "I'll be ready," I said, anyway, knowing I'd eat whatever he made and probably love it to distraction, like I loved him.

We said our good-byes, and then I mentally made

a list of all the things I wanted to talk with him about tonight. I needed a different set of eyes on this picture, ones that hadn't seen the actual house and didn't have anything to compare it with. He'd seen the pictures once already, but maybe seeing them again revealed something I was missing. I had to be missing something, or I would have found that missing wall.

Out in my car, I turned the engine over and watched as Mrs. Petrovski and Burton came out the front door. Mrs. Petrovski was first, full steam ahead, as if she had places to go and things to do; and Burton trailed along behind her, as if he'd rather be anywhere else.

She was still talking, so I rolled down my car window, just in case I could get a hint of what they were talking about.

"There is no such wall. I've been in and out of this house for almost seventy years. I would know if there was such a wall. Let that go for the moment and get me a killer. Do your job as you're meant to, and leave the frivolous things alone. Tallie is not my first choice of people to help. She shouldn't be yours, either."

And then there was that saying that you never heard anything good about yourself when you eavesdropped.

I rolled up my window, but Burton still caught my eye. He shook his head, but I didn't know if it was because he was ashamed of me for not having left already or because he didn't agree with what Mrs. Petrovski had said. I didn't stick around to find out, since Mrs. Petrovski looked like she was about to head my way. Probably to tell me I should have already be working on her other property. I could just see her doing that. But a thought kept circling through my mind: How would Mrs. Petrovski not know about the half wall, unless she was lying?

I pulled out of my parking spot near the front of the house and eased my way down the driveway. I needed these moments to think about what I had seen and not seen since I'd found Audra dead. I still felt horrible that her life had been cut short. The few times we interacted, she'd seemed like a really nice person, someone I would have wanted to become friends with, but sometimes it turned out that people were not at all what they seemed. So we'd have to see what, if anything, Max had found, while digging into her background. Burton had said she was a peach, but that didn't always mean he'd tell me everything. He'd proven it before with his comments about being a concerned citizen, not a vigilante. I hoped Max had been able to find something on Audra that maybe Burton had missed or was keeping from me. So I'd ask Max about any progress he'd made on his Audra search. And also the boyfriend. And maybe that helper of hers, though I'd have to remember her name first.

I also had an absurd curiosity about Preston Prescott. He seemed to be following people around like a bloodhound. Though that was not unusual, it also wasn't usual, unless he thought he could get something from you.

But what did he want from me?

I knew what his aunt wanted—for me to clean that house. And I wouldn't get any peace until it was done. In fact, my phone dinged on the seat next to me, and I had little doubt that it was her trying to tell me to hurry up.

Cleaning a house that was nearly clean was never a hardship. From the info I had already got from Letty, the tenants of this rental property were always very fastidious about keeping things clean. I wasn't sure why Mrs. Petrovski wanted us to do this house, but I supposed it was that gift horse thing and not looking in its mouth, because you might find cavities. The property was in the next town over, so about two miles away, and was easy enough to find.

Pulling into the driveway, I was gratified to see everyone else's car here, except Bethany's. She was off today, and I had let that stand. I had left her a message, just to make sure the pictures were all of the house, and hadn't heard back from her yet. There was no need to pull in another person when I didn't know what all needed to be cleaned, and she was on vacation.

I wished I were, too.

Instead I was here, checking up on my ragtag crew and hoping that I hadn't taken on more than I could handle just to play nice with those I used to air kiss before I'd performed my swan dive from the upper crust of our small society by divorcing Waldo.

Letty greeted me on the front steps.

"Did she say what she wanted us to do with the place? I swear there's not a lick of dust in the whole place. Like nothing at all, anywhere."

That was strange. I'd have to see this for myself. Wandering around for ten minutes, I found nothing. Nothing in the corners, nothing on the ceilings, nothing anywhere. I had never seen a place that was this immaculate before.

"Well, what are we supposed to do with this?" I asked no one in particular.

I got three shrugs in return.

"I can't charge for us being over here when there is nothing to clean," I noted. "Did you check the lint trap in the dryer? Under the utility sink? Mud on the back porch?"

"Everywhere, Tallie, as in every single place, and there is nothing." Letty shrugged. "Why do you think she sent us out here?"

"Let's ask." I pulled out my phone and hit the number for Mrs. Petrovski.

She answered on the first ring. "What?"

Okay then. "I, uh, just wanted to check in with you. I'm in the house, and there is literally nothing to do here. The place is absolutely spotless."

"Are you sure you're in the right house?"

I put my hand out, and Letty gave me the piece of paper with the address of the house we were supposed to clean. I rattled off the address, and Mrs. Petrovski scoffed at me.

"I most certainly did not send you there. Why would I send you there? I just had poor Audra clean that the other day, so it is absolutely perfect. Go next door. That's the house that needs to be cleaned. And don't take all day. You've already wasted an hour by being at the wrong place and taking way too long to leave the Astercromb mansion. Please do this right, or I will not be above asking for help from someone else." With that, she hung up.

I gathered the troops around. "I know I wrote that address down right," I said to my crew. "But whatever. Okay, I don't know what this woman is doing, but apparently, we're supposed to be next door and getting our hustle on. Let's move."

I led the way. I locked the door behind us and opened the front door to the house next door, where we found a special kind of chaotic mess. I couldn't help but think, *Hoarder*, when I saw it.

"Holy cow." Letty put her hands on her hips.

My thought exactly.

At that moment my phone rang, and I didn't know what more I could handle at the moment. I almost wished we were next door, trying to pick up miniscule pieces of carpet fluff off the shiny tile floor.

"Hello?"

"What time are you coming back?" My father did not do pleasantries unless you were a client or the relative of one.

"Uh." I looked around the front room and could not even begin to calculate how much time this was going to take, even with four of us working. "I'm not sure. We just got a huge job, and we have to come up with a battle plan."

"Well, I really need you here today. Francine just called out sick—some bug going around—and I have no one to drive the hearse. Normally, I could do it myself, but Jeremy is going to be doing that ceremony, because I just got a new client in, and we have three days to get her ready for the service. Another is coming in this evening, and I have a third funeral booked today. I don't know how we overbooked, but I can't tell the relatives that today is not a good day to say good-bye, and therefore they'll have to wait until tomorrow."

My dad was a pretty succinct guy, so that was a lot of words for him. Sometimes he communicated only in grunts. To have him go on and on about the schedule was shocking enough. To learn that we were overbooked was astounding. I could not recall a single time that had happened in the past.

I looked at the room before me again and at the women, who were picking through things to make a path to the back of the house. This wasn't like a former suspect's house, which had been filled with knickknacks and doodads. This house had serious clutter and junk, and some things had been thrown around willy-nilly, while other things had been stacked all the way to the ceiling. I couldn't leave these women here to handle this all by themselves. But I also couldn't leave my father in a bind.

"Let me call you right back. I know that's not the answer you want, but I have to talk to Letty. I promise to call back within five minutes."

"Please do." He hung up without saying good-bye. That seemed to be a running theme today.

"Letty, can I have a moment?" I did not want to do this, and under normal circumstances, I would never walk away from a job to do something else unless that job was life-threatening. But whereas Burton had sounded defeated earlier, my dad sounded frantic, and a frantic Bud Graver was not something I thought I had ever heard before.

"Sure, boss. This is going to be quite the cleanup.

We might want to divide and conquer, because this is going to take days. I hope you tell the old broad that."

The old broad . . . Yes, I'd have to deal with her and her demands soon, but I had other things at the top of my list at the moment.

"I hate to do this to you . . ." I didn't even know where to start, so I dove in, even as her eyes narrowed. "My dad really needs my help. There's some confusion at the funeral home, and I can't leave him hanging, but I don't want to leave you guys hanging, either. I don't know what to do. I wish I could be two places at once." Wasn't that the truth? "Can you take the lead on this one? I promise to give you all a bonus. I won't take a single penny, even though I'll be back to help as soon as chauffeur-to-the-dead duty is over. I promise." I seemed to be making a lot of promises today, but it was the best I could do, and I only hoped I could keep them all.

"Is that all?" She smacked me on the arm. "I could have sworn you were going to say this was too much for us and call it quits. I want my hands on all this stuff. This place is going to shine when I'm done with it. Me and the ladies, that is."

I breathed out a sigh of relief. I hadn't realized I'd been holding my breath in and had been like a balloon about to pop. "Seriously? You're not mad? I don't want to cut out, but I have to help my dad as best I can."

"Tallie, I wouldn't say it if I didn't mean it. Go. Go now. I'll talk to everyone, and they'll all be fine with it. I'll make sure. And if you want to spend some time with Max instead of coming back later, I guarantee you we can handle this ourselves. No problem."

"I feel horrible, though. This place is a mess."

She laughed and tapped me this time instead of socking my arm. "I'm telling you, it's a challenge, and it's going to be fine. Now go, and I'll talk to everyone."

"You're the best."

"And don't you forget it, even when you become the queen of Squeegeedom, with a battalion of awesome women at your back."

I couldn't help it. I laughed at the image of me standing with a squeegee held high, going into battle with my ladies armed with caddies. "Okay. Let me know if there are any issues, or if anyone needs to talk to me about why I left. I'm in this as much as you all are. I might write the checks, but I also do the work." It still smarted that Mrs. Petrovski had said I was above all this and messed things up deliberately. But once we finished cleaning this house and showed her what we could do, then she'd have to eat her words. I'd tie the bib around her neck myself.

In the meantime, I had a hearse to drive and some assistance to give to my father.

I called him back on my way out to the car and told him when I'd be there. I'd have to go change first, I thought as I looked down at my grimy jeans and faded shirt. I could check in with Max as I buzzed through. I hoped that we could be together later. In the meantime, chauffeur duty was calling.

Chapter Twelve

Dressed in a black skirt and a jade-green top, I kissed Peanut good-bye and waved to Mr. Fleefers, who was sitting on top of the fridge. I didn't know if he and the dog were having a fight or just taking some alone time, but as long as my apartment wasn't destroyed, I wouldn't worry about it.

Max was still out at the job, so I simply texted him that I'd see him later and went to do my duty. The funeral parlor was a hive of chaos if you looked close enough. But if you didn't know what you were looking for, then it looked like smooth sailing on a glass-clear lake.

My father roamed the floor, fixing a tissue box and making one small adjustment to the arranged flowers in order to achieve perfection. My mother made sure all the chairs in the blue room were organized correctly and were aligned with the discreet marks on the floor that showed where they belonged, in order to provide enough leg room but still be intimate. Jeremy straightened his tie in the oval mirror in the foyer and then slicked his hair down.

"Looking good, brother of mine. Where do you want me, and how long do you need me for?"

I was completely not expecting him to grab my arm and drag me into the little alcove behind a big old urn of flowers that stood almost seven feet tall.

"You have to help me. I don't know what's going on with Mom and Dad, but it's like they've lost their minds. Mom is the one who double-booked us, and Dad agreed to have the deceased delivered without making sure we even have room in the basement. I had to run down and check that the space was open. It was, but only because another person we were supposed to get has been delayed for toxicology reports. I'm losing my mind here, Tallie, keeping track of them."

Uh-oh. This was where I resolutely did not get involved and instead encouraged everyone to hire a new helper.

"When did this start?" I asked and wanted to slap myself on the forehead. What had happened to not getting involved? But this was my family. No matter how many squabbles we had had, and would have, I was not going to walk away if there were some serious issues going on. "Do we need to bring in Dylan?" My other brother was a groundskeeper and a landscaper, but Jeremy and I could count on him to help us in a pinch.

"I don't think so yet, but it's not off the table. They both seem so scattered, and I don't know what to do with them." He blew out a breath and then straightened his already straight tie. "Thank you for coming in. I know you don't want to be here, but I really appreciate it." He walked away, and I watched his shoulders slump. Because he felt defeated or because he was sincerely relieved to have the help? I was going with the second one, for all our sakes.

Jumping into the fray had never been so easy. Still, I took my mom upstairs and went over the calendar for the next few days to make sure there weren't going to be any more issues. I also put myself down for hearse duty, as necessary, after noting other funerals were scheduled for the next few days but had no assigned driver, as one of the regulars was taking off those days and the other was on vacation. I texted Letty to let her know and was rewarded with a thumbs-up.

I also texted Max to let him know I was going to be a little later than I had planned, and he responded with a thumbs-up too.

Okay, then, things were running again. We could all breathe.

I checked my black skirt and my standard jade-green shirt, which everyone at Graver's Funeral Home wore, and trotted back down the steps in my low-heeled black pumps. I met my dad at the bottom of the staircase and smoothed down his comb-over, which was covering his ear.

"What's going on?" I knew this probably wasn't the time to press the issue, but if he was here, and I was here, then maybe we could have a moment to talk.

"We've had more deaths in the past few weeks than normal, that's all. I just got caught up in wanting to make sure everyone was taken care of. Some of these contracts we've had since your grandfather ran the place. I can't turn them away. I just can't, no matter how stacked up the bodies get."

"Can you space the funerals out a little more?"

"Not when there are religious reasons that make it impossible for a funeral to be on a different day."

There were a number of things I didn't know about the business. The religious aspect was high up on that list, I admitted. I wouldn't press about that now, because I didn't need to know, and it was time to drive the big old behemoth of a hearse and play chauffeur.

After adjusting the seat once I was in the shiny black boat, I waited for the casket to be loaded, made sure I knew which church I was taking it to, and then got on the road.

It was extremely important to go the speed limit in this thing. I watched the speedometer, keeping the needle under forty-five once I got outside the borough. The church sat on a piece of property nestled in the hills south of town. My job would be to pull up to the front door, pull out and set up the cart, then wait for the helpers to unload the coffin. Not much else to do after that except wait for the ceremony to be over. As the driver, I didn't have a part in the actual funeral, and that was fine with me.

I figured I'd take the time to go over the events of the past two days and sort out what could have happened to Audra to lead to her murder and ending with her rolled up in a carpet, where that mystery wall was, and why Mrs. Petrovski seemed bent on selling several of her big assets in such a short time.

Unloading went fine, and the cart rolled on well-oiled wheels. Squeaking was not an option with a Graver funeral. As much as my dad could be a pain, he always did right by those he served in his capacity as usher to the afterlife.

As everyone went inside the church, I exchanged sad smiles with people I knew and brief nods with anyone who nodded at me. I kept my eyes forward and didn't engage those who looked like they were about to fall apart, unless they came directly up to me.

After everyone had filed into the church, I checked to make sure everything was clear and then got back into the hearse, where I cranked up the heat and checked in with Letty. She sent me an emoticon of a smiley face sticking out its tongue and told me she had things under control. *Fine, fine, fine.*

So now thinking . . . And there was a lot to think about. I had originally considered that she'd been pushed out the window, but figured now that the body must have been carried down the stairs instead of dropped from that height. The body would have been more damaged and the carpet would not have been so neatly arranged if it had been pushed out a window. So in my estimation, it had to have taken more than one person to get Audra not only wrapped up in a carpet but also down the stairs and then hoisted into the Dumpster. I didn't know anyone big enough or strong enough to do that by themselves. Even my cousin wasn't that buff, and he was a weight lifter. So two people, but who? I couldn't think of any pair that had had it in for the sweet woman.

Frustration bit me in the prefrontal cortex, so I moved on to the next thing, the wall. I didn't even know where to start. How could a wall be there in a picture but not in real life? I'd had run-ins with secret doors and secret rooms, and with doors that you didn't know were there or that you didn't remember. But this was a completely different kind of thing. Scrolling through the pictures on my phone again, I just shook my head.

I'd checked out the dimensions of that room with Burton, and I couldn't fathom how a half wall would fit there, no matter what story the pictures from Bethany told. One wall of the room was also an outside wall, and it was as solid as anything else, since the interior walls were made out of horsehair plaster. Thank you, 1820s builders.

An idea struck me at that moment. I pulled my phone out and checked the pictures again. Could the half wall I'd been looking for actually be some kind of half door instead of a wall? Something to ponder.

But since the pictures weren't clear enough to show if it was a door or wall, and I didn't see any kind of doorknob, I moved on to the next thing, Mrs. Petrovski and her selling. Was she in trouble? Was she having financial issues? What exactly made her want to get rid of all her property at the same time? There would be wagging tongues if she decided to get rid of much of the property she'd inherited over the years. She had no children and had never married, so anything she did not sell would go to whomever she had deemed worthy in her will. Who was that? Preston Prescott? Another relative? All of the relatives?

But if she did not intend simply to bequeath her property to her heir or heirs, then she had to be experiencing money problems? It had to be money problems, though I hadn't heard anything about that, other than a faint whisper from Mama Shirley and Audra's warning to cash any checks immediately. Of course, since I was no longer part of the upper crust in this area, it was possible that rumors were running rampant and no one thought I was worthy of hearing about it.

Going from being married to Waldo and in the inner circle to being kicked out on my fanny had not been fun, but it had been so worth it, and I never regretted it a single day.

I'd gotten lost in my world of questions and nonanswers for a little too long. The knock on the window and the frown on my brother's face told me he'd been standing there for longer than he liked.

After throwing my phone on the seat beside me, I hopped out of the hearse, then popped the back door open. A *thunk* was not the sound I had hoped to hear. Sure enough, the back door had knocked into the coffin, which was now sitting at the back of the hearse. My face flamed; I could feel the heat rising like I was being scalded with hot water. Instead, I was going to be scolded, just as soon as my brother got me alone.

Fortunately, the rest of the funeral went by without a hitch. I was able to drop the casket off at the cemetery without any other issues, and by the time Jeremy got ahold of me, he'd obviously decided not to look this gift hearse in the mouth. He simply thanked me, yanked at his tie, and walked across the street to Gina's.

After running upstairs to change into jeans again, I followed behind him, hoping I could catch Mama Shirley, while Gina soothed whatever ills Jeremy was going to complain to her about.

"Tallie, caffeine?" Mama Shirley called when I came through the door. She already had a steaming mug on the counter, and I was both pleased and surprised to see Max sitting next to it.

"Oh, yes, please!" I sat down and laid my head on Max's shoulder. He stroked his hand over my hair, then kissed my crown.

"Long day?" he asked.

"Uh-huh. And I still have no answers. I can't seem to figure out why Mrs. Petrovski is on the warpath to sell everything she owns. Or am I just making too much out of two buildings being sold, the mansion and this additional house she gave us while we're waiting for the mansion to be released from investigation? I have no idea how much she owns. Maybe she just doesn't want to be a landlord. Or maybe she's tired of paying all the taxes. Or maybe she wants a big vacation, including cabana boys, with her little Pomeranian, and it will cost an entire mansion to do it right."

He stroked my hair again. "I have no idea, but why don't you put it away for the moment? We'll go eat some dinner after you're caffeinated and then call it a night in."

That sounded heavenly, except that I still had to check in with Letty and my crew to see how they were doing, and I should check back in with my parents to see what they were up to. I watched in the mirror behind the counter as Gina and Jeremy put their heads together and murmured to each other, holding hands. If Jeremy wasn't concerned enough to go run after my parents, then I could take the night off, too. And with that last text from Letty, the one with the smiley face with the tongue sticking out and the assurance that she was handling everything just fine, I was pretty sure I could let that go, too. I had a whole month with Max, but I really wanted to spend it *with* him, instead of watching the days run by until they were gone.

"We should take a walk after dinner," I offered.

"Anywhere in particular? Are there any leads you need to follow up on that can be handled with a walk around town?"

I mock punched him in the arm, which got a smile from Mama Shirley as she sidled up to the counter.

"Actually," she said softly, "if you go on down to that house your girls are cleaning, you might be able to find out quite a bit of stuff. I heard that your friend Audra was supposed to clean it out and set up an auction of the furniture and valuables, but instead, she donated a few pieces of furniture to the community place and threw the rest of the stuff into the house next door."

"That would explain why it's so packed."

"But apparently, she told Marg that she sold everything, and she even had bills of sale, so she could get her cut of the profits. She asked for them to be given to her before the buyers had even written their checks."

"That doesn't sound like the Audra I knew." I

shifted in my seat, decidedly uncomfortable with the direction of the conversation. Mama Shirley was to be trusted, but nothing she was saying coincided with what I knew of the sweet woman who'd been found dead.

"How well do you think you knew her?" Mama leaned farther over the counter and gave me the squinty-eyed look.

My feathers got ruffled right then and there. I knew enough to know that she should have been able to live out the rest of her life in happiness, to be with her boyfriend, and to clean with wild abandon if that was what she wanted.

Instead, I said, "I liked her a lot, and I think something really wrong must have happened. She didn't have any rivals, she hadn't done anything wrong, and someone cut her life off way too early. She was getting married and was so happy and nice. That's all I need to know."

Mama leaned back against the counter behind her and crossed her arms over her chest. She fwapped her ever-present towel against her upper arm a few times, as if debating whether to tell me something I wouldn't want to hear.

I was pretty sure I didn't want to hear anything except what I had just said. I was also positive that she was going to decide to tell me no matter how nicely I asked to be kept in the dark.

"I wasn't going to tell you this . . ."

"And you don't have to now," I said, jumping in when she paused.

"It's for your own good."

I hated when people said that. It was like telling

me to eat kale or brussels sprouts, both of which I couldn't stand.

I kept my mouth shut, because she was going to tell me, anyway.

"She was going after your jobs, hon, deliberately."

My mouth dropped open, but no words came out.

"Stacia Covington came in the other day and was complaining about how Audra wouldn't leave her alone about moving from your services to hers, because you weren't good at what you do and you charged too much. Why have a girl do the job when a real cleaning woman could do it?" Mama Shirley's face didn't change. She wasn't smiling, she wasn't frowning, she didn't look sad, but she looked resolute. Like she was telling me brussels sprouts were good for me, and I was going to eat them whether I wanted to or not. *Just choke it down, Tallie.*

And I tried to. I clamped my lips together in an effort not to say anything, even though I felt like I was going to burst.

"Betty Ann Justice came in, too, when she picked up her cake from my Gina. She said she received a mailing with very specific language against you. It stated that Audra would be more than willing to undercut your prices for anyone who would move over to her service. I think it was thirty percent off the life of the contract."

"Bah!" I finally released the breath I was holding in. "Both of those women have a nasty habit of telling lies, and they're the kind of people whose checks I cash before I even go home. Betty Ann watches my every move, and Stacia lies on the couch, directing me to do all the things while eating bonbons and watching soaps."

"Nothing wrong with watching the stories."

Max laughed at Mama Shirley's words, until I glared at him.

"There is something wrong with trying to speak ill of the dead when it comes from two women who love to make waves," I continued. "Did Betty Ann show you the flyer? Maybe she was just trying to get me to cut my prices. She did mention last time that I was too pricey and might want to think about lowering my prices."

I bit my lip, because I knew I was wrong about Audra. Something had clicked when Mama Shirley told me about that flyer and about the undercutting. A bunch of my clients had recently been telling me what a great job I was doing and how they'd never leave me. As if assuring me of something that I hadn't known was wrong. I had thought they were all just incredibly grateful for my services and happy that I was doing a good job. Instead, they had been telling me that they weren't falling for another cleaner's shenanigans.

A cleaner that I had been going all over the place for, asking questions for, and defending endlessly. A cleaner whose murder I had been investigating tirelessly and whose demise had me wringing my hands. A cleaner who I had thought was my friend, or at least had the potential to be my friend, and instead had been badmouthing me not only to my clients but to anyone who would listen.

Instead of bursting this time, I felt like I was

boiling. Of course she still hadn't deserved to die, and she definitely had not deserved to have her dead body wrapped up in a carpet, but come on! Why did I keep believing people were inherently honest? When was I going to stop believing that people were naturally good until I was proven wrong? Had Audra gone after my cleaning service to build her "side business," as Caleb had called it?

"I'm not going to apologize for setting you right, Tallie, but I will say that it's a shame you weren't told earlier. I just thought Audra was being a pain. And I know those two ladies enough not to believe every word out of their mouths, but both told me unsolicited information, and I just keep seeing you exhaust yourself to get justice for someone who was out to gut you."

"I understand, and I appreciate it. I guess I should start thinking about going to all my customers and thanking them for staying even through the slander campaign." I shifted in my chair again, not sure how I wanted to go about that. I'd come up with something, though. Maybe little tokens of gratitude I got from my friend Monty at the florist.

"Pshaw. You'll do no such thing. They know they're getting a good deal and that you have the best crew out there. They would have left if that wasn't true. But maybe you can back off from trying to find this girl's killer. Leave it to Burton. He might be a pain, but he does know his job, too."

"But I promised Letty. Her nephew is under suspicion, and he's just trying to start over. He really loved Audra, no matter what she was after. Plus, you wanted me in this."

Max played with my fingers on the counter as I

drummed them next to the untouched coffee. "You could back out."

"I could, but Burton is so overworked, and the whole police department is understaffed. She still deserves justice." And wasn't that a full one-eighty from what I used to be like as Mrs. Waldo? Then I had been as cutthroat as the next person, always looking to get ahead, be bigger, be seen more, have the best of everything. I was not proud of that time, but I had been in it up to my eyeballs with Waldo as a husband.

Now I had finally arrived at a place where it was about what was best in general, where things like lives and justice mattered more than anything, and where I could look outside myself to find what had to be done, instead of what I *wanted* to be done.

Talk about growth! *Go me!*

But that was for another time. For now, I was going to take the night off, hope that Letty didn't hear these stories about Audra's wrongdoing, and have dinner with my boyfriend. I was going to relax and think only if I wanted to. Tomorrow was soon enough to get back into the race for whodunit. Until then Burton could possibly solve the whole thing, and I would be completely unneeded. Wouldn't he just love that? Maybe this time.

Chapter Thirteen

I groaned after eating a bowl full of the best beef and broccoli I'd ever had. Max had even taught me how to use chopsticks, or at least he'd tried. I could run a vacuum like I was waltzing with it and use a squeegee like a baton girl, but chopsticks were not my forte. They never had been. He still got points for trying.

I glanced at my computer over on the coffee table and then quickly glanced away. I did not need to do any searches on Audra or on the nephew of Mrs. Petrovski or on Mrs. Petrovski herself. I was no longer in the game, at least for tonight, and I wanted to spend time with my boyfriend.

"You know, I did a search on the whole family today, but I don't know if now is the right time to talk about it or if we left that over at Gina's for the night. Some interesting stuff there." He played with the wrapper of a fortune cookie he'd bought at the store to go with our dinner.

I stared at him until he looked up, with a smile.

"You know you want to know, and I wanted to know, too. Can I be John Watson this time? I don't really think I'd make a good Shaggy or Fred."

I laughed and laughed. "You will always be my Watson, but doesn't that make me Sherlock, who was a self-professed high-functioning sociopath?"

"Never that. Just brilliant and good at putting the pieces together when you have them. So let's start laying them out on the table."

I rubbed my hands together and wiggled in my seat with glee. "So what do we have?"

"Well, first there are Mrs. Petrovski's properties, and there are a lot of them. It seems that almost every single one is either on the market or going on the market soon. I know you originally thought that maybe she was going to keep you on to clean the mansion on a continual basis, but she wants them all gone. I haven't been able to find out why she wants them all sold. The guy I asked to look into her bank accounts didn't see any outstanding debts or deficits in the cash flow. I don't see any way in which she needs a bunch of money."

I blew out a breath and pulled a notepad and a pencil on the table toward me. "So nothing except that she wants cash, instead of the properties that have been in her family for years. That's not a crime in any way, and there's nothing wrong with not wanting to have a bunch of places, for which you have to pay taxes and upkeep. She might get snubbed for deciding to be cash rich instead of land rich, but I'm pretty sure she can handle that. She's older, she's high up on the scale as far as upper-crust society around here, and she'll be fine."

"However, there's a brother."

"Really? I thought her only brother was dead." This I wrote down on my notepad.

"It's a half brother, and the money came through the father they don't share, not the mother they do."

"Hmm." I crossed through the *half brother*.

"However, there's an issue with three of the properties."

"Oh?" This could be good. I wanted it to be good so that we could start down a solid path to the killer.

"Yes. Word is that there's an issue with the titles. I wasn't able to get more than that through the grapevine, because I was working."

"Oh. Can we do more to find out about that?" I felt like this might be something. "What if someone wanted the properties and thought they belonged to them? What if he or she was at the mansion when Audra was there, did something he or she shouldn't have done, and Audra saw the whole thing, and so this person killed her and tried to get rid of her before anyone knew about it." I was rambling in my excitement, and my imagination was getting away from me.

"I'm already on the fact-finding. As for the scenario, I don't know. Do you think that makes sense?"

I sank back in my chair. "Not really. Why would killing someone get you the three properties or even one? That doesn't make sense at all, Watson. Thanks for pulling me back to reality." I laid my hand on top of his, and he turned his palm up to lace our fingers together.

"We can keep thinking about it. In the meantime, my information is that the aunt pays for everything for the nephew but has removed the majority of the money from that account and has opened another one."

"When did she do that?"

"Today."

"Interesting." I rubbed Peanut's head. She'd just come over to see if I had any food to drop on the floor for her. "Could he be bleeding her dry, and that's why she has to sell everything? He said he wanted money for some kind of investment that he needed to make right now. Maybe he thought if he killed Audra, then his aunt would sell the house for whatever she could get so he could have the money now."

"I don't know if that makes sense, either. He'd have to wait for the investigation to be over. And he had to know that Mrs. Petrovski would give the cleaning job to you, which he was adamantly against."

"But when it happened, he didn't think there would be an investigation. He'd called the truck to come pick up that Dumpster before anyone knew that someone had been killed. He might not be big, but he could have moved Audra from the house. But how did he kill her, and why a carpet? It was so big and bulky. Why not a big black trash bag? As for me and the job, maybe he had someone else lined up already. After he sabotaged me, there was a very good chance that Mrs. Petrovski could have been swayed to hire someone else."

"Carpet to be able to hide the body. And you're right that he did think no one would be at the mansion when the truck arrived to pick up the

Dumpster. As for the cleaning job, I don't know what would have happened. She did choose you, though. Maybe she realized that you were more reliable than she had thought."

We both sat in silence for a moment.

"You know, I promised myself that I wouldn't let this case mess up my time with you, that I was just going to be the concerned citizen, not the vigilante that Burton accused me of being. And yet here I am," I said.

"Vigilante looks good on you. Maybe we should get you one of those long leather dusters and a pair of cowboy boots."

I burst out laughing. "Yeah, I think if I put that on my résumé or in my work queue, my dad would have a fit for sure."

He held my hand across the table and massaged my fingers. His warmth was everything I'd ever need. "Are you that worried about what your parents think?"

I remembered that his parents had not wanted him, had, in fact, shipped him off to live with his stern and unforgiving grandmother when he was a teenager. This issue with my parents could be a tricky quagmire, and I did not want to drag him back into it.

"Not worried so much as I appreciate my parents and love them, no matter how much they annoy me. They've been there for me from the beginning." I watched his face to see if it would go blank at my admission. But he just smiled at me. He loved them, too, he'd told me when I'd caught him pretending to be a flower delivery guy all those months ago.

"They've been there for me, too. It's hard not to want to please them."

I shrugged. "It's also hard to please them sometimes. I got married to get away from this place." I really meant the two floors below me, where the dead bodies were kept and then displayed for their loved ones to say good-bye.

"And do you still feel that was the right decision?"

I gave that one some serious thought. My marriage had been a disaster from pretty early on, and yet I hadn't left until it was leave or go down with him. I hadn't been happy for years. Now I could honestly say I was happy, but was that in spite of having to work at the funeral home part-time? Was I happy because I was back in the arms of my friends and family and with Max? Was I still putting up resistance to the funeral home because I always had? Or did I really hate working there that much?

"Marrying Waldo might not have been the best decision, but I think I had to go through all that to understand where I am now and appreciate it. I can't deny that I wouldn't be sitting here with you, that we wouldn't be talking all this out over delicious beef and broccoli, if the rest hadn't happened. Even if he were alive, I don't think I would be able to thank Waldo for being a jerk just yet, but I can look back and see the path that got me here. And I am extremely thankful for it."

He squeezed my hand. "I'm obviously happy to be where I am with you right now, too. The answers for the rest of it will come later, I'm sure." And he smiled at me, not one of those beaming smiles that made you feel like you had to go do some rainbow dance or something, not even one that made me feel like he was patronizing me, until I got my stuff together and decided that I had been wrong all along. No, it was one that made me feel that he was here for the journey with me and that whatever I decided would be right.

I couldn't help myself. I got up, went around the table, and sat on his lap to snuggle into his chest. Of course, Mr. Fleefers did not want to be left out, so he jumped on my lap and proceeded to climb up my chest to get to Max's shoulders, where he draped himself, with his back paw stuck to my nose. Then Peanut came over and rested her head on my knees.

Max and I looked around at the animals, which were making sure they were noticed, and then back at each other and laughed.

"We might need better chairs," I said.

"Or maybe more room."

Maybe. I wanted him up here, but I kept going back to the fact that I'd have to move to Washington, DC. I couldn't ask Max to move to my tiny town in central Pennsylvania when his work life was based in DC. But I didn't want to leave my small town. As much as it could be a pain to have everyone know me to the point that I couldn't get away with anything, as a call would be placed to my mom, and as much as I balked about working at the funeral home, I'd started building a life here, one I really loved, finally, after all these years. I just wasn't ready to let it go yet.

Although I did wish people would stop killing each other in our area so that I could retire my deerstalker hat.

"We can discuss that later," I finally said and snuggled back in, removing Mr. Fleefers's paw from my face. He put it right back, but at least I'd tried. "Right now we need to figure out this murder thing and get to the place where we can point a finger at someone, with evidence to back it up."

"I thought you were leaving the finger-pointing to Burton."

"Well, yes, of course, but he's so busy with everything that if I can help, I'd like to. If you still want to do that." Oh, I so hoped he was going to say yes, but I wouldn't press if he didn't.

"I find it fascinating, to be honest, and a whole lot more interesting than running numbers every day sometimes. I love my job, but recently, it's been getting to the point where I'm asking for the more in-depth things, because it's getting old."

Could Max want to change careers? Oh, that would open up the possibility for him to move up here! But I wasn't going to press that issue, either. We had all the time in the world, unless you listened to my mother, who had recently started lamenting that my biological clock was ticking so loud it kept her up at night.

I jumped off his lap and got our computers. After placing his in front of him, I grabbed my notepad. "Okay, we need more information on business dealings and current life situations for the family. Background checks are good, but I think we need to know more about them at this moment instead of in the past. I feel like I need a filing cabinet to keep everything together."

Looking around the tiny apartment, he frowned.

"I don't think you have room for one, unless you're planning on becoming a private eye."

I'd had that thought when Matt mentioned Burton wouldn't be able to shut me out if I was licensed, but I shuddered to consider all the people I'd have to interact with, people with secrets or bad deeds in their past. It was one thing to complain about picking up dirty socks, but sifting through people's emotional dirty laundry would break something in me if I did it on a permanent basis.

"Nope, no private investigator stuff. I might be curious and not know what I want to be when I grow up, but I'm pretty sure it's not that."

"Still, we need to do more research."

"Yes, why don't we take tonight off, and tomorrow you take the computer stuff while I go ask some questions? If I run into Burton and get the lecture about the concerned citizen again, I'll just tell him I'm asking after people's well-being. He can't argue with that."

After our discussion, we went to bed, but I was up early the next morning. I gathered my purse and my notepad, then headed toward the door.

"Don't let Burton deter you, unless you're not going to be safe," Max said as I exited the apartment. "I'm sure he'll try."

"No doubt, but that's part of the game. I'll be fine."

"Just make sure you're safe."

"Will do. See you later."

I had left my laptop on the kitchen table, just in case Max wanted to run two searches at the same time, and then I went looking for the pool of people I usually asked for dirt.

Mama Shirley was the first one who popped into my mind, but I had tapped her already, and she might not have anything new. There was my uncle Sherman, but I wasn't sure what he might know or if it was worth having to listen to him berate Burton yet again for not doing his job fast enough.

Trotting down the stairs, I listened for sounds of my mom. In two hours I had a funeral to drive for again. Letty and the rest of the crew were already at Mrs. Petrovski's house and were making good progress, and the mansion wasn't open for cleaning just yet, so I wasn't needed for the next two hours.

Perhaps I could go back to the mansion and look for more clues, not that we'd found any yet, but anything was possible.

However, my phone rang before I made it all the way down the stairs. It was Matt. What had we done without phones before now? They were both a curse and a blessing, but lately I felt like my whole life depended on this electronic device in my hand.

"Where are you?"

I looked around and told him, "At the foot of the stairs at home."

"Well, I want you to be careful. We just found Audra's car, and Burton wanted me to check in with you. See? He doesn't think you're annoying, and he wants you safe."

Right.

"What about the car makes him think I'm not safe?" I sat down on the bottom step and rested my feet for a moment. This could take two minutes or all day, depending on what kind of mood Matt was in.

"Not you in particular, but he's concerned because whoever did this is still out there and could be getting nervous about being found out. The whole thing was wiped down meticulously. It was parked at Caleb's apartment complex, in the back, on the other side of a Dumpster, where we might not have seen it, except that a woman called to report it because her son cracked the windshield and she didn't want to get into trouble with the owner."

"What does 'wiped down' mean?"

"There isn't a single print anywhere, and no fibers, no dust, no lint, nothing at all. It's like someone set off a Roomba in there and let it run for hours."

"Again with the hiding and the Dumpster. It's just weird that whoever is doing this seems to be drawn to the big metal cans. That and keeps doing everything he or she can to make sure any evidence is never found."

"Yeah, you're preaching to the choir. Burton's fed up to his eyebrows. Every time we think we have a lead, it disintegrates like it's on fire."

"Do you think it's the boyfriend again?"

He sighed, and I felt his pain and frustration. "No, we think someone is trying to set it up to look like the boyfriend is guilty. We found an ex that lives in the same complex, and we are bringing him in for questioning." I heard his teeth snap together. "Don't tell Burton I told you that. I don't want to get into trouble for bringing you in."

But now my curiosity was piqued again. "I

thought Audra was single when she first moved here. She said she met Caleb, and they hit it right off. In her words, she was so glad that she wasn't tied to anyone, because that way she could do anything she wanted."

"She might have been single at that point, but she originally moved here with a boyfriend, who paid all the bills, until she got the job with that commercial cleaning company. Then she dropped him like a hot potato. My information is that he was not exactly happy. As it turns out, her ex and Caleb live in the same apartment complex. She and Caleb always met at her house, just in case they came across the boyfriend in the parking lot. That must have been awkward to have your ex and your current boyfriend in the same apartment complex."

"Well, at least that was thoughtful of her."

"Ha! Not her. Caleb," Matt said. "She wanted to come over as often as possible, and he just always made sure that they went to her house."

"Trying to make the ex-boyfriend jealous?" Man, I wished I had my laptop with me. This was someone else to look into, if I could get Matt to give me the guy's name.

In the end, he wouldn't, but I still wanted it. Surely someone would know. Maybe Caleb would tell Letty. I'd have to call Letty to see if she could get him to give her the guy's name, which she then could give to me. It was a brilliant plan, and one I was about to execute when my phone rang again.

Lo and behold, it was Letty.

"Hello, my favorite lady. How's it going over there?"

"We're getting things moved around and out onto the sunroom, but, man, this is grueling work."

"Are you sure you don't want me to come over and help? I feel terrible that I'm not doing anything at the moment. I was going to go dig up any dirt on the players in this wonky murder but I think I need to find Burton, instead. Other than that I'm open."

"You can come over if you want and haul furniture. Actually, we might want to ask your brother Dylan and Max to come move some of the bigger stuff, if that's okay with you. We're strong, but some of this stuff is gigantic and old. I don't get how they moved this kind of furniture around when they just had a horse and buggy."

"Me, neither, though I've never thought about that. Maybe it was like the people who built Stonehenge. A lot of back-breaking work."

She snickered, and that was much better than the exhausted sound of her voice at first.

"So what can I do for you? And then I have a favor to ask," I said, still sitting on the steps. At some point in the near future, I could just imagine my mom coming in and wanting to know why I was there and not with Max. She'd ask if we had had a fight and what I had done wrong. I was not going to borrow trouble, though, so I tuned back in to Letty.

"I thought Bethany would be back by now, but I haven't seen her. Any chance she's called you?"

"Weird. No, I haven't heard from her. I would have thought she would have reported to you at the house. I left her a voice mail about the change of plans."

"Yeah, I did, too, but she doesn't seem to be answering her phone, and it goes right to voice mail, then says the voice mail is full."

"That's not good." Of course my brain started whirling through the possibilities. Was she hurt? Had she gotten stuck on vacation without a charger? Had she had a run-in with Audra when she was at the house that first night, taking pictures, and forgone her vacation and come back to kill the woman?

That last one seemed far-fetched, but at this point anything was possible.

"Have you checked with her boyfriend?" I asked.

"I don't know his name or his number."

"We should have a contact on her employment sheet. I can go run to get that, and I'll call you back once I have something. Speaking of boyfriends, though, Matt just called to tell me they found Audra's car at her boyfriend's apartment complex, and that her ex also lived there. I never heard of an ex. Do you think Caleb might know his name? He might bear looking into."

"Concerned citizen, huh?"

"The most concerned."

She chuckled. "I'll call him, and when you call back with Bethany's info, I'll give you the name."

"Deal."

When I rose from the stairs, I was just in time, because I heard my mother rummaging around in the kitchen and singing to herself. I did not need her to come out right now, unless she had snickerdoodles in her hand. Most likely, she was making them now. It would be fine enough to see her later, just not at this moment, when I was on a mission.

I rushed back up the stairs and surprised Peanut and Max by bursting through the door. Mr. Fleefers, being his usual self, barely glanced my way.

"Hey, everybody! Sorry to buzz in and out, but I need an employee folder."

"Did you leave, then come back?" Max asked from his place at the table. I really needed to think about getting some kind of desk for him. I just had no idea where I might put it in this small studio apartment without cluttering up the tiny space.

As I rummaged through my box of files—I really should get a cabinet for them too—I finally came up with Bethany's information. I didn't have a lot of employee folders, just the four, but I had also been putting receipts in this box, too. I had a feeling Max was not going to be pleased with my organizational skills when it came time to do taxes.

Max stopped me on my way out the door. "Do you have to run right now? I just need a few seconds of your time."

"Of course." I put the paperwork down on the table and joined him, sitting in the chair next to his.

He turned the computer toward me and used a pen to tap the screen. "I hit on a few things for Audra. She actually has a rap sheet for stealing and the misuse of company funds."

Chapter Fourteen

"You have got to be kidding me. I really thought she was a great person, and now that's two different things I've heard that don't jive with the picture she painted of herself. Plus, Burton said she was clean."

"Not everyone is as transparent as you are, Tallie."

"Well, they should be. Just let those warts hang out so I can see them. But how did she get the job at the commercial place if she has a record of misuse of company funds?" That was incredibly puzzling. I hadn't held a job for which I had had to fill out an application in a long time, but even I knew a record of misusing company funds would be a black mark on an application for employment.

"I'll have to do some more digging. Maybe she was able to convince them that she was a changed person, so it wasn't an issue any longer. Maybe the court sealed the record. It doesn't show when the

misuse of funds happened, only that it did. I'll
look into it more."

"I told Letty that I need to find Burton, and I
also planned to make the rounds and try to dig up
some dirt on Mrs. Petrovski and other people, but
I think I'll go help Letty instead and talk with her.
The thing is that we have another potentially serious matter on our hands. Apparently, we've lost
contact with Bethany, who should have been back
to work by now."

"I've been told to take another break today
from the job, so I'll be here if you need me. Good
luck out there." He flipped me a salute.

"Good luck in here," I said, doing the same
thing.

After hustling back out the door, I got into my
car and called Letty. My phone battery was going
to be dead soon, given how much I was using this
thing, and I hadn't even gotten to Burton yet.

"Jason Huntington," I said when she answered.

"Yeah, that's the boyfriend's name. How did you
get it before I did? I thought you didn't know who
to ask, and that's why you had me ask Caleb."

"Wait, are you saying Audra's ex-boyfriend is
Jason Huntington?"

"Yeah. Isn't that what you're saying?"

"No." I drew out the word, my mind pinging all
over the place. "I'm saying that Jason Huntington
is Bethany's boyfriend and contact person."

"Strange coincidence?" she asked, her skepti-
cism coming through the phone loud and clear.

I shared the same feeling. "I don't think so, but
let's call him to check things out. I'll get back to
you soon. I was going to come over and join you at

the house, but I think, as a concerned citizen, I need to get this information to Burton."

She snorted. "Good luck with that."

"Yeah, thanks." We hung up, and I sat there for a minute. So Jason was Audra's ex and Bethany's future. How had those two women felt about the way their lives had overlapped? More information kept coming in that suggested that Audra was not at all the person I had thought she was, so was it safe to say that she might have hated Bethany for being with her ex? If Audra had tried to rub her relationship with Caleb in her ex's nose by seeking to parade around with Caleb at the two men's apartment complex, then it wasn't hard to imagine that Audra might not like her ex's new woman, who might drive her ex to distraction and lessen her jealousy.

Bethany was a sweet kid. I knew that for sure, especially since Letty liked her, and I trusted Letty implicitly. Besides, I'd already run a background check on her, so unless she was super good at hiding things, she did not have a rap sheet. But if Audra had caught her out at the mansion, taking pictures, and had taunted her enough, would Bethany have killed her to shut her up?

Did I have a murderer on my payroll?

Before I got too far ahead of myself, I reviewed the facts and put together a mental checklist of what to say when I spoke with Burton. I would speculate. I would not hypothesize, unless he asked me to.

But I did know that Burton should be at the station. I rang over there and got Yolanda, Letty's friend who was filling in for Suzy. After some small talk, I asked for Burton and was patched right through. That was quite different from Suzy's normal efforts of protecting Burton from the likes of people like me.

"What now, Tallie?"

"As a concerned citizen, I'd like to share some information with you."

He sighed but then told me to hold on while he got a pen.

I spilled it all out for him, letting him know that I appreciated the call about the car and his concern for my safety.

"I shouldn't ever worry. You'd probably survive a massive nuclear war, like a cockroach."

"Grouchy, are we?" I didn't take offense, since I knew he had a lot going on right now.

"Overworked is what we are, and it's not getting any better. I have got to figure this thing out, and you keep handing me tidbits that I should be able to get myself. It's appreciated, believe me, but it's also frustrating."

"Do you want me to stop?" Not that I would, but I felt it was appropriate to at least show him some courtesy by asking.

"No, don't stop, or this might become a cold case, but please be careful out there. I don't need someone to find you dead."

"Yeah, me neither."

After the call was over, my phone chimed at me. Dad texting. Honestly, what had we done before without this level of communication? When I was little, I had to be at home if I was expecting a phone call, or I could listen to any phone messages when I got home. Cell phones and being available twenty-four/seven could get old, but in instances like this, they were very much appreciated.

But it was my dad texting, so this could be great or not so great. He hadn't yet given me the lecture about staying out of things, so I kept thinking that this was going to happen at any moment and thus was on edge with anticipation.

But it was a text asking me if I could work a funeral and keep someone out of the room while my dad tried to do his job.

I texted back, asking if I had time to change my clothes. He responded that he would make the time. I could not come in jeans.

Fine then.

When I buzzed up into the apartment for the second time in an hour, I caught Peanut off guard, but no one else.

"Hi again!" I announced.

"I heard you on the stairs," Max said.

"Oh." I snickered. "If my dad didn't need me right now, I bet I'd hear a lecture on my elephant-sounding tendencies."

"No doubt. What is it this time?"

"We appear to have someone who is causing trouble downstairs, and my dad wants me to keep an eye on him. I have to get dressed quick and get back downstairs."

"You're a busy lady, while I'm just hanging out here, doing research and eating your mother's snickerdoodles."

"Snickerdoodles? Where are they? Tell me now!"

He pointed at a plate on the counter, and I ran over to it and grabbed a cookie. After shoving the snickerdoodle in my mouth and thoroughly enjoying the cinnamon and sugar greatness, I turned back to him. "Speaking of research . . ." I dug into my closet, thankful I'd done laundry yesterday, so most of my work clothes were clean and ready for the funeral home. "I need you to look up a Jason Huntington." I rattled off the address and the few things I knew about him. I also handed over the folder with Bethany's employment info.

"Sure thing," he said as I whisked into the bathroom, where I threw on my clean clothes and ran a brush through my hair. I didn't know whom I was going to be handling downstairs, but I figured it didn't matter. My dad trusted me to do this, and so it would be fine. I could do this. I *would* do this, and it was good that I had the time.

After hauling tail back out of the bathroom, I gave Max yet one more kiss and pulled the door closed behind me. I took my time getting down the stairs, though, since even though he might need me, my dad might also lecture me if I really made an entrance while sounding like a herd of cattle.

I was at the bottom of the stairs and tucking in the bottom of my shirt when my mom found me.

"Oh, thank goodness you're here. Daddy's about to blow a gasket. I hate to see him like that. Please be nice and do all you can to keep this guy out of his hair."

Who was this person? Had I been too quick to think I'd be able to handle the situation to my father's standards? Before I could start second-guessing myself, I patted her hand, told her it would be fine, and strutted my way out to the front foyer to deal with whatever my dad had for me.

Unfortunately, I came face-to-face with Preston Prescott and almost immediately turned back around.

"Tallie, thanks so much for coming down." Bud Graver gripped my upper arm when I was in mid-turn, and swiveled me right back in front of one of my biggest nightmares. "If you could answer Mr. Prescott's questions, I'm sure it would be a great help, while I handle the funeral next door."

I cleared my throat and squelched my urge to yell and smiled. "Of course, Dad. We'll talk later." I gave him the evil eye, but he either missed it or it didn't affect him, as his smile did not change. He walked away then, leaving me with a nemesis I hadn't had to interact with on a steady basis for years. Now I couldn't seem to get rid of him.

"I don't want you," Preston said instead of hello.

I had better manners. "It's nice to see you again." *Even though you are the one who tried to ruin my chances of cleaning your aunt's house, you jerk.* Fortunately, that was said only in my head.

"It is not, and you know it. I have some questions only your father can answer, if he'd just take a moment to help me."

"While I'm sure he'd like to do that, we have a funeral going on. Can I show you into the office? I'll get us some coffee, and then we can talk. Anything you need to ask, I can probably answer."

He gave me a skeptical look. I didn't blame him for that one. I didn't know much about how things ran around here, but I'd try. And he wouldn't know if I gave the wrong answer, anyway.

I held my hand out in front of me to show him the direction of the office. My mother stepped out of the kitchen at that moment, and I asked her for coffee for two. She had a horrible look on her face until Preston turned, and then she was all smiles.

"Of course, of course. Would you like some cookies too?"

What I wouldn't give for another snickerdoodle. "Yes, please. We'll be in the office."

"Coming right up."

"Hopefully, your mother is a better hostess than you used to be," Preston muttered.

My smile almost gave way to a snarl, but I held my expression in place with every ounce of professionalism I could muster. "If you'll follow me, we can get to your questions."

"No pithy rejoinder? Ah, it must be that your father would ream you up one side and down the other if you did anything unseemly to a potential customer." He smirked, and I wanted to smack the expression right off his face. I didn't, so I mentally congratulated myself and sat behind the desk while I waved to a chair across from me.

"You had questions?"

"Fine. I need to know how Audra's funeral will be taken care of and whether or not we'll be liable for anything since she died on our property."

I was pretty sure it wasn't his property at all, but I didn't know for sure, so I avoided that topic. "Unless the family files a claim against the property, there should not be an issue. Beyond that, Audra's company would have some sort of injury and accidental death insurance to cover things. We don't generally handle that kind of thing, since that's between the company and the deceased's estate, so that's about the best I can do for you. You'll want to talk to your aunt or her insurance company for confirmation on that."

"Except, according to my information, the death wasn't an accident. I don't think she fell over and rolled down the stairs in a carpet, then bounced into the Dumpster by herself. Do you?"

I cleared my throat. "No, of course not. Her employer will have insurance, though, for liability, and your aunt should have had her sign the same release I signed."

His forehead wrinkled. "A release?"

"Yes. Did Mrs. Petrovski have her sign a release?"

"No, not that I'm aware of. I got her into the house and asked that she be given the job. I don't know why Aunt Marg felt the need to include you also when we already had a wonderful cleaner, but there you have it."

Another dig at my abilities. As far as I knew, he didn't know what I could do with a dustpan and a scrub brush, though I was very tempted to ram either one down his throat to show him. Instead, I cleared my throat again. It was getting dry. Where, oh where, was my mother with the coffee and the cookies?

She entered the room with a tray at that moment, thankfully, giving me a second to compose myself and get rid of the fantasy of Preston with a handle sticking out of his mouth.

I smiled at her as she looked at me nervously before turning a blindingly bright smile in Preston's direction. "Please know we are here to help. I'm sorry Bud was occupied, but you're in good hands with our girl, Tallie." She set the tray down and handed Preston his cup of coffee.

He snorted, and her hands fisted at her waist, where she'd clasped them together. I had to get her out of the room before she used the tray to bean him over the head. I came by my violent tendencies honestly, as my mom tended to be brutal when pushed.

"Thanks so much for the coffee and cookies, Mom. I can take it from here."

"I know, sweetheart." She exited the room without giving Preston another glance.

"I see it runs in the family."

I ignored him and continued our conversation. "So Audra was supposed to get the job, and I wasn't supposed to be on the scene at all?" Now seemed as good a time as any to see if I could nail him down about what had happened that day.

"I told Aunt Marg that it was covered. We didn't need a stupid competition, but she was insistent about bringing you in. I wanted Audra to get the job so that she'd be around."

"*Around* as in you could visit her at the job site?"

He didn't say anything, just shoved a cookie in his mouth. *Interesting.* I'd take that as a yes. Had he had a crush on her? Designs on her? I wasn't going to ask, because he wouldn't answer, and that question would tip my hand.

"When you're done munching on that cookie, I'd like you to at least be honest with me about the fact that it was you who messed up my room and made sure your aunt saw it so I would get disqualified."

He swallowed and took a sip of his coffee. When he set the cup down, he had a sly grin on his face.

"How very astute of you. She was considering giving the job to you and had seen what a good job you were doing, whereas Audra was leaving it up to that ridiculous girl with the mop of hair. I don't know where Audra got her from, but Audra was trying to start her own side business, and I was just helping her get out of the corporate world. As you've seen, we have quite a few places that need to be cleaned and sold. It would have been the perfect opportunity for Audra to begin getting more business in the area."

"Ah." *Rotten jerk!* I knew it was him, but the confirmation was at least something I could share with Burton, to see if it had anything to do with the investigation. "So you destroyed my room, brought in your aunt, and made sure she saw it. Did you also tell Audra your demands for getting her the job, like, say, a date with her, even though she was engaged?"

He sat back in his chair and steepled his fingers. "I would never do something like that. Audra and I had an understanding way before I assured her I would get her the job."

"So you were dating?" But how did that fit in with her engagement to Caleb and her efforts to make her ex, Jason, jealous?

"We're getting off topic. I want to make sure that we won't be liable for the costs of the funeral. Has her family set something up for when the body is released?"

"I'm sorry, but I can't tell you that. It's personal and confidential." And even if I could have, I wouldn't. "You'll have to ask her family or wait to read about it in the paper."

"We're done here." He rose from his chair, so I got up, too. I was not going to let him walk himself to the door and take a detour to corner my father.

"I'll see you out, if there's nothing else."

"Oh, there's plenty, but you aren't going to answer anything, and I'm not wasting my precious time. Do not under any circumstances send us a bill. It won't get paid." With that, he stormed out of the room. I was close on his heels, in case I needed to intercept him on his way to the front door.

He didn't deviate, fortunately, and went straight through the foyer and outside. I was able to catch the door before it slammed from the force he'd put behind closing it after he stalked out of the building.

Score one for me, or really a few, since I had some more info to share with Burton and a reason to seek him out now, instead of just hoping to bump into him. Time to go back upstairs for a third time and change clothes to get this show on the road. I still had an hour before I needed to drive the hearse, and I had a police chief to find.

More importantly, I had an idea about who had taken Audra's life; now I just needed to figure out how to prove it.

Chapter Fifteen

I made it out to the hallway and then to the stairs. I didn't see or hear my mother, but that didn't necessarily mean she wouldn't dive-bomb me at any moment.

I was at the bottom of the steps, ready to go up to my apartment one more time, when she snuck up behind me. "Thanks for handling that nasty man, dear, first of all. But second, you're in and out a lot. What's going on? I heard about that dead girl over at Astercromb mansion. Wasn't she your friend?"

I almost said yes, then really had to think about the answer. Was she my friend? I barely knew her, judging by what I had learned about her. And I had certainly not learned much about her that showed her in a good light. In fact, she had been trying to take my clients and had perhaps been trying to take over my queen of Squeegeedom crown.

"I knew her, but I wouldn't have called us friends.

I've found out all kinds of stuff that I didn't know before that has changed my opinion of her."

"Oh, Tallie, you're not investigating this one, too, are you? Daddy is not going to be happy about that."

Daddy didn't have any say in what I did, and I hated when she called Bud Graver that. It was useless to try to get her to stop, though, because she had almost forty years of calling him that under her belt.

"Dad hasn't said anything to me, and I'd rather he didn't. I'm only helping Burton if I hear something. No vigilante here."

"Well, okay. I won't say anything to Daddy, then, but please be careful. I don't want you hurt, and as much as Burton can irritate me, he's a good guy and knows how to do his job."

"I don't doubt that, yet sometimes he doesn't know how to get the info that I can."

"So you *are* investigating." She gripped my arm. "You know we talked about this. I'm just going to put it out there now that you are not going to go join the force or anything. I can't handle having a cop to worry about over and over again. It's bad enough that I have to worry about your brother out there with a weedwhacker, which could cut his leg off at any point."

I was not successful at keeping my eyes from nearly rolling into the back of my head at that comment, but at least my mom didn't see it. I would have been lectured for days. "I'm sure Dylan is very good at using his equipment. He's been doing this for years and has had only a few nicks and cuts. He's never come close to hurting himself like that." Or at least I didn't think so. There were those years when I had been married to Waldo and hadn't been around, but I was pretty sure that even I would have heard if he'd done something that devastating to himself with a mower or a tree trimmer.

"Anyway, Mom, I have to go. I need to talk to Max." And to find Burton, to share my theory.

"Oh, sweetie, I'm so happy he's going to be here for a whole month. What a pleasure that will be. I'm going to set up a big family dinner this weekend, and we'll celebrate him being here and show him what it would be like if he was here all the time." She beamed at me, and I choked.

I knew for certain that if Max lived here, we would not be having dinner with my parents all the time. We did so monthly now, and this particular dinner she was planning would be okay as a special one, but I was not committing to more than that.

"Thanks, Mom."

"And then we can figure out how to get him to stay. I'd really rather he lived up here, instead of three hours away. Anything could happen in that big city of his, and we'd never know. But if he was here, he'd be much safer, and happier, too, I bet."

There was not going to be any way I could get around her on that one. Max had a job in DC, which I couldn't ask him to leave, but if I told her that, then she might jump to the conclusion I'd already come to—that I'd have to move down there—and I just wasn't ready for that argument yet.

"Okay. Heading upstairs now. I'll see you later."

"Oh, I have to go, anyway. I have special dog and cat treats on order for those precious pets of yours. I figure since they might be the only grandchildren I ever have, I should spoil them rotten when I can."

This time I groaned, and she giggled as she passed me by.

I took the steps up to the first landing and was about to turn the corner when my phone rang in my pocket. Well, it vibrated, not rang, since that would have broken the rules of Graver's Funeral Home. It was bad enough I had the phone in my pocket, even though I was supposed to leave it up in my apartment, according to my dad. I had been a popular person lately.

But I was glad I had it on me, because it was Letty. As I answered, I had a flash of hoping that things were going well and no other bodies in carpets had been found.

"What's up?"

"Are you still working through the info I gave you earlier?" she asked, with something in her voice that I couldn't quite identify.

"Um, yes, but only as a concerned citizen."

"Right. Anyway, my nephew called me again after we hung up, and this time he was in tears, and I thought there was info I should give you."

"Why give it to me? Why not call Burton?"

"First, because I trust you to look into this without pulling the poor guy in. Caleb is distraught and can't think straight right now."

Because he was the one who'd actually killed her, and the guilt was eating him alive, despite his supposedly ironclad alibi? Maybe my theory was wrong. I didn't have proof, and if her nephew's alibi wasn't as solid as he'd led everyone to believe, then I'd have to go down a whole new avenue. I, of course, didn't want to ask Letty about the alibi. Instead, I waited for what she'd say next.

"Second, because I trust you to do the right thing, and some of this has been sitting on me for some time. I just can't keep it to myself anymore."

Okay, now I was confused. Did this have to do with the nephew or the murder or something else? I had a momentary panic that she was going to leave me with a crew I didn't know, and was going to tell me she was walking to do something else, like wash cars or be a receptionist or go back to school to be a lawyer. I just couldn't take it. I gulped. "Just spill. I can't take the uncertainty or the angst I'm feeling in my head right now."

Letty snorted. *The brat.* "It's nothing like what you're probably fretting about. Just hear me out, and then we'll go from there."

That didn't sound good, so I sat on the second to bottom stair and gripped the carpet just in case.

"For one thing, Caleb told me that he and Audra were not doing well. He was actually going to the mansion on the day Audra's body was found to find out why she was going around town with a ring on her finger. He didn't propose."

"No proposal? But she was so quick to flash that beauty around."

"And he has no idea where she got it. She either bought it for herself or was engaged to someone else. But it definitely wasn't him. He'd just found out that she had been seeing someone else, or had been seen around town with someone else, but he couldn't figure out who it was. For such a small town, it's surprising what people can keep under wraps if they want to."

"No doubt about that. So Caleb did not propose, and the rosy stories she told about her boyfriend were either not true or were about a different boyfriend?"

"Did she ever say it was actually Caleb?"

I tried to think back, and I realized that all Audra had ever said was that her boyfriend had given her the ring. I had taken that to mean Caleb, since that was who I thought she was dating. Could it have been someone else? "Not that I can recall," I answered after a few seconds.

"Exactly. He was going to confront her about the rumors, because she wasn't returning any of his calls. He knew where she was supposed to be, because she had texted him that she got the job at the mansion, just like she had told him she would."

"So she thought all along she was getting the job, even though it's a smaller property than she was used to and we were both in the game? I told everyone that the best person would win and that this was fine with me."

"That is not what she was telling everyone. Apparently, she was super confident that the job would be hers. Several people have said that she very blatantly and vocally wondered why they had even let you compete for the job, because they had known they were going to give it to her from the beginning."

I wasn't sure what to say to that, so I just said, "Huh."

"Which then leads to the next part . . ." Letty allowed that to hang there for a moment, one in which I gripped the staircase tighter. Was she going to leave me?

"I've been hearing from clients for the past few weeks that she was approaching them about taking over their cleaning." She blew out a breath. "I'm sorry I didn't tell you, but I wasn't sure what to do, and since no client left us, I figured it would be okay to just keep this to myself, instead of burdening you with something that wasn't a real issue."

That was a lot of words with no breath, but I understood, because I'd held mine the whole time she was talking. Now I let out my breath. "So you're not leaving me?"

"What? No! Why would you ever think that? You're the best boss I've ever had, and you totally don't micromanage. Plus, you're always so supportive. I would never leave you as long as you want me around."

"Phew! I was worried there for a moment that you were going to decide to go out on your own." I released my grip on the stairs and stood up. I could go to my apartment now that I knew I wasn't going to be hit by the two-by-four of being left behind.

"You're so silly, Tallie. I don't know what I'd do without you, and I can't tell you how thankful I am that you saved me from Darla. I'm not going anywhere."

"Promise?"

"Pinkie swear. Now, what do you think about the Audra thing? I'm sorry for not telling you sooner."

"Meh. Don't even worry about it. I actually heard the same thing from Mama Shirley earlier, and I got over the anger pretty quickly. Audra might have been trying to get in the door, but she wasn't having any luck."

"You know, your clients actually like you a lot and were nervous about telling you about Audra. They told me because they didn't want to hurt your feelings."

That statement caused me to sit back down on the stairs. Fortunately, it wasn't far to go, since that had rocked my world. "Really? I thought it was all just a game to them to see me brought low."

"Maybe at first, but in the end they think you do a great job, and really like having you there. Most often I hear that they can trust you and don't have to worry about anyone stealing the silver or leaving the house half done, because they have something else they'd rather be doing than keeping a close eye on their possessions."

"Huh." I wasn't particularly proud of the fact that I seemed to have lost my ability to say actual words, but I couldn't quite wrap my head around the fact that all the people who had hired me to come clean their houses respected me and cared enough about me not to want to hurt my feelings. I was sure there were a few who didn't feel that way, but those didn't count. The ones who stuck around and worried about hurting me were the ones I was going to concentrate on. So strange, but in a really nice way.

"I feel bad now. You're at a loss for words," she said.

"Oh gosh, no. Please don't worry about it. I'm just stunned. I really thought I was just being tolerated as the swan-dive survivor that they wanted to watch flounder in their own homes. Since they have the cash, I just thought they were willing to pay money to see it happen. I never really considered that they liked me."

"You need to get over that. Now. You're valued by a lot of people. More than you know. Max, me, Gina, Mama Shirley, your uncle, your dad, your brothers, your mom. Even Burton values you, though he'll probably never say it."

And yet he had. And that was a big list of people.

But Letty wasn't done. "And far more people than that, but I don't have time to list all of them. Except you are also valued by those who have died and no longer have a voice to tell us who did it or how. I get that you don't want to be a vigilante or interfere with Burton, but I also think you have a knack for finding things out and piecing them together in a way no one else does."

"My head is going to expand to the point that I can't get out the door," I said, laughing.

"Well, let's not go too far, but I think it's time you looked at what all you have going for you, instead of always looking for that something else you could be doing."

Okay, a little bit of a smackdown, but that was allowed and wouldn't burst my bubble. "So what am I looking at as far as Caleb? He said that he didn't put a ring on it, but he doesn't know who did? Does he at least have any ideas?"

"I don't know. Oh . . ." Her voice dropped to a whisper. "Mrs. Petrovski just walked in, and she does not look happy. You might want to come down here and use your valued talent to talk us out of a bad situation. Like now. Bye."

I had wanted to find Burton, but it wasn't a choice at this point. Letty needed saving, and she was more important. Burton would still be there when I had time. And if I could approach him with real proof, I'd much prefer that over a theory.

Time to be the boss.

Chapter Sixteen

When Letty sounded the alarm and it involved Mrs. Petrovski, I was ready to jump. I did not want the ladies handling her on their own if they didn't have to. I'd seen her tongue-lash a poor butler once, when I was married to Waldo, and the guy had left looking like he had just been drawn and quartered yet was still breathing.

Fortunately, the house was only a few blocks away. Unfortunately, when I headed to my car, I stopped short when I realized it was blocked in by the hearse again. I knew I had not parked the hearse like that earlier, so who had been out in the behemoth? It didn't matter. I could walk to the house and get there faster than if I went back into the funeral home for the keys to the hearse, moved the thing, and then got my car out.

I walked and texted Max to let him know where I was heading, then picked up the pace once the message was sent. It wasn't easy in my heels and skirt, but it had to be done.

I flung open the door to the house, then called out to see where everyone was, hoping to catch Mrs. Petrovski in mid-haranguing without coming across that way.

It worked, I was pleased to say. She turned to me, with her eyes burning, her mouth turned down, and her fists clenched.

"Ma'am, to what do we owe the pleasure of your visit?" I said.

"I don't need you to patronize me. I know you weren't here when I arrived, and I want to know why. I saw your car over at your father's. I'm not paying you to sit upstairs with your boyfriend and neck while your crew is here cleaning this monstrosity."

How did she even know about my car? My low-slung car was parked in the drive-through portico at the funeral home's entrance, and the hearse, parked right behind it, towered over it and made it impossible to see from the road. *Not important*, I told myself and soldiered on.

"I'm here now, and my crew is more than capable of doing all we have on our plate. With this new house that you gave us, we've had to rearrange some schedules." I was not going to address the necking comment.

"Fine, but I want to know how soon you can have this place cleaned up."

I looked around and was honestly astounded by the amount of work everyone had done so far. The floors were bare, if dirty, in the front room, and as

I looked through the doorways in the shotgun-style house, I could see that the other rooms were in pretty much the same condition.

"I think you should be pleased with how much progress we've made so far. This place had a heap of junk all the way to the ceiling when we got here, and now we're almost down to just the cleaning."

Mrs. Petrovski scoffed. "It was not a hovel when I gave it to you, and the floors are dirtier now than they were when I was last here. I don't know what you're trying to pull, but I will not pay you for extra time just because you want to gouge me."

Okay, so she was not one of those people who didn't want to hurt my feelings, but that was okay.

Letty signaled to me over the woman's shoulder. I had no idea what she was trying to tell me. She kept mouthing a word, yet I couldn't for the life of me figure out what it was, though I knew what she was saying was important. Her shoulders dropped after three seconds, and she took her phone out of her pocket. Was she going to text me? I couldn't look at my phone. My life depended on behaving right now.

Letty waved her phone at me, like that was supposed to help, and I gave a slight shake of my head.

"What do you mean *no*?" Mrs. Petrovski barked at me. Oh, man, she had still been talking.

"I'm so sorry. I felt a hair tickle my ear and was trying to get rid of it without interrupting you." I frowned and then shot the same look at Letty.

"Fine. That's acceptable. I do want this place cleaned up as soon as tomorrow, though. There is no reason why this should look dirtier than when I

left it. Don't make me regret that I let you in to do
the work you say you and your crew can do."

I seriously thought about telling her to stuff it
but couldn't. The ladies of the crew were depending on me.

Letty's shoulders dropped farther as she shook
her head. I wished I knew what she wanted, but I
had no clue.

Finally, she stepped forward. "Tallie, I have
those pictures we took of the house before we got
started cleaning, just in case we had to remember
where something went."

Oh! There were pictures on the phone she had
been waving at me. That made sense now.

"What pictures? And who gave you permission
to photograph my house?" Mrs. Petrovski was on
the warpath, no matter what was said.

I was quicker on my feet this time. "We photograph every house before we start housecleaning,
in case there's an issue down the road, as sometimes happens with the more intense jobs." That
was a total lie, but if she bought it, then I would
sell it with everything I had.

She harrumphed but didn't say anything else,
so I took the phone from Letty and scanned
through the pictures. Once I found the photo of
the exact room we were standing in, I turned the
phone toward the sourpuss woman.

"What am I looking at?" She pulled the glasses
hanging on a chain around her neck up to her eyes
and stared through the lenses instead of putting
the glasses on her face.

"This is the room when we first arrived. This
room, actually." I carefully picked out a place on

the wall that matched the wall in the photo exactly, because I just knew she was going to tell me that I was lying. I beat her to the punch as she opened her mouth. "If you look right here, you can see that the wainscoting is the same color as in the photo and placed at the same height at the push-button light switch."

Her mouth snapped shut, and her glasses dropped as she stuck her hands on her hips. "You must be mistaken."

So she was going to try, anyway. "I assure you I am not mistaken. When we came to this house, it was stuffed to the rafters with furniture and debris. There was some question about the person who cleaned next door just shoving things over here, instead of handling them, as she'd been asked to do." It hurt to say that, because I didn't like to speak ill of the dead, and Audra had been my friend, or at least I had thought so. But there was no hiding the truth, and it was best to come clean about the whole thing right up front, especially if this was going to make us look better.

"I . . ." She grasped her throat and coughed and for a moment, I thought she might choke. "I don't know what to say. When I handed you the keys, I certainly didn't expect to have you walk into this. Where is everything?"

"It's in the sunroom at the moment, unless it was trash, and then it went in the bin near the garage. We hadn't discussed what you wanted to do with everything in here. You simply said to clean. When we got here and saw the amount of work, we just got to it, instead of calling for further instructions." Because the woman would have had a fit and would have told me I was trying to get out of doing the job. . . .

She closed her eyes and took a moment, either to calm herself or to figure out how not to apologize—I wasn't sure which—but either was fine as long as she didn't get angry again, at least not at us. "Well, as I said, I did not expect this. I can, of course, give you additional time to do your job correctly since this place will be on the market soon also. How much time do you need?"

I looked over at Letty, who raised a hand. Again, I did not know what she meant. We'd have to work on our telepathic skills. I took the safe route. "I'll speak with the crew and consult the calendar. I should be able to text you tonight with an answer to that. In the meantime, what would you like done with the contents of the house that are in the sunroom?"

"Donate. Just donate it all, unless you find something that you believe has value and could be sold at auction. There shouldn't have been much in here. I did ask that dratted Audra to donate everything before, but now I'm thinking that the receipts she gave me were fake. I already handed them to the man who does my taxes."

"You might want to get them back or at least verify with the various places they came from that they're real."

"Yes, no doubt. I'll leave you to your work, then, and I expect a phone call this evening to let me know when you will be done. I have high hopes that Chief Burton will be closing up this case shortly. I gave him the identity of the murderer just this afternoon, before I came here, so things should move swiftly now."

My breath stopped in my throat. "You gave him the identity of the murderer?" I squeaked. Why hadn't I heard this? Max was home doing research, when he could be with me, and instead I was alone, facing the dragon lady, while the murderer lazed around in jail. Why hadn't Burton called me?

That was the big question, and one I was going to ask just as soon as I could get away from this house and phone him.

"I most certainly did. Preston Prescott got it into his head that he was going to take over things and had decided that he was going to marry that woman. I told him he would be cut out of the will, and apparently, he thought that if he couldn't have her, then no one could. They should be picking him up now, and they'll deal with him. He's dead to me already."

I nearly choked. Preston Prescott had been the number one suspect on my very short list. I'd wanted to talk to him again to see if I could get him to spill his beans, and now Mrs. P had just handed his name over to the police.

But nothing I had on Preston would be necessary now. Preston had been dating Audra and had given her that ring? And then, when his aunt had told him he'd be cut out of the will, he'd killed Audra instead of just breaking up with her? Or, even better, telling his domineering aunt where to go and marrying the woman he loved, anyway?

To say I was shocked would be an overstatement. Yes, I had thought he was the murderer, but it was still a theory, not something I would have completely bet on. He was a jerk, and I could see him thinking about actually doing Audra in when his inheritance was in jeopardy. But he'd given Audra a ring even when she was dating Caleb? How had she kept her two lives running concurrently?

Here was where the shock came in: Who knew he had it in him? Even I had been struggling with that part of my theory. He might talk a big game, but he always let other people do his dirty work. Then again, I guessed anyone could be pushed to kill for something. Or at least that was what all the podcasts about murders I'd been listening to lately seemed to say.

I had to get out of here, though, and see if I could talk with Preston before Burton caught up with him. I still wanted to know how he had done it. I didn't want to wait for the newspapers to print the story, because I knew they'd never report the whole thing, and I wanted to know what had actually happened. Call me morbid or just overly curious, but I wanted to see what Preston would tell me.

I walked Mrs. Petrovski out of the house after telling her we'd be done as soon as possible. Once I came back into the front room, I planned and made detailed lists with Letty about how we would get this monstrosity cleaned, then realized I was twenty minutes away from having to drive the hearse for a funeral this evening.

After wishing my crew good luck and waving good-bye, I ran home as fast as I could. I didn't try to text anyone on the way, as I did not want to stumble into a light pole or trip over a crack in the sidewalk and make myself late.

I buzzed into the apartment after shouting to my mother that I'd see her in a few when she tried to stop me on the stairs.

"The cops have the perp on their radar and are looking for him to question him," I told Max as I entered the apartment. I went right for the closet. I shooed Mr. Fleefers out of the way when he came through the back of the closet. I always forgot that door to the other side of the building was in the back of the closet. He had a toy in his mouth, but he dropped it long enough to hiss at me, then picked it back up and sauntered away. Peanut ran in circles around the cat, then lay down for the cat to knead his claws into her back.

"Who?" Max turned around on his kitchen chair. He had spreadsheets and a ton of windows open on the laptop. I doubted it was our case he was researching.

"Preston Prescott, if you can believe it." I pulled out a blouse and a black skirt, then zoomed into the bathroom to change, leaving the door open a crack so I could continue to talk while I dressed. The dirt in that house had clung to my clothes. Even though I would just be driving the hearse, I still had to be up to Graver Funeral Home standards.

"Really? Preston? I just don't see him being able to do something like that."

"He could be cruel after he'd been drinking. I would think he could conjure that up all on his own without the vodka when dear auntie told him that he'd be disowned if he married a girl not of her liking." I yanked my blush and eyeliner out from under the sink and reapplied both as quickly as possible.

"He wanted to marry Audra? But I thought she was engaged to Caleb."

I told him the whole sordid story about how Caleb had never proposed to her and how she had suddenly shown up with a ring on her finger. One he hadn't given her and one whose origins he had no idea about. I also explained that Preston hadn't wanted anyone to have her if he couldn't have her, according to his aunt.

"That must be why he kept hanging around and showing up during the investigation. He wanted to see if anyone knew that it was him, so he could cover it up. Not a bad idea, actually, but it didn't work this time." I chuckled. Stupid people who thought they could get away with murder. The identity of the murderer almost always came out at some point.

"And he's the one who called the truck to pick up the Dumpster?"

I poked my head out of the bathroom as I brushed my hair into a bun. "I guess so. I haven't had a chance to talk with him or with Burton. By the time the aunt left and I got the brigade in order, it was time for me to hustle back here." I placed the brush back on the counter and stepped back into my heels. "I'm sorry to run again, but I have to drive this evening, and then I'll be home. At that point, I promise we can talk all we want and also have some time together without a murderer on the loose. Won't that be nice?"

He chuckled. "Be safe out there driving that beast."

"I took my driver's test in that beast. It's my kitten. Bye. I love you." I ran up to him, gave him a quick kiss on the forehead, stepped away, then stopped, turned around, and laid one on his lips. "I'll see you soon."

"I'll look forward to it," he said.

After taking the stairs two at a time—which was a feat in heels—I scooted past my mother again and went right for the hearse. The body would have to be loaded in, so I pulled into the drive-through portico and waited.

I didn't have long to sit there, since I was right on time, and so were my father and brother. I smiled at them both and got a side-eye from my dad and a frown from my brother. Let them have their doubts about my happiness. I, for one, knew that I was not going to have to face a criminal before he was caught. I would not have to have that showdown where they delivered a monologue about the ways in which the world had done them wrong, and that was why they thought they had to kill to make their life better, but instead they only made it worse. It was a good day in my book. And Burton would solve the case, and maybe that would make him happy enough to smile once in a while.

Like I said, a good day.

My dad thumped the top of the hearse to let me know I was locked and loaded. I carefully pulled out into traffic, knowing that I would have a long line of cars behind me with their lights on, announcing that this was a funeral procession.

There was something so quiet and solemn about

this part of the journey. No one talking to me, no one demanding anything. I didn't even turn the radio on, though I could have. Instead, I drove slowly to the cemetery on Sycamore Street, winding through the streets of our little town to the top of the hill and turning left. I kept an eye out behind me to make sure I still had a car right behind me with its lights on. Some people in the procession would get held up at a light or two, but there was nothing I could do about that, and it was to be expected. They all had maps to where they were going in case they got left behind. It was part of the program my father drew up in the office on the second floor.

Most vehicles would wait for our line of cars to pass, not wanting to get caught in the middle of a funeral procession. Today one car did not, and its tires squealed as the driver got right in front of one of our cars. I shook my head, knowing there was nothing I could do about that and it would just come down on their head. Karma was only a jerk if you were.

After about ten minutes, I pulled up along the curb of the service road at the cemetery and parked the hearse. The pallbearers got out of the two cars behind me with a chorus of slamming doors, and we moved the coffin smoothly out of the rear of the hearse. I didn't have any other part to play in the burial, so I got back in the hearse. I'd wait until the pastor had begun the burial service before I pulled out of the service road and onto the street to freedom. I'd done my duty for the day. I could soon go back and hang with Max.

Then again, when I checked my phone, I saw

that Max had texted that he was going back to work and would see me later. So scratch hanging with Max. Maybe I'd see how the ladies were doing with the cleaning. I needed to do something until I could call Burton and ask what the heck was going on. I could call him now, but I was afraid that would be crossing the concerned-citizen line and going straight into nosey-parker territory, which my cousin Matt had recently accused me of doing.

I turned on the engine, engaged my seat belt, checked the rearview mirror, and had about two seconds to register that something or someone was in the back of the hearse before I felt a very hard jab of a cold metal object to the back of my head.

Chapter Seventeen

I'd never felt the barrel of a gun anywhere on my body. I had certainly never felt one on the back of my head, no matter how many times my ex-husband had threatened to kill me because I irritated him. But even I thought the object was a little too big and a little too cold to be a gun, once my brain started working.

I looked in the rearview mirror and could just make out the shape of a cravat. Not a bow tie, not a tie, not an ascot, but a cravat. Either that or the man behind me was wearing some other kind of neck adornment made of soft material.

"Really, Preston? Is that a freaking can of soda?" Inside I was shaking, because even with a can of soda, he could do some damage, but this was Preston, and as much as he could be a jerk, he was also a cowardly bully. You stood up to him, and he backed down or trounced off.

The cold cylinder was removed from my head

with a sloshing noise, which that affirmed my guess that it was indeed a soda can, but he did not refrain from leaning menacingly over the seat.

"Don't tempt me to hit you with this, Tallie Graver. I'm on the run for my life, and you're going to help me, or I swear I'll hurt you and your petty little amateur-sleuthing behind."

Okay then. "What on earth do you think I can do, and how did you get in here?"

The walkie-talkie on the console squawked, and Preston and I both froze.

"Tallie, you okay in there? I need you to head home. The hearse has to be serviced, and Michael is picking it up in an hour." Michael was one of the other drivers for Graver's Funeral Home.

"I have to answer, Preston, or my dad will send someone over here to find out what's going on." Then again, maybe I should have let him, and then I could have hauled off and whacked Preston myself before scrambling out of the car. I didn't know what I'd hit him with, but it was worthwhile consideration.

"Fine. Answer it," he grumbled. "But no telling about me. I will hurt you."

I had no doubt about that, since his aunt had said he'd killed Audra and rolled her in the carpet. Now my shaking went to my hands, instead of just staying in my abdomen. Preston noticed.

"Good. We understand each other. Keep that fear, Tallie. You're going to need it in a moment."

I picked up the walkie-talkie and depressed the switch. "All's fine here, Dad. I was just making a call before getting on the road. Wanted to make sure I didn't break any laws on my way back to the shop."

"Um, okay. I'll see you when I get home. Just leave the keys in the hearse when you get there. Michael knows how to find them."

"Okay. See you. Love you. Bye." And I let go of the button. I could have screamed for help; I could have yelled something about needing to be saved. But I really thought Preston was not going to hurt me. Then again, I'd also thought I wouldn't have to endure the customary bad-guy monologue, yet I seemed to be right in the middle of that, after all.

Now I just had to figure out how to thwart him, as I had the others before handing them over to the police.

"Drive," he said in a low voice that brought the shivers back.

I would survive this. I would, and then I would beat the crap out of this guy for scaring me.

I put the hearse in drive, took the road slowly, and made a full stop at the end of the service road. "Where to?"

"Turn left. We can go to the cemetery up the road, that Lincoln one."

I knew exactly where he was talking about, but I didn't want to go. It was secluded, out in the middle of nowhere and on a dead-end road. It had been a place of burial for hundreds of people of color from 1806 until the end of the Civil War. It was a site of great historical significance, and the Vietnam vets in our area had started taking care of it to make sure it was given all the glory and honor it deserved. But since it was a Sunday, it was likely to be deserted. Which might work for Preston, but most certainly not for me.

But the road either way was clear. I had to decide what to do. He might have used a can of soda to threaten me, but that didn't mean he didn't have something else to hurt me with if I tried to challenge him and go a different way. I also gave brief consideration to speeding and then slamming on the brakes to throw him off balance, but the hearse didn't stop that fast.

So I turned to the left and hoped for the best.

It took only about three minutes to get to the cemetery. The area was well cared for and beautiful, but sad. It hadn't seen any new residents in years, and the headstones showed age but also care. It was beautiful. I just hoped I wasn't about to become a new resident.

"Move over," he said from behind me when I pulled to a stop.

This skirt was not exactly the best outfit in which to slide over the console, but I did my best. He scrambled into the front. I had hoped for a second that he would get out the back, open the front door, and get in. I would have locked the doors in a split second, then sped off.

It was not to be, though. I did, however, take a second to grab my cell phone and turn the recorder on as he fell over the front seat and tried to get himself organized in the driver's seat.

"Okay," he said breathlessly. He straightened his cravat and then smoothed down his hair.

"What do you want? And why do you think I am

going to give it to you when you just hearse-jacked me?"

"You always did get straight to the point, even when you were a vapid airhead."

"Look, we're not here to make small talk. You kidnapped me with a can of soda and then made me lie to my father, and I have less than an hour before I have to have this beast back to the funeral home, or I'm going to get in trouble. So what do you want? I highly doubt you wanted to give me something to drink to quench my thirst." Although, on second thought, I could really use some caffeine right now. "Hand over the can." I stuck my palm out and waited for him to do what he was going to do.

Surprisingly, he laughed and handed over the soda. No caffeine in it, but it would do in a pinch.

"Now talk," I said as I cracked open the tab.

He closed his eyes and rested his head back on the seat. I was very tempted to bean him with the Sprite. However, now my curiosity was getting the better of me. I wanted to know what he thought I could do to get him out of answering for a crime that his aunt had turned him in for. I certainly couldn't hide him, and I couldn't clear his name if he had done it. I wasn't going to say I had killed Audra to get him out of trouble. So what did he want?

He opened his eyes and turned his head to look at me. "I didn't do it."

"That's what they all say."

His neck went red, and a vein throbbed in his temple. Okay, maybe I had pushed it too far, too fast.

"I swear to you, I didn't do it. I don't know why someone told Burton that I did, but I swear I did not kill Audra, and I need you to help me clear my name."

"I'll reference again the hearse-jacking." Interesting, though, that he didn't know it was his aunt who had turned him in. I debated whether to tell him or not and decided in the end that it was not info he needed. Plus, I wasn't going to be the one who was blamed if I told him and he went after her. Better to keep it to myself and see where this went.

"Come on, Tallie. I know that we've had our differences."

I snorted, because *differences* was a mild word and didn't speak to all the times he had been rude and to his most recent attempt to get me disqualified for a job that I wanted for my crew.

"Okay, fine. More than differences. I've been a jerk, a scoundrel, a bastard, if you want, but right now I swear to you that I am not a murderer. I need help to get the real killer, or he or she will still be out there running around, capable of taking another life and maybe eager to do it again, having gotten away with this one."

Shoot. Now he was speaking to my curiosity, and I could almost feel myself leaning toward him. It was like when I didn't want to adopt Peanut, and yet I took her with me. And that had worked out okay, except for when I didn't have any room to sleep on my own bed, or when she drooled on my clothes a moment before I had to get out the door. But all in all, it had worked out. And I really didn't want a real murderer to get away.

"Explain to me how you think I can clear your name."

He sighed and flicked his thigh. "I don't have a clue. I just know that I didn't do it. I don't even know how she was killed. I don't have an alibi, though, since I had left the house and had just driven around."

"Why did you need to drive around?" I turned more fully toward him, tucking my feet under my rear end.

"I just had a lot to think about. Aunt Marg is selling all these places, but they need so much work before they can go. This business opportunity isn't going to be around forever, and the longer I wait, the more I'm going to have to pay." Tugging on his chin, he groaned. "There's just so many things that are wrong with this. And I don't know where to start."

Neither did I, to be honest. So I shrugged. I was curious, sure, but I didn't want to be involved with this guy. However, an idea was forming in my head, and it would take some serious maneuvering on my part to see it to fruition.

"Where did you drive?" I asked to keep the conversation rolling.

"I don't even know. I was just wandering around. Of course, I didn't see a single person while I was out. I eventually went back to the house."

"When was that?"

He hesitated, making me wonder why. "That's not important. Besides, I don't remember. I just know I did go back there, and then I went home. That I can verify, but other than that, I have time unaccounted for."

"I can't do anything with that at the moment, Preston. I mean, you have unaccounted time, and someone has said they know you were the one who killed Audra. Why would they have said that?" I really needed to get out of the car. My legs were cramping, and the skirt was cutting off my circulation. "If I promise not to go anywhere, can we take this outside? I need fresh air to think."

"You promise not to go anywhere?"

"I do. You don't have to accept my word for it, but I'm getting out no matter what you say. You want my help, then this is my game now."

He growled, and I didn't care. I opened the door before he could hit the automatic locks, then got out and stretched my legs. I took a couple of steps back and forth and was very happy that I had chosen the skirt with the pockets. There was a chance that I wouldn't catch all the conversation—I knew that—but I had to get out of the car with my phone so I could continue to run the recording app.

He met me around the side, and we sat on the hood of the hearse. I kept my phone in my hand as I put it in a pocket, but I held my hand over it. I didn't cover the microphone at the bottom and hoped that would be enough to continue catching the conversation.

"So tell me what someone thinks they have on you," I said.

"I don't even know." He shook his head. "There's nothing they could have, as far as I can tell. I don't even know why they think it was me at all."

"But they have enough to make Burton come for you."

"I overheard two of the men at my gentlemen's club talking about it when I was in the restroom. Someone started a rumor that the cops should be looking for me, and they were discussing that it wouldn't surprise them if I'd sunk that low. I waited for them to leave, and then I snuck out the back door. I hid in my house for a little while, then thought I had to get out of town. Leave until the threat died down and they found the right person."

"I'm pretty sure they stop looking when they find the person they think did it," I said, looking out over the grounds and into the trees. There was no way I'd be able to make it through the trees and away from him in my heels. Heck, even in tennis shoes, I couldn't outrun many people. Especially those who were fit and trim, like Preston.

I looked down into my pocket and snuck a peek at my phone, and it was still recording, though nothing useful was actually being said. I did, however, also notice that my hour was slipping away. It was not going to be possible to get back to the funeral home on time if I didn't get moving soon.

"I'm still not sure what you want me to do, Preston. I can't clear your name if I have nothing to work with, and quite honestly, I still don't understand why you think I would do this."

"Because I'm desperate. I might be a jerk, but you always like to figure these things out. I was going to ask you to look into it before I was accused. I liked Audra. I would never have killed her."

"How much did you like her?" I thought about my initial gut reaction to the fact that he was the one who had put that ring on her finger. He had denied it before, but with Letty's info, I could see if he'd be honest with me this time. And I still wanted to know what he had done when he went back to the house after Audra was killed. I had noticed that he'd sidestepped the question altogether.

His eyes glassed up, and he sniffed. "I wanted to marry her, if you really want to know. We'd talked about it. Getting her that job was one of the things she wanted before she would say yes. When Aunt Marg brought you in, Audra was extremely angry and threatened to cut me off altogether. That was why I ruined your room when you were competing for the cleaning job at the mansion. I had to be able to ensure that Audra got that job, or we'd be over."

"Why would you want to be with someone who would hold that over you and make sure you stayed in line, or they would leave you?"

"Come on," he said. "Tell me you don't know what it's like to stay with someone who you know is wrong for you."

Touché. "This is not about me and my disastrous marriage to Waldo."

He chuckled. "Do you know how much it pissed him off that you called him that?"

"Yes, I do, and that's precisely why I did it." I was softening toward him. If he'd loved Audra—no matter how much I didn't understand it—then why would he have killed her? "Look, I have an idea, but you're probably not going to like it." I wasn't going to be able to trick him into anything, and trying would only get me hurt. So far he hadn't threatened me again. I wanted to keep it that way.

He turned toward me eagerly. "So you'll clear my name?"

"Well, it's not going to seem like that when I tell you my idea, but in the end I believe it will get both you and me what we want." It would take some fast talking on my part in the end, but I was confident I could convince him.

"So what is it?"

Chapter Eighteen

And so, after that fast talking I was confident I could pull off, I found myself at the police station, with the hearse parked around back. I'd called Michael and asked him to give me a half hour more to get the hearse back to the funeral home. He'd said that was fine, since he was finishing up another job, anyway.

I was currently standing at the receptionist's desk, waiting for Burton to come out of his office. I'd heard him grumble after Yolanda, Letty's friend, had gleefully announced my name and winked at me.

Finally, Burton came out to the front. I'd asked to be taken back to his office so that we could do this in private, but apparently, he did not think enough of me to give me that courtesy. *Whatever.*

"What now, Tallie? Some more concerned-citizen information?"

I frowned at him. "I seriously think this would be better done in your office."

Yolanda frowned and shook her head. I was just going to have to disappoint her. I walked past Burton and headed for his office. He could either follow me or remain standing out in the waiting room, like an idiot.

He chose to follow me. Thankfully.

I sat down in the visitor's chair in his office and waited for him to come in and close the door. Once he did that, he sat in his chair and steepled his fingers under his chin.

"This had better be good. I have a man to find for murder, if I can just figure out where the heck he is."

"Is it good that I have Preston out in my hearse, and he's ready to turn himself in?" I said.

He jumped out of his chair. "You left him out in the car without any supervision? He might be gone by now."

"I zip-tied him to the bars in the back that keep the coffin in place."

He laughed. Like an actual real laugh that shook his shoulders. "Why on earth did I even bother to doubt you?"

I shrugged. "I have no idea." I took in the office and looked over the books on his shelves and the penholder on his desk. He had mountains of paperwork next to his flat-screen monitor. He looked like he'd been here for hours, and his shirt was rumpled. If I could help, then maybe he would be able to sleep or at least go home for a little bit.

"So you have Preston Prescott zip-tied to the

bars in the back of a hearse in the parking lot. Dare I ask how you managed that?"

"Is that important? Don't you want to go get him?"

"No. I think we'll wait just a moment, then go out to get him. I'd like to hear how you managed to catch him when I found out only today that I should be looking more closely at him."

I walked him through the events of the day and told him about Mrs. Petrovski fuming over the housecleaning and about her accusations against her nephew. He shook his head at me.

"She was supposed to keep that to herself."

"Yes, well, I think you had better remember the town you live in. Hardly anyone ever keeps anything to themselves." He frowned at me, but I kept on going. I told him about my happiness over not having to have my near-fatal showdown with the bad guy, as had happened previously. He smiled his way through the whole thing. So then I told him about Preston hearse-jacking me. That finally got a frown.

"I told you to stay safe."

I groaned. "And how was I supposed to do that better than I tried? I had let everything go. Max was still at home, doing some follow-up, but I swear, I was out of it. I was going to let you handle everything. I was doing my actual job, not even being a concerned citizen, since I was sure you could handle the case, and then I get kidnapped with a can of soda. I didn't ask for this."

"You never do." He sat back down, only to lean forward in his chair. "You never do, and yet here we are again."

"This time, though, I don't think I brought you the killer." I bit my lip when the storm clouds started scudding across his face. It was no more than usual, but it still made me cringe a little. "Let me explain, before you blow your lid."

"Maybe we'd better go get Preston, because I do not want to lose him, and you can explain to your little heart's content after I book him."

"Whatever you want, but you might want to hear this before we get him, so you know what you're walking into."

He rose from his chair and shook his head. "At least let me pace while you're telling me how this is going to be messed up yet again."

I took offense to that statement but let it ride, because it would gain me nothing to get in his face about it. "Look, I know you're not happy, but he swears he didn't do this. He has no idea who did, but I talked him into turning himself in and staying in jail until we find out who the real killer is. You get your man until we get the right one. I get to look around some more, and we get a killer—the real one, not the one that it seems the aunt wants to get rid of, enough to turn him in without the blink of an eye and with a smile. He doesn't even know it was her, only that the police were looking for him, which he overheard at his gentlemen's club."

"He says he didn't do it, but he has no alibi."

"Yes, he was driving around and no one saw him and he didn't see anyone. He says he doesn't remember where he was driving, but eventually, he came back to the house. He won't tell me what he did there, only that he left again and went home.

His plan was to leave town, but he decided to come find me instead and try to force me to clear his name."

Another laugh, this one bigger. "Does he not know who he is dealing with?"

"I guess not." But I did smile at Burton. That was almost a compliment, or at least I was going to take it as one. "So I convinced him that if he would turn himself in, he could be protected at the station while we went and found out who really did this, and then he would get out of jail. I don't know if he's completely clean of this whole thing, but I'm a little surprised that he is thought to be the killer. I just don't think he has it in him."

"We'll see about that. In the meantime, I guess we've made him wait long enough."

"Well, at least it's not hot outside, because I didn't leave the car running, and I left the windows open just a crack."

He chuckled some more as he led the way out to the back parking lot. When I opened the back door, of the hearse, I saw that Preston was sweating profusely and his cravat had gone completely limp and was draped across the floor.

"God, Tallie, I hope you never do that to your dog. You could have at least left me some air running. I was afraid I was going to die in here, and it was going to be your fault."

"Yes, well, beggars can't be choosers, and when you chose me to help you, you should have considered who you were asking. Burton has agreed to take you in, but he'll have to process you and interview you, as if he is really booking you with the crime," I told him, then paused. "It's the only way it's going to look authentic," I rushed to say when it looked like he was going to protest. "You'll be protected here, and no one can come for you. We'll figure out who really committed the murder, if it wasn't you, and then we'll be able to let you go."

Not that I was really part of that *we*, but it sounded better than putting words in Burton's mouth.

Burton got a utility knife off his belt and cut the plastic keeping Preston Prescott in the hearse.

"Efficient," the chief said while sawing through the thick material.

"Useful," I said. "I also have some other info that I can send to you on your cell once I get this hearse back to the funeral home. Give me about fifteen minutes, and it's all yours. Better than any scraps of paper I've ever given you."

He cocked an eyebrow at me as he grabbed Preston's elbow and hauled him out of the back of the hearse. "I'll look forward to it."

After giving a small salute and a nod to Preston and Burton, I watched the chief escort the now prisoner into the station. I had no idea if Preston would ever leave, but it really wasn't my job to make sure he did or didn't. He'd held me captive and forced me to do his bidding. But then again, I had taken matters into my own hands and had made it turn out all right for me.

He had been belligerent when I'd first told him my idea of letting Burton house him, which would cause the killer to think he or she had gotten away scot-free. He did not want to be in jail and did not want to lose face in front of his friends and associates by sitting for even a moment behind bars. But I was persuasive about the benefits of doing it this way, and in the end I threatened to leave him in the cemetery, tell Burton where he was for pickup, and refrain from interceding on his behalf if he didn't do what I told him to. Not a proud moment, but at least it wasn't a deadly one.

And now I had to get that phone recording I'd made to Burton and drop the hearse off for Michael to pick up. I then wanted to check in with Max and maybe Gina. I hadn't heard anything from her about being cut out of this particular investigation, but she'd had a lot going on recently, what with an upswing in business, and probably wouldn't have had time to help, anyway. Or at least that was what I was telling myself and would tell her if she decided to get nasty about not being involved.

And it was time for some actual caffeine. I'd finished that soda a while ago, and since it was caffeine free, I was starting to get a headache.

After leaving the keys in the hearse visor, I trotted across the street to get my fix and to see if Mama Shirley had heard anything about the arrest of Preston or had any more info that could be useful. Max had been called into work and had texted me to let me know he was going to be out until later this evening. I didn't feel it was appropriate to send him a text about how I had been taken hostage in a hearse, so I decided instead to share that with him over dinner. At least that way it would be more personal, and he could actually see that I was okay, instead of me just reassuring him over the phone.

I hadn't exactly promised Preston that I'd clear his name in the end; I had been careful about that.

But the more I thought about his story, the more I wondered who had actually killed Audra and who would have had a motive.

"We haven't seen much of you," Mama Shirley said as soon as I opened the door.

I should have known that this was going to happen. "I was just in here yesterday."

"Yes, but you're not keeping us up to date about the investigation, and we're being left out in the cold on the details. Gina is sad. You know how I get when Gina is sad. Plus, I could be the absolute number one on the gossip tree, and you're cutting me out."

An answer was on the tip of my tongue—maybe not a smooth or witty one, but it was there—when Gina saved me.

"Mom, knock it off. Tallie is doing the best she can. If I needed more information, I would have called her. She's been running around like a lunatic lately. Cut her some slack, instead of cutting her with that sharp tongue of yours."

Oh, that was a burn, and I was interested to see how Mama took it.

"Pssh," she said, smacking Gina with her towel and then laughing. "Fine. You weren't sad, but I still could be the absolute center of the gossip pool here."

"You already are," Gina said. "What more could you want?"

"How about the details on how I was abducted at cold soda point and Burton has the suspect in custody and he is singing like a canary?" I offered as I sat down and rested my elbows on the lunch counter.

"Do tell." Mama started my favorite whoopie pie latte and smiled over her shoulder as the milk steamed.

"Yes, do tell, and don't leave a single detail out," Gina urged. "I've been trying not to be nosy, since I have my own stuff going on at the moment, but I can't say I didn't want to be Velma from *Scooby-Doo* again."

"There wasn't much Velma-ing to do this time. I thought I was out until Preston Prescott decided to hijack me in the hearse at a funeral."

"Wait, wait," Mama said, turning from the machine. "I'm not going to be able to hear you over the noise of making this thing. Gina, get her a cruller while I finish up, and then we can sit and discuss."

The place was empty, as it tended to be at this time of day. The lunch crowd had gone, the early afternooners had gone, but the after-work crowd hadn't yet come in for their daily dose of coffee and talk.

I staked out a table while Mama finished her coffee magic and Gina warmed up a cruller and put it on one of her pretty purple plates.

Once they served me the latte and the cruller, they both sat opposite me at the four-top and folded their hands on the table in front of them. I would never tell Gina how much she looked like her mom, because it would get me walloped, but, man, did they resemble each other.

"Spill." Mama pushed the plate toward me. "You have all you need to get this all out to us. Now get moving."

So I told them what had been going on lately, about the cleaning jobs and the overly cluttered house and the additional info I'd learned about Audra from Letty. I told them about Caleb and Jason Huntington, and about Mrs. Petrovski telling on Preston, but Preston not knowing that. I also triumphantly crowed about tying up Preston in the hearse with zip ties after he had decided that taking me hostage at a funeral was a good idea and had demanded I help him. I still was on the fence about helping him at all, but if it would bring in the killer, then I wasn't against looking for more information.

After about an hour, I was done, and they sat, staring at me in wonder.

"You're a busy girl." Gina swiped at the table with a white cloth she always had in hand.

"Yeah. Sorry for not coming to get you, but so much of it was random conversation or people seeking me out that I wasn't really able to do much more than react this time. And I have spent so much time on the phone I thought the thing might meld with my hand."

"But now you're going to have to find the killer while Burton has this guy in custody. This guy can't be seen out and about, trying to find someone else, if you want the real killer to believe that he's off the hook for the crime, without a single issue," Mama said.

I hunkered down over my lukewarm cup. "I know, but I just don't even know where to start. What if Preston really is the bad guy? Mrs. Petrovski turned her own nephew in. Why wouldn't she know for certain it was him before she made that kind of declaration? That seems like pretty heavy stuff to do on a whim."

"Oh, I don't know," Mama Shirley said. "I could see several reasons why she'd be happy to have him out of her hair. And if she's been looking for an excuse, then this would be the perfect one. If nothing else, he'll be tied up for months, during which she can sell all her property and cut him out of the will, like she's been threatening to do for years. She wants to leave everything to her precious Pomeranian, but she has been having trouble doing that because of some legalities with the properties themselves and the way they were passed down to her."

Her desire to put the Pomeranian in the will and cut Preston out of it, regardless of whom he married, was new information. Unfortunately, Max texted that he was on his way home and the after-work crowd had started coming in. Gina got up to serve, but Mama stayed seated across from me.

"She can handle it for just a moment," Mama said. We both eyed the line at the counter. "Or at least for the next minute or two." Mama shrugged and then leaned forward. "I've heard something about Marg Petrovski that might help you with your case."

"It's not my case. Don't let Burton hear you say that, or he'll have a fit."

"Bah. He's my cousin, and I'm older. I'll handle him if I have to. Now listen up." She leaned in even closer, and I was afraid she was going to be in my lap at any moment. "Now, I heard that she's been dealing in some shady stuff, and there's some question about where those properties came from in the first place. Maybe you should have your Max look into some of the property records to make sure that she bought them on the up-and-up. There were rumors years ago about a bank heist. People thought it might have bankrolled the whole thing. That family has been up to their eye-balls in nasty things for years, and I wouldn't be surprised if the missus is in on it somehow, too."

"Mrs. Petrovski?" I wasn't sure what to think about that or what she could possibly be into. She wasn't the nicest of people sometimes, but I just couldn't see her being nefarious. At one time we had considered the family friends, but now I wondered if I had just remembered that wrong.

"Yes, but keep your voice down. You know how she's been selling everything off? They say that if she got the properties through illegal means, then it will all be confiscated, and she won't be able to do anything about it. I thought she had to sell due to money trouble and wanting to get out of debt, but that was bad information. So if she isn't in financial trouble, then why else would she all of a sudden have to sell everything off? Monroe down at the bank let it slip at bingo that the woman has a bank account that's bigger than ten of those socialites' up on the hill, and it has to be enough. Why now? Look into that." She rose from the table. "I'd better go help my Gina. She's giving me the evil eye. I can feel it on my back. Good girl for being so strong, but I'm not going to tell her that."

Sure enough, Gina's eyes were squinted, and her spine was ramrod stiff. I hid my smile behind a cough and waved to her on my way out.

So now I was looking into Mrs. Petrovski's bank records? I didn't know if I was going to be able to do that. She was untouchable in many circles, and I no longer had many friends that I could sidle up to and ask about her business. In fact, I had no friends like that, and I couldn't ask any of my cleaning clients, because they all knew better than to mess with a woman who could cut you with a look and had on plenty occasions. Invitations had been rescinded to parties that weren't even at her house if she said the right words to the right people. But did that mean she was dirty? I guessed I was about to find out.

It might not be pretty, and I might not be happy, but I was dedicated to figuring this out, while Burton grilled the man I didn't think had committed the murder.

Chapter Nineteen

For the fourth time that day, I walked up the stairs to my third-floor apartment. I was absolutely going to count this as exercise and not worry one bit that I'd stopped at the kitchen on the first floor and raided my mother's unending supply of snickerdoodles. I deserved them.

Opening my door, I was greeted by Peanut, who tried to jump up and almost knocked me over. I gently scolded her and told her to get down. She sat on her rump, then gave me the goofiest smile. I loved that dog and was so happy that in the end she was mine, even after the turmoil of how she had come to be in my house in the first place. I guessed I should have been thankful that she was used to living in tiny places, since my space was small and tight and quaint.

I maneuvered around her and put my plate of cookies on the kitchen table. After turning around, I showed Peanut that I had her treats, and as I knew would happen, Mr. Fleefers then deemed me worthy of a visit. When I'd picked up the snickerdoodles downstairs, I'd also raided the animal treat jar. This one was new, about three months old, and my mother was very pleased with her garage-sale find of a cat and a dog nestled together and napping in ceramic.

Hey, at least she hadn't been bugging me too much about kids now that she had these two adorable children to spoil.

I handed out treats, then got down to business. After pulling my laptop over, I smiled when I saw the folder Max had put together of the information he'd been looking into at my request.

Nothing much on Jason Huntington, though. I was definitely going to pay him a visit and find out if he knew where Bethany was. She still hadn't answered her cell phone. I was starting to get worried about her. She should have been back at work, and there had still been no word from her today. I wasn't willing to fire her as a no-call, no-show just yet, at least not until I found out what had happened and why she hadn't gotten in contact with us.

But Jason paid his taxes, was an upstanding citizen, was underpaid, and had never had any issues with the law. He was an outlier in the murder case, and I knew that, but I wanted info on all the players, and he was a player given that he had been involved with both Bethany and Audra at one point. From what I could tell, he didn't have a big enough motive; however, that didn't mean he hadn't held a grudge about the way Audra dumped him and moved on so fast. Then again, he had moved on, too, so I almost had to be willing to cut him out of my investigation altogether. I wasn't ready to do that, though.

But why would Jason have gone out to where Audra was working to kill her when supposedly she was no longer in his life, and why would he have chosen now? I made a note on the pad next to me to ask these questions when I went to talk with him. I was hoping to drag Max along with me just to be safe, in case Jason was the killer.

Then I had Bethany herself. I didn't want to think she could have done something heinous like this, but why would she be out of communication for so long? What if Audra had been there with her the night she was taking pictures? Maybe that extra something in the picture wasn't a wall but a hand or a piece of paper that had obstructed the camera lens. I'd thought about that on my way home from talking to Mama Shirley. I hadn't considered the pictures in days, since I had so much else whirling through my brain, but if there was no missing wall at the mansion, then it had to be something else. I made another note on the pad, to ask Burton if he had been able to make any progress with the pictures I'd texted him at his request.

Which made me move on to Caleb. I didn't want to look into him too much, because he was related to Letty, but his story could just be a convenient fabrication. He had known where Audra was around the time of her murder and had run when questioned by the police. I'd believed him when he said that he hadn't murdered Audra, but I had been known to be wrong before and had to put everyone under the microscope.

And then there was Mrs. Petrovski. She wasn't a tiny thing, but I didn't think she would be capable of actually moving a body wrapped in a heavy carpet to the Dumpster. How would she have managed that, and why would she have done it? Unless she'd had help. But who would have helped her? Unless she really was part of some kind of central Pennsylvania underworld and had been able to call in one of her goons to make the move for her.

Another note went down on the pad, and I honestly didn't know where to start. With Jason? But I wanted Max with me. Caleb? I wanted him to be last, so as not to irritate Letty. Bethany was not really on my suspect radar, and I could maybe find out about her from Jason. Mrs. Petrovski I was going to need help with.

Okay then, Jason it was. I'd start there and go on. I was nervous, to say the least. I didn't mind asking the tough questions, and I wasn't afraid to take people to task, but I also didn't know these players well, hadn't even met most of them before this whole thing started. Then again, I had thought I'd known the players before and had been totally wrong—in fact, I had almost drowned once and had been put on the train tracks, to get run over, like a character in a cartoon—so there wasn't much to be gained by *knowing* people, anyway.

At that very moment, Max opened the front door, interrupting my train of thought. Peanut rushed to greet him, and of course, so did Mr. Fleefers, the brat cat.

But I stepped into the middle of all the chaos and offered him something better than panting dogs and purring cats. "You want to go start the inquisition?"

He smiled and kissed me. "I thought you'd never ask."

We took his truck, just so that no one would know it was me, in case anyone was looking. With Preston in jail, I figured most people would think the murder case had been solved and they could go back to their regularly scheduled lives. Or at least that was what I hoped. I needed them pliant and unassuming, if I was going to ask the hard questions.

After pulling up in the apartment complex, we chose a parking spot that was between Jason's apartment and Caleb's, because if we didn't get anything from Jason, then we might as well just check in with Caleb to see what was what.

I hadn't heard anything from Burton after I texted him to find out about what had been found in the car that was in the parking lot or about the pictures. I had left Matt a message, too, but he'd texted me back that he was on the hunt for a drug dealer and couldn't talk at the moment. Totally understood. We'd catch up later.

And again I thought, What did we do without cell phones? So much contact, so much availability. It wasn't always awesome to be able to be contacted at any time, but right now I was blessing the cell gods and thanking them for everything I had.

"Okay, so when we go in, what are we asking

about?" Max had a hand on the small of my back, following my lead but right next to me. I loved it.

"We're going to ask about Bethany and find out if he knows where she might be. They're supposed to be dating, and he's the emergency contact on her employment form, so I at least have a right to be at his door, since he isn't answering his cell phone, either."

"Am I the silent partner? The heavy along for the ride, in case things get nasty?"

I laughed out loud. "Heavens no. You're going to be right there beside me, and if there's anything that you think we should ask, then go for it. You do this with money all the time. I don't think this will be much different. Interrogating is interrogating."

"I don't know what you think I do, but rubber-hose interrogation is used only for special occasions."

I tucked my arm into his elbow. "We'll do just fine. I left my rubber hose at home, so we'll just use our words."

I knocked on the second-floor door and waited. I heard someone moving around inside, but no one answered the door. So I knocked again and called out, "I'm just looking for Bethany! I've been trying to call her, but she's not answering her phone. I'm her employer."

Still no answer, but more footsteps scurrying around. I was not above breaking the door down if he was doing something he shouldn't be. Maybe Max would have to be my enforcer, after all.

I raised my hand to knock again, and the door opened, almost making me bop the man, who I thought must be Jason Huntington, in the nose.

"Sorry about that, sorry. I'm just heading out." He hopped on one foot while getting the other one into his sneaker. "I fell asleep, and I was supposed to be at the hospital thirty minutes ago. I'm sorry."

He wasn't wearing scrubs or some kind of uniform, just jeans that had seen better days and a T-shirt that looked like it had either been slept in or picked up off the floor.

"Are you going to visit someone?" I asked as he ran farther into the apartment, stuffing his keys and wallet into one pocket while he smoothed his wild hair down with his other hand. The guy was a mess, and I felt like I should keep him for a moment just to calm him down so he didn't drive like this.

"Yes. Bethany. Sorry. I really have to go. I don't want her to wake up, and I'm not there. She'll be sad, and I can't stand to see her sad." He rushed the door, but Max stood his ground in the doorway and put his hand out.

"Slow down for a second," Max said. "You're going to end up in the hospital yourself if you don't calm down and take a deep breath."

Max could be authoritative when he wanted to be, and he commanded a room without being domineering. He was strong, intelligent, well spoken, and mine.

Jason stopped in his tracks, bent forward, and inhaled a deep breath. I wanted so badly to ask him what had put Bethany in the hospital, but I was trying to follow Max's lead and let this poor guy catch his breath.

"Take another one, and take a minute to just rest. Bethany will be okay. She has staff caring for her, if you are going to see her at the hospital. You can make your excuses, say Tallie was looking for her and just wanted to make sure she was okay," Max said.

"I'm just so exhausted," the younger man said. "I've been doing this for days. I tried to sleep at the hospital, but I just can't get comfortable, and I had no clean clothes. I'm not even sure if these are clean, but I overslept, and I want to get back to my girlfriend."

"It's okay." I patted him on the shoulder as he straightened back up. "I'll vouch for you, and from what I know of Bethany, she is not going to be angry that you're a little late. She cares about you a lot. She wouldn't want you to hurt yourself."

"I know, but I feel terrible about the whole thing."

Again, I wanted to ask what had put my employee in the hospital, but I felt that demanding answers right now would only backfire on me. But had he hurt her the same night he'd killed Audra? Had Bethany seen him kill Audra, and had he tried to hurt Bethany, too, but couldn't bring himself to do it? Maybe he had killed Audra and had made assertions that he had just found the body, and then maybe something happened to Bethany, and now she had amnesia. I told myself to hold on a minute, because I was going to a far-off land, with no known facts, and that never did me any good.

"Why do you feel bad?" I asked.

"I was supposed to pick her up from that huge mansion outside of town, and when I got there, she was crumpled in her car, with her eyes closed. I couldn't find anything wrong with her, but I also couldn't wake her up. Her speech is slurred at the moment, because whatever drug they gave her at the hospital is still messing with her system, but they tell me she's going to be okay now. Because they can't figure out what precisely it is that affected her, they have to keep her for observation. The doctor couldn't even have her system flushed. It's been a huge mess and worry. But seeing me comforts her, so I don't like to be away for too long."

"Is that why no one is answering her phone?" I asked.

"To be honest, I don't even know where her phone is or if she still has it. I rushed her to the hospital as soon as I found her, knowing it could take a while before Bethany's friends or family got there. I'm a paramedic, so I knew what to do to make sure she was safe. I brought her to that hospital because, no offense to your West Shore hospitals, but I like that one better and my dad's on staff, so I could make sure she was getting the very best care possible."

That all made a lot of sense, but I wanted to see Bethany for myself. "Do you mind if we tag along for a visit? I really do just want to see her to make sure she's okay and to assure her that we're thinking of her. Her job will be there when she's ready."

He looked me over and shrugged. "Actually, she would probably love to see you. Your name was one of the first things out of her mouth when she came to the first time."

"Does she know who did this to her or how it happened?" I asked. This information would, of course, be invaluable.

"We haven't been able to piece together much of the story. From what I can tell, she said she was going to take pictures for you, and while she was doing that, someone must have drugged her and knocked her unconscious, and she went down. I think they dragged her down the stairs, because she has some bruising on the back of her thighs, and they must have stuffed her in the car. Until she's fully awake, I don't have much more than that."

I needed her to be fully awake and answering questions. Jason's cell phone rang at that moment, and he apologized, with a look, as he yanked it out of his back pocket.

"Yeah? She is. Okay. I'll be right there. Is she crying? Tell her I'll get there as soon as I can."

He turned to us with his mouth set. "I really have to go. She's awake and not crying, but she's asking for me, and she's scared. Why don't you come with me? Maybe she'll feel better for having seen you."

"We'll be right behind you," I assured him.

We got there in record time. Obviously, Jason did not worry about getting pulled over by the cops like I did, and Max was right on his tail the whole way. Harrisburg Hospital had tricky parking, so we momentarily lost him in the parking garage, but we caught up with him at the elevators.

"Has anyone been able to tell you what drug they gave her?" I asked as Jason jabbed the elevator button thirteen times in a row. I put my hand over his. "It's going to be okay."

"I just want to get there."

To make sure that Bethany didn't talk to anyone and tell them Jason was the one who had drugged her? Because he wanted to figure out how to finish the job? Although why would he have brought her to the hospital in the first place if he had meant to kill her?

Sometimes I hated my own mind, as I was always imagining bad things about people who probably hadn't done anything wrong at all. But I couldn't take the chance, and I was in full amateur-sleuth mode at the moment.

Perpetrators, watch out!

Chapter Twenty

Finally, the elevator doors slid closed, and we stepped on and rose quickly to the fourth floor. Jason shot off the thing as soon as the elevator doors started opening. I was not small enough to squeeze through behind him, and neither was Max, so we waited for the doors to open fully, then exited. I had no idea where he had gone. We stopped at the reception desk to ask for directions.

"Oh yeah," the woman sitting behind the desk said. "I just saw Jason shoot by. I have never seen a more devoted boyfriend in my whole life. He's around the corner. Room five-fourteen."

"Let's be careful. I don't know if I believe his story," I said quietly to Max as we walked down the hall and turned right.

"I do. I've seen that look before, and I have felt that concern myself when you were in trouble. I think he's okay, and he checked out fine as far as any sinister things in his past."

"I'll take that under advisement, but I'm still going to reserve judgment."

"Fair enough."

After rounding the corner, we arrived at the correct room and found Bethany sitting up in bed, hugging Jason, with her hand clasped around her other wrist, which had turned white, despite her tan, from her own grip.

"Someone's here to see you," I heard Jason say into Bethany's hair.

The girl looked up and squealed, then winced. "Maybe not my best idea."

"Maybe not," I said, smiling. "I'm so sorry. I didn't even know you were here. Are you going to be okay now?"

She nodded and winced again. "Not a good idea, either."

"Take it easy." Max stood behind my shoulder, with his hand on my hip. "Tallie's here when you're ready."

"Oh, I am so ready."

"So what happened?" I couldn't help but ask, just to get the conversation rolling.

"I was taking pictures. I remember it so vividly. The place was ghastly, and I really hoped we were going to be able to handle it. Between the pictures, I almost texted you that it wasn't worth it. Did you get them? My phone was acting wonky that night."

"I did. The last one I have is of a room with some kind of weird wall that doesn't seem to exist."

"Oh my God. So it did go through when I sent it. I wasn't sure, and the staff here just told me they don't have my phone. I have no idea where it might be, but whoever hit me must have taken it with them. Jerks."

"Wait. I thought you were poisoned or drugged?" Jason said.

" 'Hit me,' as in 'drugged me,' sweetie." She patted his hand. "I was taking those pictures, and then this smell hit me that I couldn't identify, and then a white cloth came over my face, and I don't remember anything, until I came to in this bed. I must have hit SEND on my phone just as I was falling to the floor. Go me!"

I smiled, because what else was I supposed to do when really I wanted to go rip someone's head off? "Go you. So you didn't see anyone?"

"Nope, not at all, but they smelled like the ocean, or the beach at least. It was the last thing I got a whiff of before I inhaled whatever was in that cloth."

Jason put his arm around her shoulders, and she snuggled into him.

It couldn't have been him. The look in his eyes and the way he treated her? I just couldn't believe he would do something like that. And I couldn't come up with any good reason as to why he would. I put him lower on my list of suspects . . . at the bottom, to be precise. I'd come back to him if I didn't find anyone else, but for the moment, he was looking lovingly at the woman, who was staring back the exact same way, and I just couldn't picture him harming her in any way.

"So the extra wall is probably the cloth they used to knock you out?" I asked.

"It has to be. I don't remember any extra walls."

"One more question and then we'll leave." I

didn't want to do this here, but I had to know. "Jason, did you still have anything to do with Audra before her death? There are stories going around that you might have still wanted her after your breakup." I wasn't going to mention the ring unless he did.

"God, no," Bethany said fiercely.

Jason patted her hand this time. "No, and I've already been questioned. I promise I wanted nothing to do with that vicious woman. I don't know why I never saw her for what she was until we broke up. I guarantee you I had nothing to do with her or her death."

"Okay. We'll go. Thanks for letting us see you," I said. "Just in case, I wanted to check up on you when you didn't come back to work. I'm glad we found you, and I'm sorry this happened. Whenever you're ready to come back, just give me a holler, and we'll get you on the schedule, but no rush. And, hey, from now on, maybe have someone call to let me know if you're hurt. I would have come a lot sooner."

"Oh, Tallie, I'm so sorry. I've been in such pain, and Jason's been by my side, and I didn't even think of it. But your offer means the world to me. I really like working with those women and with you. As soon as I get the okay to leave the hospital, I'll get a new phone and call you."

"I'll be waiting to hear from you. And let Jason take care of you. Don't get going too soon if the docs want you to stay."

She saluted me as Max and I took our leave. We waved to the woman at the receptionist desk, then got on the elevator.

"Thoughts?" I asked as he hit the button for the lobby.

"He didn't do it. I have extensive training in spotting a liar, and he was not lying. No dipping of the eyes, no slow blinking. He showed the appropriate emotions, and there was anger under that concern, not guilt. He wasn't lying about Audra, either."

"You know how to spot liars?" *Dang.* I would have to make extra sure I didn't ever tell even a white lie. How was I going to hide Christmas presents from him if he asked what I had bought him?

"I can, Ms. Tallie Graver, so don't forget it."

I hugged his arm to me as the elevator door opened to the lobby. We stepped off and came face-to-face with Letty.

"Oh my God, I tried to call you after you texted about Bethany being in the hospital. I hustled over to see her. I got her flowers." She held them out, as if I couldn't see them. "I'm a horrible manager."

"Knock it off, Letty. I didn't get her anything, and I pretty much interrogated her while she lay in bed. I also warned her to let us know what happens from now on. Flowers are going to make her day. You're a wonderful manager."

Her shoulders fell from her ears a little. "Really?"

"Yes, really, and it's not your job to keep track of everyone. This is a special circumstance. I've been trying to call her since yesterday. When I couldn't find her, I decided to go to the one person who might know. You've been super busy, and you are the best manager ever. Don't doubt that. Plus, you came right over with presents when you got my text."

"Okay. I'm better. I didn't do anything wrong. I'm good."

"You are amazing. Now go take those flowers to her, and let me reimburse you from the company. I'd like them to be from all of us, if you don't mind."

"I already signed the card that way." She grinned. "Good management material."

"The best, and you deserve a raise as soon as Max figures out what our profit is. Make sure you turn in that receipt, or I'll dock your pay."

Now she laughed. "Thanks, Tallie. No matter what you think about yourself, you are the best boss ever."

Max held the elevator door open until Letty had got on. We waved as the door closed, and then headed back to the car.

"You know she's right and wasn't lying at all," Max told me. "You are good at what you do. Any more thought given to what you want to be when you grow up?"

"Honestly, I just want to solve this whole mansion thing, and then maybe I'll give it some more thought. I really wanted to own a restaurant or a tea shop, but I get more pleasure out of driving the hearse and running this cleaning crew than I thought I would." *Oh crap.* I had never told Max about the hearse-jacking.

"Something you're not telling me?" he asked, pulling me aside as people streamed by to get to their various destinations.

"Um, no."

"Yeah, lying. See right there? That twitch in your eye right there is a telltale sign that you're not being honest with me. So spill. I'm not taking you home until you do."

I sighed. This whole "telling lies" thing was going to be a problem. "Can we at least get something to drink while I tell you?"

"Café's right through here." He gestured to the door behind him, and the place was more of a cafeteria than a café, but it would suffice. And honestly, if we were going to talk about this, it was probably better done away from the funeral home, where my mom could accidentally hear something. And I didn't want to talk about it in his truck, as he might swerve off the road.

We sat after getting to-go cups of coffee, and I told him about Preston and his soft-drink shenanigans.

"That doesn't sound like a shenanigan to me. That sounds like something I want to beat the snot out of him for," Max said when I was done.

"Oh, he's not going to get away with it. Even if we find a different killer, he's still going to get smacked with a charge for kidnapping. I'll see to it."

"Either you do or I will."

"Down, boy. I've got this."

He massaged my fingers and looked into my eyes. "I have never, nor will I ever, doubt that, but you're going to have to put up with me wanting to protect you. Not in one of those 'I am man' ways, but more in the way that I care about you and don't want anything ever to hurt you again."

I laughed nervously. "Maybe the next time I have a hangnail, I'll call you in DC, so you can come cut it off and yell at it for making me cry."

"Or maybe I should just move up here, and then it won't be an issue of a three-hour drive."

God, was I ready to do this now, in a hospital cafeteria? Of course I was. If I could face down murderers and can-wielding idiots, then I could do this. "I would love that."

"Really? No eye twitching."

"No eye twitching, and really. I would love for you to move up here. I've been trying to think up a way to ask you, but I didn't want to have to move down to DC just yet. And it felt wrong to ask you to uproot your life when, in the scheme of things, it would probably be easier for me to uproot mine." I raised my shoulders and spread out my hands.

He grabbed my right hand back and kissed my knuckles. "Absolutely not. DC is just not ready for you. I don't know if they'll ever be, but here would be a perfect fit for me. I loved living here when I was younger, and it will be even better now with you."

"We might want to think about getting a different place if you're going to be here all the time. Cozy is one thing. Cramped is something altogether different."

"Do you mind if I handle that? I have a few ideas. I'll run it by you before it's final, but I think I know the perfect place."

The perfect place? That would be wherever he was, no matter how schmaltzy that sounded. However, the prospect of getting out of the funeral home and living with Max somewhere in town, but not that close to my parents, sounded divine.

"Surprise me," I said, knowing I could trust him but hoping he knew what he was doing.

* * *

We made it back to the apartment and then split up to do some things. Max wanted to look into the properties again and see what old Mrs. P had up her sleeve with all these house sales, and I wanted to check in with Caleb. Instead of going back to the apartment complex, I decided to call him. He answered right away.

"I was hoping you might call," he said.

That was not the usual response I got from people I was trying to get to trip themselves up, but I'd take it on this weird and wacky day of everything seeming to be different than I had originally thought. "What's up?"

"I heard they took Preston Prescott into custody, and I just wanted to thank you for getting me out of the spotlight. I had a feeling he was the one who had proposed to her, because she kept crowing about some kind of yuppie guy. I kept thinking that maybe we could fix things and try again. That's why I was frantic when I couldn't find her. But I realized eventually that it wasn't going to happen. She wanted to string him along until she got what she wanted. Mainly, to take over all your jobs and any new ones, and then she was going to drop him, and she wanted me to stay around until everything happened the way she wanted it to."

"Is he the one who gave her the ring?"

"No. I think she gave that to herself, but I could never confirm it. She chuckled a few times about how his aunt was livid about him even considering marrying someone beneath him, but she got such a kick out of him squirming to keep dear old auntie happy while also trying to keep Audra happy."

"Why didn't you tell me this earlier?" I asked, baffled. This could have helped me so much.

He shrugged. "I felt like an idiot and just wanted to get her killer found so I could get out of the spotlight. It felt like that information would just make you look harder at me."

I shook my head at him. "I don't think it would have, but that leaves another question. Why on earth did you stay, Caleb? You sound like a pretty smart boy, and you're related to Letty, so you must actually be brilliant. Why on earth wouldn't you have left her earlier?"

"She was a manipulator, and I didn't see that until the end. I think she was actually more of a narcissist, and it seemed fine, before she started gloating."

"Do you think that was why she was killed? Because she was trying to manipulate people?" I had to ask.

"I don't know, and before you ask, I swear it wasn't me. I was trying to leave her and just wanted out. Not enough that I would have harmed her. I just wanted to walk away, and I was doing that. She was the one who couldn't handle being walked away from."

We signed off, because I really didn't know what else to ask. I believed him, too, even though I didn't have Max's superpower of liar detection. But this also left me completely without any other clue and with nowhere else to go with all of this. Man, this sucked. I wanted to be able to find this killer and have him or her nailed to the floorboards.

But why couldn't it be Preston? He was in the right place at the right time. He wouldn't tell me what he had gone back to the mansion for, and he wouldn't

tell me when he'd gone back. So had he gone back
and told Audra that with this housecleaning job
having been given to her, they should now wed,
and had she laughed at him? Told him that he had
served his purpose and she was moving on?

"I have to go see Burton with all this," I told Max.
He sat on the floor, with Mr. Fleefers wrapped
around his neck and Peanut trying desperately to
fit herself into his lap. What an incredible life I had
with those three. Yes, even Mr. Fleefers was wonderful, the darn cat.

"We'll be here when you get back, and maybe
we could do dinner. After that coffee, I realized
how hungry I am. Is it okay if we order in instead
of cooking?"

"Always. You don't have to cook, though I love
when you do, but ordering in is totally fine with
me. Maybe we can discuss that kind of thing when
I get back."

"I'll look forward to it."

Smiling, I headed out the door. My life was
marching in a direction that I would never have
guessed it would eighteen months ago, and I
found myself extremely pleased with the twists and
turns, which I had not realized I could love.

I even kept my smile as my mom tried to waylay
me at the door, and I continued to smile as I decided to walk to the police station instead of get
my car out from around the hearse, which had
blocked me in again.

Walking along the sidewalk, I composed what I
was going to say to Burton, and I gave careful
thought as to how I would word my questions. I still
didn't have the murderer, but that would come

soon enough. I was eliminating people left and right. I didn't have anyone to fill in the gaps, but that would come. Some piece of evidence would snag me, and I would know exactly what to say and how to get the confession. I just knew it.

Not really, but that was what I was telling myself when a white cloth landed over my face and I passed out without another thought but *Yikes*.

Chapter Twenty-one

My first thought was that I was surrounded by the smell of the ocean. I didn't know why that struck me as funny, but I snorted at my own laughter before clamping my hand over my mouth.

What the hell had just happened, and where in the world was I? This was not good.

I jerked around to find any piece of furniture or sight that looked familiar. Obviously, I was not in my house. I wasn't in a hospital bed, like where Bethany had woken up. I wasn't in any place I knew, except that my gaze landed on a picture frame that I knew I had seen before. I was in the house Mrs. Petrovski had sent us to clean after the mansion was closed down for the investigation, the one that was way too clean to need to be cleaned.

I thought about calling out, but then I realized that one of my feet was tied to the chair I was sitting on and that I was not going anywhere, unless I planned on hopping out of here with my hands tied in front of me and with a chair attached to my leg. *Holy crap. So not good.*

"Well, at least I got the dose right this time, unlike with that stupid employee of yours. I ended up having to hit her more than once to get her to drift off, and then I had to give her something a little special to make it all end."

That voice. I knew it, and I did not like it one bit. It had told me I was worthless, and it wouldn't let me speak when I had something to say. It had talked down to me, as if I was less, and ultimately, it had told tales that obviously were not true, which was a given if I was tied to a chair in her house and was just waking up from something like chloroform.

Mrs. Petrovski. How had she drugged me, then dragged me in here?

I closed my eyes, then opened them again, hoping that I would find myself in a different place, thinking that I had been having a nightmare of epic proportions.

But no, it was definitely real. The knot at my ankle was digging into my flesh, the one around my wrists was pulling at the fine hairs on my arms, and I was staring into the eyes of a madwoman. *So not awesome.*

"No words, Tallie Graver? Usually, you're full of words and questions and too much information, but not enough smarts. So here we are. You had one job and one job only. To leave it to Burton to arrest my nephew and get him out of my life, and you couldn't even do that right."

"I—"

"No, don't start talking now. Let me tell you a

story, and then I'm going to have Jackson take you out and get rid of you."

Jackson? I looked frantically around the room but saw no one else.

"He'll be in after I'm done. I'm thinking about an even more special cocktail for you, one that will make you tell me all the things I want to know and then cause you to forget it all before Jackson's turn." She paced in front of me, with her heels and her pearls and her perfectly made-up face. She clicked across the room with the exactitude of a metronome, staring at me and then staring at her nails and then staring at me again. I was too scared to be bored this time. Whereas I had not feared Preston and his can of soda or his threats, this woman was altogether different and not the militant but manageable old lady I'd thought she was.

"Why are you doing this?"

"I said no questions, but I'll answer that one, because it goes nicely with the little story I have to tell." She paused and fingered the pearls at her neck. "Do you know what it takes to run an empire, Tallie?"

Was I supposed to answer that? I didn't know what it took to run an empire. I couldn't even think up a good name for my cleaning crew. But since she had said no talking, I just shook my head and waited for her to continue. I was going to have to start thinking of a way to get out of this predicament, long before Jackson came to do his duty.

"It takes a smart woman and an army of dumb guys. That's what it takes."

"Okay."

"But then somehow I got an idiot of a nephew and no one to help me move to the next level and a cop who didn't know when to look the other way."

"Who should have looked the other way?"

She towered over me in a flash. "Burton. He was supposed to look the other way, over at my nephew. And he would have done it if you hadn't taken Preston to jail and then tried to dupe me out of my perfect setup. You know, he might not have killed her, but I know for a fact he was the one who wrapped her up in that carpet and took her out to the Dumpster. Him and that woman he hired to work for Audra during the competition. I watched them do it from behind the half wall Bethany took a picture of, before I could close it, the dimwit."

"What?"

"You see, there is a secret wall, but I couldn't tell you that, or it would give away too many of my secrets, so I scoffed and I pooh-poohed and you believed me, you silly twit. The half wall isn't where you thought it was, but it does exist. It's there for me to use at my discretion."

A light blinked on in my mind. "It's that soft spot on the wall in the room upstairs, isn't it?"

She smiled but didn't answer my question. Instead, she continued her story. "Preston moved the body because he was afraid that if someone found her in the house, it wouldn't sell, and if it didn't sell, then he wouldn't be able to buy into a little proposition that I'd asked one of my men to approach him with. It was brilliant, actually. I'd have him pay me through one of my goons, and he'd never know that the money he made was coming right back to me. Stupid man."

"And what was the proposition?" I hadn't come up with a way to get out of this, but I was fascinated by what she was saying.

"Drugs, my dear. A lot of lovely drugs. Burton shut me down without knowing who I was. I was selling all these properties to start up somewhere new, now that he was onto my staff of dealers. I killed that girl so he would look the other way while I made my escape, but you had to get involved and do your little nosy thing and then start interfering, and he didn't take it as seriously as he needed to. I tried to encourage him to do his job, but why should he when he has an unpaid, stupid woman to go floundering around, trying to find clues for him like a little dog?"

Now, that was going too far. I was not little, and I wasn't a dog. I puffed up my shoulders, because I really wanted to take a swing at her, even with my hands tied, and the chair moved a little. An idea started to form in my head, but I'd need to work out the logistics before I attempted it. Since she was still delivering her monologue, I felt I had a little time to get all the info I possibly could to nail her for all her crimes when I got out of this.

When, not *if*. When.

"And then my idiot of a nephew touched the corpse before I had a chance to dispose of it. And because he was so afraid of getting in trouble, as he'd left his fingerprints on her, and was also afraid that the house wouldn't sell, he decided to throw her away and call a truck in to take her to the dump, so people would just figure she went missing. I almost killed him, too, that day, but when you found her, I decided he would be the perfect scapegoat."

I scooted a little on the chair again and found that it was heavy but not too heavy. She walked away, and I scooted a little more. This was doable. All I needed to do was wait for her to get close to me again.

Frustratingly, she stayed out of reach while she delivered her next monologue. "My family has been running drugs for years. I took the small-time business and made it into something magnif-icent in the past few years, putting my education at Harvard behind it to make it bloom like no one had even conceived. But it all went downhill when Burton caught a whiff of what was happening in his little burg. I tried to get someone to pay him off to keep quiet, but he was having none of it, that ridiculous do-gooder. And then Preston started playing with that floozy and thought he'd marry her. We were not going to marry beneath us. We just don't do that in this family. That's why I never married. There was no one who was worthy of me."

Good Lord. Not only a monologue but a self-aggrandizing one. *Awesome.*

"And so she, too, was the perfect scapegoat."

I took a breath right before I challenged her. It might be my last one ever. "Perfect, except for the idiot nephew and the idiot cop and the idiot you, who thought you could get away with it."

She came for me, just as I had hoped she would. In a flash of movement, I stood, kicked out my leg with the chair attached to it, and nailed her right in the chest with the wooden seat. I was against violence on a daily basis, and I sometimes had a hard time watching action movies, because they made me wince, but when she went down, I did a little cheer inside, right before I hopped and hobbled out of the house and started yelling like the place was on fire.

To echo Bethany's sentiments, maybe yelling was not my best idea, but I was not going to get far with this chair attached to my leg. I reached down to untie it now that I was semi-free, or at least free from that house and that woman, but a hulking figure came toward me from my right. Could this be Jackson? I was gearing myself up to take another swing with the chair when I recognized my cousin, Matt.

"Why in the world are you screaming, and what is that attached to your leg?" he asked, running toward me.

"No time for questions. Go arrest the old biddy on the floor in the house behind me and I'll tell you everything I know."

He did as I asked, but by then a crowd had developed. Max was there and my father, and even Burton stood near me. He took the utility knife off his belt again and sawed through the rope binding me to the chair.

"Not so efficient," he said.

"And definitely not useful," I answered as I fell into Max's arms.

I woke up on a couch in the funeral parlor, the blue room, to be precise. My mom fluttered around my head as if she were a butterfly and I was a flower, but her face said she was likening me to a Venus flytrap.

"Don't you ever do that again! Never! My heart can't take this!"

"Stop yelling, Mother." That was my dad, and I didn't like him calling her that any more than I liked her calling him Daddy. But my head ached, so I let it pass.

"I'm going to need all of you to step out of this space," Burton said, finally coming into view, as I tried to sit up. "Just stay where you are, young lady. I have questions, and you'd better have answers."

Flopping back on the couch made my head pound more, but then Max was there with a warm washcloth and a kiss on my knuckles. "It's going to be okay. I was so scared, but it's going to be okay."

I wanted to reassure him. I really did, yet the words wouldn't come out of my mouth, and I must have passed out again.

This time when I came to, I was still on the couch, but in Max's arms. I snuggled in, not sure why we were on the first floor of the funeral parlor but willing to take his embrace anywhere I could get it.

Until Burton cleared his throat and everything came rushing back to me.

"Oh my God! Did you get her? Please tell me she didn't get away from you. I think I hit her hard enough to make sure she didn't move until someone got there. Oh, but Jackson could have carried her off. I didn't think of that! Crap!"

"Slow down there, Tallie," Burton told me. "Everyone has been caught, and even a few bonus guys, just for good measure. Once Marg started talking, she did everything she could to get out of the charges, but they're going to stick like superglue. And we picked up the girl who helped Preston throw away the body, so no worries there, either."

I sighed in relief, not wanting to have any loose ends that might come after me again.

"You can rest easy," he added.

"And maybe you can now, too," I answered.

"What?"

"You were working too hard. You were a mess and your shirt was rumpled and you were so stressed. When I was making my way to the station, I so wanted to be able to give you the name of the killer, but I was afraid I'd hit a dead end. Then Marg kidnapped me, and if nothing else, I was happy to be able to help."

Burton shook his head and stared up at the ceiling. "You're killing me."

"No, I saved you. Now, what do you need from me? She did her unloading of all the information, so if there's anything she isn't telling you, I bet I can fill in the gaps." I sat up with Max's help. "Is she singing like a canary?"

Burton burst out laughing. "My God, you can be annoying, but you also are incredibly thorough. I have everything I need, but if I come across anything I'm unsure about, you'll be the first person I ask. For now, rest. We can talk tomorrow. It'll be soon enough."

He left the room, and it was just Max and me.

"Sorry about all this," I said. "I didn't mean to get drugged and tied to a chair."

His laughter wasn't a burst, more a puff of disbelief. "I'm just so happy to have you back and un-harmed. You are unharmed, right?"

I rotated my shoulders and shook out each leg, then rolled my neck. "Other than a headache, I'm good as gold."

"You certainly are, and no matter what Burton says, he was extremely worried about you and in-credibly grateful for all the info he now has."

"He'd better be," I said, but I didn't actually mean it. He was a good cop and did a good job. Sometimes I just got there faster.

"Now, since you're a little incapacitated and shouldn't move for at least the next ten minutes, and the bad people have been caught and Burton has things under control, I thought I'd take a minute to talk to you about my plan for moving up here."

"I'm all ears." I had already heard everything Marg Petrovski had to say, and I knew most of the Preston story. I could get the rest of it tomorrow if I wanted it. But right now I wanted to think about happy things, and Max made me the happiest I'd ever been.

"I talked to your dad."

I groaned. No good conversation started with that sentence.

"Are you hurting? We can do this later. No need to rush if you want to lie back down."

I reached over to kiss his cheek. What a sweetie. "That groan was more for the 'talking to my dad' thing, not pain. I'm actually feeling pretty okay right now. So tell me what you and my dad talked about. I'm braced."

"Well, the building next door went up for sale privately this morning. They asked your dad if he wanted it before putting it on the market. The lower floor is all set up to be an event spot, and he was thinking that perhaps you'd be willing to run that instead of working the actual funerals. Like a tea shop, but for grieving people. He even said that you could hold other events there if you wanted. Maybe Gina could help with catering."

My eyes were about to pop out of my head, and my tongue was thick in my mouth. "Are you serious?"

"Is that a good 'Are you serious?' or a furious one?"

I grabbed his ears and kissed him full on the mouth. "That is totally a good question. I could be over there and still help here at the funeral home, but not be tied to the part I don't care for here. I'd be independent. Heck, I'd even pay rent for the place if he wanted me to. And I have my fabulous crew of squeegee queens to watch over, too."

"There's a catch."

I sank back against the cushions. Of course there was. "Lay it on me."

"I would need to use a corner of the space to do taxes until something else opens up in the area."

I slapped his arm. "That's not a catch. That's a bonus."

"Okay. Then hopefully, you'll like this part, too."

He paused, and I held my breath. Was he going to ask me to marry him? What would I say?

"Your dad offered to let us open up the whole third floor of this building to make it into a legitimate living area, instead of a studio apartment. I asked when I was considering what the perfect space for us to live in would be, and he was very happy to offer. Dylan could help with the renovation work."

"So we'd still live above the dead?"

"Quiet neighbors."

"Quiet neighbors," I agreed, and we laughed. After a pause, I looked him in those pretty eyes and said, "Yes, yes to all of it. And I just came up with the most awesome name for my cleaning crew. We will henceforth be called the Queens of Squeegeedom."

I should have thought of that sooner, but now it was absolutely perfect, along with every other thing going on my life.

Keep reading for a
sneak peek at
VARNISHED WITHOUT A TRACE
the next in the Tallie Graver Mystery series,
coming soon from
Misty Simon
and
Kensington Books

Chapter One

Here in central Pennsylvania, bingo could very easily be considered a death sport, filled with hurled insults, hurled troll dolls, and the occasional hurled beer bottle, depending on the venue. It could be nasty and cutthroat. And that was just in the first hour.

Maybe in other parts of the world, it was a happy, fun game, with joyous shouts of winning and prizes galore. Maybe people gathered together with dried corn and game cards that had seen a lot of use over the years. Maybe there were a lot of laughs and a lot of woo-hooing.

We, however, had a medic on hand in case things got, well, out of hand. Like that one time a bingo caller—the guy who pulled the numbers and read them off—was given a fat lip after the last game. No caller had yet landed in my family's funeral home due to grievous injuries from doing his volunteer job, but I wouldn't be too surprised if that happened.

In my town, it was kill or be killed when it came to a game dependent solely on a cage full of balls and some cards with corresponding numbers. Even if it was Christmas Eve.

I just hoped the rash of fires we'd had recently wouldn't interrupt the game. Then again, maybe that was exactly what was needed to get me out of what could be an awful evening. We'd have to wait and see.

On Christmas Eve my grandmother, my mother, and I walked into the fire hall, prepared to enjoy this traditional form of entertainment, at about six. By 6:05 p.m., I knew from looking out over the sea of bingo players sitting in their historical seats that it might not be the bowl of jolly laughter my mom had hoped for to distract my visiting grandmother.

We walked up and down the aisles of long tables, empty-handed, when others had whole luggage carts of things with them. We finally settled on a table halfway to the back of the room and sat down to play the traditional Christmas Eve bingo game, with me between my mom and my grandmother, like the buffer I'd been signed up to be.

And then I was promptly assaulted by an angry woman with a bingo bag.

"Tallie Graver, you move your tushie right now. This here is my seat!"

I jumped up before anything else could be said, and found another seat another row back. Then I was moved again. By the third move, I was ready to take on any of these grandmas and chain myself to one of the folding chairs, even if my headstone would read TALLIE GRAVER, DEATH BY DAUBER. I was sure my dad would direct a beautiful funeral and have Mortimer Smith down the road carve me a lovely headstone.

I wasn't complaining too much, though. Since I'd already been moved away from my mother and my grandmother three times, I was out of harm's way. I hadn't counted on those women who had been playing for fifty-seven years, every Tuesday without fail, and always sat in the same seat, but I should have.

My grandmother was old enough and had lived here her whole life, before moving to Florida five years ago, to simply turn around and give the first demanding "You stole my seat" accuser the mom eye. She had backed away, apologizing. Grumbling the whole way but still apologizing first.

With her steel-gray hair pulled into a severe bun, my grandmother was not to be trifled with. It was probably one of the reasons my mom could be such a softy. I would be, too, if I'd grown up with someone who could stop someone in their tracks with one disdainful glance.

I, however, was not in that age group, nor had I achieved the level of evil eye that Jane Moreland had at eighty-five. For many reasons, I had never gone up against my mother's mother for anything, even when I was too little to understand what that meant. There was just something about the forbidding woman that made you walk on tiptoes. So I had made my way through life preferring to stay under her radar. Even my ex-husband, Walden Phillips III, had never tried to take her on, and that was saying something.

But I was supposed to be the buffer between the two women this evening. She was my grandmother, and I had agreed to support my mom, Karen Graver, while Jane was here for the next ten days. Ten long days.

Getting moved meant I still got points for being in the firehouse, playing bingo, but I didn't have to be next to Grams while she kvetched about every person in the room and even some who were long dead.

I ended up between Alice Mudge, the sweetest woman in town, and Ronda Hogart, probably one of the meanest. Sweet Alice was also a little crazy, but I'd take that any day over the constant sneer on Ronda's face.

This was going to be so much fun.

I almost wished I had put my foot down and told my mother I wasn't going tonight. My boyfriend, Max Bennett, was here for our first Christmas Eve, and I wanted to spend it with him and just him. Instead, he had come with us and was currently wandering around, looking at all the food on the laden tables against the walls. My best friend, Gina Laudermilch, had outdone herself, along with the pizza shop down the street and the diner at the edge of town.

"It's so nice to see you, Tallie," Alice said, straightening her hunter-green cardigan with its snowman pin and smiling with her whole face.

"Just stay out of my way, girl," Ronda barked. She was also my great-aunt, or something like that, on my mom's side. Really, anyone older than you that you knew was related became an aunt or an uncle, and anyone your age was usually called a cousin.

I'd lost track of how many people I was related to and how I was related. I knew only that the same blood ran through our veins, and that made us family, to some extent. And it was expected that you would tolerate, if not exactly cherish, those blood relatives. So I had to be nice to her, even if she wasn't someone I specifically wanted to spend any time with.

"Happy holidays to both of you," I answered. "Hopefully, there are some good prizes tonight."

Alice's smile widened, and Aunt Ronda just snorted, then said, "Why did Christmas have to fall on a Wednesday this year? All you interlopers playing at my game and cutting my chances of winning. It's a disgrace. They should have closed it to all you toe dippers and left it to the people who are committed. There'd better be some cash prizes, or I'm taking it up with Howard."

Howard Allerman was the mayor of our little burg. And I had no doubt she'd do just that. Christmas Eve tended to be more of a basket bingo event, where instead of money, you walked away with a basket full of goodies. I would have preferred cash, too, but I probably wouldn't win tonight, so it didn't matter. Part of me hoped to win just to make Ronda mad, but the other part wanted to get out of here without the wicked queen of bingo breathing venom down my neck.

Looking around the huge fire hall, festooned in swags of evergreen branches and red ribbon, I zeroed in on my boyfriend. When we'd walked in, I'd sent Max on a mission to buy me something to munch on to get me through sitting between my mother and my grandmother. Now I might need him to head down to the bar on the corner if I had to sit between these two.

Mom turned around at that point, with her brow crinkled. I could hear Grams talking from here, even though I couldn't make out what she was saying. It must have been something mean, because my mom looked like she was going to scream. I shrugged at her and pointed to my two seat mates. The little hooligan smiled like the Grinch standing at the top of the mountain, making plans to ruin the Whos' Christmas.

Well, at least I didn't feel so bad now. . . .

So here I was, sitting in a metal chair at a plastic table, waiting for the girl to come around with the bingo cards. On either side of me, the two ladies started pulling out all manner of things from their custom tote bags. Bags that were emblazoned with the words *bingo queen* in very precise and brightly colored embroidery. Bags that had holsters stuffed with all their good luck tokens. Bags that were their lives.

Why did I have to get stuck next to the bingo queens? And how many queens could there be in our little town? It was a nightmare come true. And then a third one walked over, with her own bag absolutely bulging with all manner of things.

"Why, hello, Ronda," Jenna Front said, lowering her bag to the table, next to the older woman. This was one bingo queen I wouldn't mind fraternizing with.

"Seat's taken. Go away." Ronda didn't even look up at her.

Jenna's face went stony. "There's no one here."

"There might be, and I'd prefer it to be anyone but you." Aunt Ronda placed her bag on the chair. "I have four kids, not five and certainly not six. Whatever that rat of a husband of mine has said or done before, that's not going to change just because of what he wants. Now, we've had our words. Go bother someone else."

Jenna left in a huff, and I almost got up to follow her. She'd recently signed on for my cleaning crew, so I felt responsible for her. We could commiserate about how mean this woman was, and maybe she would be better company.

I had put my hands on the table and was starting to rise when Ronda's heavy hand fell hard on my shoulder. "Don't you dare. Tina should be around soon with cards, and I won't have you making the game later than it already is. She'll be fine. She's just in a tiff."

"But she's a friend, and that way you and Alice can sit next to each other, like you normally do." I tried to make it sound convincing, but she wasn't buying it.

"You need to make better choices in friends. Now sit and stay."

My mother chose that moment to turn around again and shook her head at me. Fine, but I was going to leave as soon as I could, then.

Tina Metzger finally came around with the cards, thank heavens. Alice pulled her six with wild abandon, almost flinging them all over the carefully setup table. I took the top one from the stack when she was done.

"Thanks, Tina. How's your son?" I asked.

"We don't have time for chitchat, Tallulah. Take your card and let her move along. She's late as it is," Ronda said.

No one but my father called me Tallulah, and that was only when he was irritated at me.

"We'll talk later, Tallie." Tina gave me a pained smile as Ronda took the whole stack of cards out of her hands and very carefully laid out four stacks of ten, then cut the stacks in half and removed the middle three cards from each.

Oh, yeah, it was going to be a long night.

But then Max dropped off a funnel cake absolutely covered in powdered sugar and gave me a kiss on my cheek just as the bingo caller at the front of the room turned on the microphone with a high-pitched whine.

Bill Jacobson, the minister at the First Presbyterian two streets up, laughed, and the sound boomed throughout the high-ceilinged building. "I'd say, 'Let's get ready to rumble,' but I think that's a different sport."

Right. One that wouldn't involve as much blood and foul language as I expected to fly around tonight.

And then we were off. We didn't have one of those fancy automatic ball machines; we still had the metal roll cage that had to be hand cranked. Jenna's husband, Nathan Front, sat with his sleeves rolled up next to Pastor Jacobson. He cranked and he cranked, and then the pastor pulled out the first ball.

"O-sixty-three."

The numbers were called out fast and furious. I had a hard time keeping up, but Alice and Ronda were throwing down the disks on their cards like they were master blackjack dealers in Vegas.

"B-seven." Pastor Jacobson held up the ball, then placed it in the slot in front of him about ten minutes later.

The woman in front of us stood up and screamed, "Bingo!" like her hair was on fire. A chorus of groans went up, and the foul language started up next to me as Aunt Ronda whisked her magnetic wand over her twelve cards, then squeezed the little chips off into her container, muttering words that would have made my mom wash my mouth out, even if I was almost thirty.

I looked around for Jenna but didn't see her. I'd catch up with her later, maybe over tea with Gina. I had to make sitting here worth it somehow.

"Oh, Ronda, watch your language. There are more games in store, and you wouldn't have wanted that basket, anyway. Look at it. It's filled with those baking pans and oven mitts. You don't even cook!" Alice reached across me to smack Ronda's hand, and I worried that it might be the last thing she'd ever do.

Instead, Ronda shook her head like an angry dog and got herself set back up. I had almost expected spittle to fly from the corners of her mouth. Ah, well, it was still early in the game.

I took a bite of my funnel cake and smiled around it, as if enjoying it, but instead, I was enjoying the moment. Maybe a little too much, as I missed the first call of the next game.

Things were hopping after that. Games were won and lost. Alice got the basket from the bakery, which made her squeal, and I found that if I paid attention for the most part, I could people watch while I played my one card. The room was full tonight, with all manner of citizens from our town and a few people I didn't know. Ronda's husband, Hoagie, who owned the hardware store, buzzed by with a smile to hand her a drink. She snorted at him and shooed him away.

I watched with a smile as my mom's cousin Velma—a real one, since she was her mother's sister's daughter—flirted with a guy at the snack table. Two men that I didn't recognize walked the perimeter of the fire hall, then greeted with a hug the woman who ran the shoe repair shop on Locust. Uncle Sherman, the fire chief, waved to me, and Chief of Police Burton sent a terse nod my way.

Fortunately, it had been months since I'd had to have too much interaction with Burton. No one had gone toes up when they weren't supposed to recently, so I had mostly been able to stay out of his hair. Of course we had people who were still passing away. My dad was as busy as ever at the funeral home, which had been in our family for generations, but for the most part, the deceased had lived full long lives, not died under mysterious circumstances. And I hadn't found them. That was a win-win situation, as far as I was concerned.

Maybe it wasn't such a bad night, after all.

Ronda was not having the best of nights, though, and her husband, Uncle Hoagie, had to force her hand down at the last moment, when she picked up one of her troll dolls and cocked her arm back to throw it at the pastor. Well, Hoagie managed only to delay her, since she chucked it hard as soon as he had walked away. The pastor knew enough to duck when the doll came zooming right at his head.

Alice chuckled from her seat next to me. "I told them they should put up the chicken-wire cage tonight, even if it is Christmas Eve, but they didn't listen to me. Pastor Jacobson is getting more agile, though. Last week it hit him in the eye, and he had to give his sermon Wednesday night with a big old shiner." She chuckled again. "You missed the B-three, dear."

She put one of her disks on my card, and lo and behold, I had bingo! I shot out of my seat like there was a firecracker under me.

Alice clapped, and Ronda gave Grams a run for her money with the death glare she sent my way. Especially since it was the last game and she hadn't won a single game all night long.

"Lousy interlopers. Shouldn't even be allowed to play. Lucky greenhorn." Each derogatory phrase, and some others that contained those words my mother would kill me for saying, was punctuated by her sweeping her arm across the table and scooping everything into her tote bag.

Stomping was a delicate word for the way Ronda pushed and shoved her way out of the hall and through the back door. It all happened so fast, I hadn't even gotten around to moving from my place at the table yet.

I glanced toward Alice, and she shrugged her shoulders. After moving my gaze to where Ronda had sat, I saw that in her fury and haste, she'd left her purse on the chair next to her.

"Did you see Hoagie?" I asked Alice, really not wanting to do the right thing here and go after Ronda with her purse. Giving it to Uncle Hoagie to give to his irate wife would be far better than chasing after her.

"Nope. You'd better go get your prize, though, before someone else tries to steal it. And I'd watch my back on your way to your house, if I were you. I know it's a short walk, but it could be a treacherous one, if you know what I mean." She chuckled and kept packing up her own things. It wasn't the same laugh as before, that jovial, fun one. This one had a slight tinge to it that made the hair on the back of my neck stand up.

"Okay then. Well, I'd better get this out to . . ." But Alice was already gone with her bag of luck.

Max approached, looking like someone I could get to do this errand for me.

"Hey, Tallie. Great win tonight. Now you can take me out to dinner." He smiled at me, and I smiled back.

"Can you go give this to Ronda?" I held up her purse. "She went out the back."

His face pulled into an adorable frown that had me frowning, too. "I promised I'd help break down the tables. Maybe you can catch her. I heard the parking lot is a madhouse."

Well, darn it. I was going to have to face the evil queen of bingo, anyway.

Better to make it quick and be done. Maybe I could give it to Uncle Hoagie if I found him first. That would work.

With that in mind, I headed toward the back door. Everyone else was heading out the bay doors out front, so of course Ronda had had to be the odd one out.

I couldn't remember what kind of car she drove, but I'd probably find her by listening for her yelling at people to get out of her way so she could get home and practice her throw for next time.

Preparing to step out into the brisk winter air, I wished I had grabbed my coat and possibly my prize. I could have left Ronda's purse with the pastor or even with Uncle Sherman, but my roots were showing, and I just couldn't leave it with someone else.

The door latch turned in my hand easily enough, but the door stuck on something. I shoved it hard to get it to open, leaning into it with my considerable weight.

It finally moved, only to have a very dead Ronda flop around the edge, with a dent in her head and a very blank expression on her lifeless face.

"Tallie, you left without your winnings," my grandmother said from behind me as I stood there with my mouth hanging open, registering very little. "I got them for you. That's very bad form when the men and women who were generous enough to put this on would like to go home to their families on Christmas Eve. We need to talk about your manners, young lady." She paused to take a breath. "Oh my heavens. Is that Ronda?"

"Bingo."

Mrs. Graver's Snickerdoodles or Tallie's Cookie for All Occasions (like figuring out whodunnit!)

All the things you need:

For Snickerdoodles

1 cup butter, at room temperature
¾ cup granulated sugar
½ cup light brown sugar
1 egg
1 Tbsp vanilla
1 tsp baking soda
1 tsp cream of tartar (trust me on this one!)
½ tsp salt
1 tsp ground cinnamon
2¾ cup white flour

For Cinnamon-Sugar Mixture

¼ cup granulated sugar
1 tsp ground cinnamon

Now here's what you do with them:

Step 1: Preheat oven to 325°F.

Step 2: In a large bowl mix butter, granulated sugar, and light brown sugar together until light and fluffy. Add in egg, vanilla, baking soda, cream of tartar, salt, and cinnamon until smooth.

Step 3: Add flour, mixing until just combined.

Step 4: In a separate small bowl mix together cinnamon and sugar until combined.

Step 5: Using a tablespoon, take out a measure

of dough and roll into a ball. Then roll each ball into the cinnamon-sugar mixture.

Step 6: Cover baking sheet with parchment paper for easy cookie removal. Place rolled dough on baking sheet about two inches apart. Bake for 10-12 minutes.

And voilà! Now, remember that you should probably share at least some of these cookies with others, although that's not a hard and fast rule!